Stone Cold

Sarah
Humphreys

Stone COLD
A NOVEL

SARAH HUMPHERYS

NEW YORK

LONDON • NASHVILLE • MELBOURNE • VANCOUVER

Stone Cold

A Novel

Published in New York, New York, by Morgan James Publishing. Morgan James is a trademark of Morgan James, LLC. www.MorganJamesPublishing.com

Proudly distributed by Ingram Publisher Services.

Publisher's Note: This novel is a work of fiction. Names, characters, places, and incidents are either products of the author's imagination or used fictitiously. All characters are fictional, and any similarity to people living or dead is purely coincidental.

A FREE ebook edition is available for you or a friend with the purchase of this print book.

CLEARLY SIGN YOUR NAME ABOVE

Instructions to claim your free ebook edition:
1. Visit MorganJamesBOGO.com
2. Sign your name CLEARLY in the space above
3. Complete the form and submit a photo of this entire page
4. You or your friend can download the ebook to your preferred device

ISBN 9781631955846 paperback
ISBN 9781631955853 ebook
Library of Congress Control Number: 2021935590

Cover Design by:
Karen Dimmick
ArcaneCovers

Interior Design by:
Christopher Kirk
www.GFSstudio.com

Morgan James is a proud partner of Habitat for Humanity Peninsula and Greater Williamsburg. Partners in building since 2006.

Get involved today! Visit MorganJamesPublishing.com/giving-back

To my dad, who inspires me to be the best possible version of myself.

PROLOGUE

Mareena clutched her newborn niece as she skimmed down the hallway, her dress billowing out behind her. She wanted to run. She desperately wanted to run. But she couldn't with so many around her. It would draw too much attention, and for her, attention was a death sentence.

Palace guards and various officials scrambled down the hallway to get to the queen. Mareena glanced back at the queen's bedroom, where she had been moments before. In the chaos, she had slipped into the room, stolen the newborn princess, for whom nobody had spared any attention, and silently snuck out. She overheard echoing voices in the hallway, a conversation between the king and whatever unlucky advisor happened to be in his general vicinity.

"This situation is awfully inconvenient," the king stated. "The queen has died. If I cannot remarry, this means I will only have two heirs."

"It's an old tradition, My King," one of the advisors explained. "Not taking another wife is a gesture of respect to the queen's family of origin."

"You're suggesting I should put my entire dynasty at risk just to honor her?"

"You have two children, the prince and newly born princess. I hardly think you should worry," the advisor responded. "Queen Ionda served her purpose."

"That's . . ." The king exhaled. "I apologize. I should contain my anger."

Mareena squeezed the baby tightly as a single tear spilled down her cheek. Ionda hadn't just been the queen. She was Mareena's twin sister, and even though their relationship hadn't been the best, she couldn't believe Ionda was gone. She was all alone now.

Of course, nobody else would mourn. Emotion was nonexistent in the kingdom of Ashlon. Eradicating emotion was the objective of everyone around her.

Mareena could clearly recall the day it started—the day that had sparked the fire still ravaging the kingdom. Eight years ago, commoners stumbled upon enchanted stones near the outskirts of the kingdom. They quickly discovered that when worn around the neck, these stones siphoned away emotions, leaving you with no pain, no hurt, and no disappointment. Even now, everyone clamored to get the stones so they could escape the irrational tide of their own feelings. People now considered it quite embarrassing, even improper and barbaric, to let one's feelings influence rational thought and judgment.

It drove Mareena absolutely crazy.

As she turned into a deserted hallway, she paused, catching her breath. As she stopped walking, tears flowed down her cheeks again, like a dam breaking. The weight of her sister's death crushed her as she crumpled to her knees, still clutching the child.

Mareena forced herself to breathe as she gradually climbed off the floor and headed to her room—the only safe place in the palace. Luckily, nobody had witnessed her emotional outburst. She wore a sapphire necklace that should have nullified sadness. Any passersby could have easily observed her tearful breakdown as seen proof that she was a Malopath, a secret she planned to take to her grave.

As she fled to her room, she carefully tilted her face away from any passersby and prayed they wouldn't spot the streaking tears. After what felt like a few eternities, she arrived at a polished wooden door and rushed into the room. As she shut the door, silence blanketed her. Mareena let out a sigh of relief before sitting on the floor with the young princess still nestled in her arms. The midwives had hastily thrown a blanket on her but had done nothing else to comfort the child, a testimony to the emotionless disregard the kingdom had for their children, even royal ones. The rabbit fur blanket felt fuzzy and soft as Mareena swept her fingers over the fabric.

She could have comfortably drifted into her thoughts if the infant princess hadn't started crying. It wasn't very loud, but the sound still jarred her. It pierced her thoughts like a sword and derailed her concentration. Mareena desired peace and calm, but that vanished with an upset baby.

An idea struck her. Her niece was crying, experiencing the primal feelings that come with life. Crying meant sadness, right? Mareena reached for the beautiful sapphire necklace around her neck. These magical stones worked on everyone, even newborns. Each stone removed a different type of emotion. Sapphires removed sadness and could stop the baby from crying. It wouldn't do any harm, she reasoned.

Her fingers brushed against the cold sapphires as she lifted the necklace over her head and touched it to the child's skin.

The princess continued to cry.

With rising frustration, Mareena repositioned the necklace so all four sapphires touched the child, but she observed no change. Then a shock of realization swept through Mareena, making her freeze. She was painfully aware of the sound of her own heart, beating like the flap of a thousand birds as her mind grasped the implications of her new discovery. Every instinct screamed at her to run away, to wipe away what she had witnessed, but she couldn't. The necklace slipped from her fingers and fell softly onto the carpet, having shattered her universe.

A sudden knock at the door made her gasp and almost drop the princess. She bolted upright, breathing heavily, and wiped the tears away with the sleeve of her dress. As the door clicked open, she prayed that her puffy, red eyes wouldn't give away her secret.

Her brother-in-law, the king, stood rigidly in the hallway. Mareena's gaze fell on the necklace he wore: a ruby, a sapphire, and an amber stone to nullify of the emotions anger, sadness, and love. She felt glad, at least, that the necklace now included an anger stone, which he hadn't been wearing while speaking to the advisor.

The king clasped his hands behind his back and observed her formally. "Hello, Mareena." His voice was neutral and toneless.

"Hello, Your Majesty," she replied, imitating the formality.

"You have the princess with you. I was surprised when I saw you leave. Did you think it was appropriate to take her?"

"I'm sorry, Your Majesty. I saw that the midwives were done with her, and since her crying was disruptive, I thought it best to remove her. You can introduce her to the court now, if you wish to do so."

"No, I see now that your action was logical," he answered. "I assume you will continue to wear sapphires this evening, due to the abruptness of the queen's death?"

She tried to make her response sound dismissive. "It wouldn't matter anyway. Even without the stones, I have no sadness to speak of. Her death means nothing to me."

He nodded his head. "Good. Then you will supervise the princess for now. I have things to attend to."

The king's order startled her. *Me? The unimportant lady with no real experience with children? You must be crazy. I only took her because she was cold and alone. I thought I would only have her a few minutes.*

Wanting to end the conversation as quickly as possible, Mareena spoke again. "Is there anything else, Your Majesty?"

"Yes, indeed. This doesn't follow protocol, but I would like for you to test the princess for Malopathy."

Mareena nodded, carefully selecting her words. "I have already completed that task for you. Nothing remotely suggests that possibility."

"That is fortunate. It would be inconvenient to execute one of my heirs since I will only ever have two." He paused. "I must go. You have your instructions."

Mareena nodded again, wincing at the lack of sympathy in his voice. The door finally closed, freeing her from the building tension. The princess was silent now. She was asleep, peaceful. Mareena smiled at her and sat on the floor again.

She couldn't help but feel both terrified and elated for the child, who apparently was a Malopath like her. Mareena had no clue what caused people with her gift—or maybe it was a curse—to have emotions that refused to be silenced by the stones. Being a Malopath was a crime punishable by immediate public execution, even if one happened to be a member of the royal family.

Her mind flashed back to the day when she recognized her Malopathy. It occurred eight years ago when the stones sapped away everyone's emotions while hers stubbornly remained. Even then, she realized the task she had to undertake: to suppress all emotion, to pretend to fit in, and to remain in the shadows.

The princess, however, was just a baby. She knew nothing about politics, social norms, or Malopathic people. If Mareena raised her without telling her of her true nature, she might as well sentence the baby to death. She already felt linked to the princess. They were both the same, an impossibility that everyone wanted to eradicate. She felt obligated to protect the child from her own nature.

I can teach you, little one. I will keep you safe. For as long as I live, I promise that no harm will come to you. I'll teach you how to conceal your emotions, to pretend that the stones work no differently on you.

And most of all, I'll show you how to blend into the background and stay away from attention.

Trust me. Being a Malopath is a dangerous game to play.

CHAPTER
ONE

SEVENTEEN YEARS LATER

"**P**rincess Syona? Are you done preparing yourself for the ceremony?" A familiar voice called from outside the door, slightly muffled by the barrier between us. I sighed, ignoring the guard.

Smooth pearls slid across my fingers as I wrapped my hands around the necklace. Carefully, I lifted it off the polished desk and fastened it around my neck. The pearls felt as cold as ice against my skin, grounding me to reality. I didn't *need* to wear a necklace, but the pearls were my favorite. I wore them to every ceremony the king insisted I attend. They helped me focus my attention where it needed to be, in my body in the present moment.

I opened my closet and selected a dress. The scarlet fabric felt silky underneath my fingertips as I pulled it out into the light. Red happened to be the most popular color worn at ceremonies, so I would blend in perfectly. Nobody helped me get ready. Though every servant in the palace was perfectly willing, I didn't want to bother anyone. And the more I kept to myself, the better.

After I finished dressing, I moved to stand in front of the full-length mirror on the wall. The outfit felt a little simplistic for a royal ceremony, especially one this important, but the king had sent no specific dress requirements. My plain reflection stared back at me: a girl in a long-sleeved red dress covered by a black silk shawl, only adorned by a choker pearl necklace. My long hair fell across my shoulders in waves, unkempt and unstyled. I didn't appear important or special. Surely I could slide by unnoticed.

Perfect.

I took a deep breath. Breathing deeply always helped calm my emotions. Mareena's words resounded my head, words she had spoken time and time again: *Other people think we're dangerous. They will kill you if they ever find out what you are. Be like ice. Cool. Composed. Nothing can crack you. Never reveal what's on the inside.*

Over the years, I had added my own mantra to my aunt's words: *Nobody cares. Nobody pays attention. You are invisible.*

"Princess? Are you almost done?" The voice outside the door persisted, the sound sending a jolt of annoyance through me.

"Yes, Officer Raynott. I'm almost done," I replied, straining to keep my voice free of intonation.

I crept across the carpet toward the door, pausing only a second to glance at the necklace stand beside the door. I unhooked one of the necklaces, four circular jewels strung onto a gold chain. The king required everyone to wear these emotion-sucking stones at ceremonies. The necklace held an emerald, a sapphire, a ruby, and an onyx stone. They correlated to the emotions of happiness, sadness, anger, and fear. People received these stones on special occasions according to position or status, most commonly at certain ages.

For instance, at the Amber Ceremony, a royal eighteen-year-old receives their love siphoning stone—a *privilege* my brother had today.

The Amber Ceremony was a major milestone in the kingdom, reserved strictly for members of the royal family and noblemen. Only the rich could afford a ceremony. Commoners received the stone at eighteen without any extravagance.

My hands trembled as I laid the necklace over the pearls. A soft humming noise winked into existence, a sound that always accompanied the stones. I was mostly desensitized to it now, but other than annoyance with the noise, the gemstones didn't affect me in any way. They never interfered with my emotions. When the officials first discovered the condition, they titled it *Malopathy*. Naturally, people became afraid of others whose powerful emotions couldn't be altered by the stones. Emotions were dangerous. Emotions were a curse. Malopathic people were unpredictable and irrational and would damage society.

So, the same year we discovered the stones, my father passed a law that made stone wearing mandatory, and he ordered the speedy execution of all Malopaths.

I pulled open the door and stepped into the hallway, observing the two guards posted against the wall, one of which I didn't remotely recognize. He must have been new to the palace. The other I could have recognized on a pitch-black night. The teenage guard was Gerrand, or Officer Raynott because I wasn't supposed to know his first name.

"Would you like me to accompany you to the ceremony, Princess?" Gerrand's voice sounded cold, like everything else in this cursed society.

My heart skipped a beat as I forced myself to breathe. "No, thank you," I answered, copying his empty tone of voice. "I am capable of walking on my own accord."

The wide and decorated corridors in the palace cheerfully greeted me. Windows on the left wall bathed me in warm sunlight. Rugs sewn with golden tassels blanketed a section of the marble floor. The carpets had swirling red and black designs, which I loved to trace with my finger when I was younger. The arched ceilings towered overhead, and beautiful crystal chandeliers reflected light into sparkling rays. Everything was radiant and intricate, but no one appreciated it but me.

Like always, the palace buzzed with activity, a kind of controlled chaos. The servants and guards calmly walked to their destinations, responding coldly if spoken to. A continuous, monotone sound echoed throughout the hallways, converging into a white noise that drove me crazy. The sound of hundreds of people's shoes tapping against the marble echoed in my ears like pattering rain. And for that reason, I always wore soft, flat shoes. My footsteps across the hard floor were always silent.

As I rushed through the hallway, I spotted my brother surrounded by people, probably congratulating and applauding him. The crowd around him parted for a split second, and I glimpsed his appearance.

He had chosen red to wear, like me and like everyone else at the ceremony. The fine black cloak he wore trailed on the ground behind him as he walked. The cloak was fastened around his shoulders with a single golden broach in the shape of a crown. The necklace he wore contained only four stones, but a fifth was about to join them.

I gathered up the fabric of my skirt in my hands and weaved through the crowd over to him. I stepped into my brother's line of sight and curtsied, my dress brushing against the floor. "Prince Davin, may I have permission to speak to you in private?"

Davin's eyes flicked across my face before he spoke. "Permission granted." He waved his hand, and immediately the crowd of people dispersed. The second they left, he stepped within inches of me. "Why do you keep doing this?" he whispered under his breath.

"What? I just want to talk to you."

"No. You want more than that." Before I could do anything, Davin tightly grasped my wrist and jerked me over to the side of the hallway. He glanced around, appraising his surroundings before pulling me into an alcove between corridors. He fumbled with the cord restraining a nearby curtain and yanked it across the space, obstructing anyone's view of us.

Once we were safely shrouded in the semi-darkness, I snatched his necklace and held it tightly in my hand. It was like opening a window to let sunlight flood in. Davin's expression suddenly melted into a puddle of emotion, an expression that was a mix of annoyance and joking happiness. He winced as his emotions flooded into him, but that didn't distract him from snapping at me. "Syona! Why did you do that?"

"You didn't need to do all this." I gestured to the curtain separating us from the crowd in the hallway. "I just wanted to talk to you."

"No. You wanted to have an *informal* conversation with me. There's a major difference. If anyone were to find out about this, it would ruin me, and people are everywhere today."

I unfastened my necklace. "Sorry, but I had to get a hold of your real personality before I lost it."

Davin rolled his eyes but laughed quietly. I guess I should have let him off easier. Informal conversations, talking without wearing any stones, were strictly outlawed. Even though we were royalty, someone in a position as high as ours could still be punished. Fortunately, it was usually only a court official reprimanding us. Nothing more serious could be done—unless someone discovered my capital crime of being a Malopath. Other than that little problem, I was untouchable.

I loved my brother. I hated it when the stones repressed his emotions. He was always extremely uncomfortable with breaking the rules. Occasionally, when he was in a good mood and if we were careful, he allowed me to have an informal conversation with him. As far as I had observed, Davin had two distinct modes. In *brother* mode, he joked around with me and expressed his emotions. In *prince* mode, he acted as strict and uptight as he would when ruling this unfeeling kingdom one day. I had learned to appreciate all the brother moments I could salvage and make the best of it when he played the prince.

"Are you, um, looking forward to your Amber Ceremony?"

Davin shrugged. "I haven't thought much of it until now."

I cocked an eyebrow. "Well, don't you usually like attention? This entire day is for you. That's something you can appreciate."

"Sure, but it's still unnerving. I usually don't have a crowd around me."

"Right. We wouldn't want you to get even *more* prideful."

"Hey!" He laughed again, pushing my shoulder playfully.

The red curtain covering us was suddenly yanked away, drenching the small space with light from the outside. I squinted into the light, studying our intruder.

Both of us winced, recognizing the face immediately. A bearded man with black hair surveyed us coldly. It was a man we both knew too well: Cyrus. Though no distinct expression was apparent on his face, I knew he hated us. With or without rubies, he hated us. As our uncle, he couldn't inherit the throne simply because we existed. I suppose his occasional eruptions of anger were fueled by both jealousy and our unroyal behavior. He was consistently against us.

"Would you mind telling me what you're doing?" he asked.

My brain ordered me to respond, but I couldn't verbalize what I wished to say. "I . . . I . . . We were just talking."

"Behind a curtain to hide you from view?"

I only managed to repeat myself. "We were just talking."

Cyrus's attention fixed itself on the necklace I held loosely in my hand. "Were you *informally* talking? Do I have to remind you that this action is *highly* illegal, or are you too ignorant to know about the edict enforced in your own kingdom?"

Davin stepped forward, shielding me with his arm. "Leave Syona alone."

Cyrus put up his arms in mock surrender. "I sincerely apologize. I meant no harm. I was simply reminding the princess that breaking rules has consequences. I'm also here to remind you that you still have an Amber Ceremony to attend."

Davin headed back into the light and the rush of the crowd, shooting Cyrus a glare before he fastened his necklace back on. Only Davin could dare to do that. He was the crown heir, outranking everyone in the palace except the king. He could do anything he wanted to Cyrus. And me? I wasn't exactly sure if I outranked our uncle, which is why Davin always ended up protecting me from him.

Cyrus's gaze latched onto me as I trailed after the prince. "Why do you always look so plain and underdressed? You're a princess, not a common farmgirl!"

Without responding, I scurried away and entered the courtroom.

Just get through this, I told myself. *Just get through this ceremony. Get through watching your brother morph into someone you don't even recognize.*

CHAPTER
TWO

"Almost since the beginning of the war, the kingdom of Ashlon has been gifted with the ability to eliminate emotion. That has been a blessing of the highest measure. It has strengthened our people and given them the morale to persevere through decades of conflict," the official droned on.

I watched from my seat in the courtroom, clutching the fabric of my dress. My pale skin made me feel transparent, like everyone could peer into my true nature. My draping black shawl felt nonexistent. Unfortunately for me, the king required the royal family to sit in the front row for every ceremony.

Rows of raised seats dotted the circular courtroom like a colosseum. Even though a cushion padded the hard, wooden seats, I could hardly feel it. The ceremonial official planted himself in the center of the room, reciting the same speech he used for every ceremony. He had been officiating for over twenty-five years, which meant dozens of stone ceremonies, and I still hadn't bothered to learn his name. I don't think I ever intended to. I absentmindedly gazed at him, only half-listening to his rambling speech.

"The war with the kingdom of Tanum has been violent and seemingly never-ending, but with the stones, we will prevail. They have made our society better than ever before. There's no more anger among us, no indecision, and no cowardice when faced with duty. These stones have saved us."

He produced a necklace with six shining gems dangling on the chain. He pointed specifically at the amber stone nestled among the others. "Amber represents the emotion of love, the most dangerous of all. Fortunately, our crown prince can escape that curse today. Please rise in respect to Crown Prince Davin of Ashlon."

I rose to my feet in perfect unison with the rest of the audience. A polite round of clapping scattered across the room. From my position, I witnessed Davin abandon his seat and stride to the center of the courtroom. He certainly *acted* like a prince, more regal than I could ever be.

I despised this version of him, which was nothing like the snippets of his actual personality I pried out every once in a while.

The official approached Davin, cradling the jeweled necklace in his hands. "Prince Davin, do you accept this stone willingly, swearing to forsake this emotion for as long as you shall live?"

"I do," he replied instantly, making me wince.

"Then we congratulate you. For you shall never endure the pain of love again." He removed Davin's necklace to thread the amber stone onto the chain, and for a split second, I saw my real brother again. His face softened, and his gaze flickered toward me. Something broke. In a split second, his expression showed all of his insecurities: the nervousness of receiving the stone, the pressure of being crown prince, and all of his inner thoughts were relayed to me instantly.

Then, the official dropped the necklace over his head, and I lost my real brother forever.

—⚬—

"Your Highness, could you at least *pretend* you're paying attention?"

I snapped out of the daydream, trying to redirect my thoughts. Usually, I loved my private tutoring lessons, but today, my thoughts drifted all over the place, mostly circling back to Davin's Amber Ceremony.

My fingers brushed against the chain of stones circling my neck. I was sure that if people could wear all six, they would, but with a limited supply, not everyone could get them. Palace workers were issued one or more stones depending on rank, but royalty had to wear three. My acting wasn't the greatest, but nobody paid much attention to me since Davin, the older and more important heir, overshadowed me. I was completely fine with that. It was a blessing. Not being heir to the throne was probably the only reason I had survived this long.

"I apologize. I seem to be distracted today because of the Prince's Amber Ceremony," I deadpanned.

"It's fine, as long as you focus from now on."

"Um . . ." I peeked at my necklace. I had sadness, anger, and happiness but not love or fear. I could probably ask without drawing suspicion. "Where is Prince Davin right now? I know that he announced it, but I wasn't paying attention."

My private tutor, Evander, glanced at me for a few seconds before speaking. He had taught me since I was a little girl and knew my tendency to get distracted during lessons. He had limited patience for answering my off-topic questions, but today he responded.

"Prince Davin announced that he was going hunting in the Southern Forest with a small group of noblemen. Without his full entourage of guardsmen, I would expect him to be gone and back in just a few hours," he answered. "That has no relevance to what we're doing right now, though. Let's get done with this lesson; then you'll have the evening to do whatever you wish." He twisted around in his chair to slide a book off of a nearby shelf.

I continued on the tangent, "But he spends all the rest of his time working."

He sighed. "Yes, I suppose so. His schedule is a lot more intense than yours. He must be ready to rule someday, so he has to travel with the king to every diplomatic engagement and peace council with the king-dom of Tanum. They're always an absolute mess. If the diplomats weren't required to wear rubies at the meetings, I'm sure they would have torn each other apart by now."

A soft knock rang out from the library door, and it creaked open. Mareena's face popped into view as she surveyed the room. "Am I inter-rupting something?"

"No. Not at all," I immediately replied, despite knowing how Evander would react to that response. A familiar wave of relief came over me from seeing my Aunt Mareena's face. She served as my sole protector. A Malopath like me, she had been steadily teaching me about our lot from her lifetime of experience.

"I didn't see you at the Amber Ceremony. Where were you?" I questioned.

"I'm not technically required to attend, and admittedly, I found a new book in the library that I thought was more interesting than the ceremony."

I held my hand over my mouth to hide the smile that threatened to break across my face. I wore an emerald, which should suck away happi-ness. Instead of manifesting anything on my face, I simply laid my fingers on the wooden desk and tapped them twice, using the code of secret hand signals we had developed years ago, a way to convey to each other what we felt under prying eyes.

Mareena mirrored my tapping signal, then spoke again: "I just wanted to check to see what you were doing, so I'd better be on my way. You tend to get distracted during your lessons, and I'm not helping." With those final words, she shut the door.

After a few seconds of silence, my tutor swiveled his head to peer out the library window. The sky was on fire, red and orange sunset colors streaking across the horizon. "Now, are we going to actually start our lesson, or are we just going to talk in the library all evening?"

—◦—

After the excruciatingly long history lesson, Evander released me out into the hallway. A few guards noticed as I passed through the relatively empty corridors. The sound of echoing voices occasionally pierced the near silence.

It was fall, so the sun had set earlier than usual. The curtains were drawn across the dark windows, so flickering candles and golden chandeliers drenched the hallways with a friendly yellow glow, casting dancing shadows on the walls. Since there were no witnesses, I unclasped my heavy necklace and tucked it into the palm of my hand.

As I turned the corner, a figure melted out of the shadows and snaked toward me. Before I could react, a hand latched onto my wrist. Cyrus's angry face raked me down, making my stomach drop. *Wait. Angry? He isn't wearing a ruby.* My gaze flicked to the necklace he wore. *Why isn't he wearing a ruby?*

"Where. Have. You. Been?" He seethed as he roughly dragging me into the shadows on the far side of the hallway.

"My . . . my lesson went long," I stammered, not used to him expressing anger. "Did something happen?"

His line of sight snapped to my neck, seeing it bare save for the necklace of white pearls. "You like this necklace, don't you?"

I didn't exactly know how to respond. "Yes?"

Without warning, his arm shot forward as he snapped the necklace off my neck. I yelped, startled. He held it in his hand for a few seconds before throwing it on the stone floor. Pearls spilled off of the broken chain and scattered across the hallway.

"Why do you have to be such a disappointment? You never follow any of the emotion edicts." He spotted the gemstone necklace in my hand—the one I was supposed to be wearing—and pried it out of my fingers, brandishing it in front of my face like a weapon. "Just one of these stones costs more than what an average person makes in a year. Having them is a *privilege*. People at the palace have the privilege to get rid of their emotions, but you go around making a mockery of our family. If I didn't know any better, I'd say you were Malopathic!" He spat out the last word like it was a curse. It was, actually.

I didn't have anything to say in my defense, so I stayed silent and hoped the storm would blow over.

Cyrus noticed my silence. "Stop being such a liability. I've arranged a meeting for you with me and the king in the morning. Look your very best—nothing plain or simple like this." He gestured to my dress with disgust. "We expect you to wear nice things, including all the emotion stones that you've been presented with. I'll send Akilah to your room in the morning to make sure your appearance meets my requirements."

"You . . . you have no right to yell at me. I'm a princess." I tried to make my voice sound strong.

"Any member of the court can yell at you as long as the lecture is necessary," he huffed. "Now go to your chambers and *stay* there. *Don't* forget the meeting in the morning," he hissed through clenched teeth.

Cyrus glared as he released my wrist. He stalked across the hallway into an adjacent corridor, out of sight. For a few moments, I stayed frozen. Then I peeled myself off the wall to slink down the hallway, my soft shoes completely silent on the cold marble floor.

CHAPTER
THREE

"Good morning, Your Highness!" exclaimed an annoyingly cheerful voice.

A soft groan escaped me as I rolled over in the soft blankets, burying my face inside the cushion of warmth. Morning light streamed through a crack in my curtains directly onto my face; the brightness seemed determined to drag me out of bed. Akilah marched across my carpet and yanked the curtains open, blasting me with more sunlight. I jerked the blanket over my head and nestled myself into the darkness.

"You're going to have to get up . . . eventually," she said, taking a few of my blankets and neatly folding them.

"I probably won't get up on my own accord, but I suppose your insufferably positive energy will drag me out of bed . . . sooner or later."

Akilah chuckled. She leaped over to my window and grasped at the ribbons, tying the curtains aside and preventing them from swinging shut again. I studied her, admiring how quickly she skimmed over the carpet.

Akilah was fifteen, two years younger than me. She had everlasting energy, with a bounce in every step and a continual melody humming on her lips. She constantly and relentlessly organized things, a skillset I had never picked up on. Even this early in the morning, she wore a meticulously clean red and white trimmed dress—her servant uniform—with her black hair styled in a tight braid down her back. For all the time I had known her, she only wore one stone: sapphires. This solitary stone created a problem. I appreciated having a person around me who could experience happiness and love, but the joy was unnatural. There was no opposite side of the spectrum, just overflowing positivity all the time, turning her personality sickly sweet and somewhat fake.

"Remind me why you're here again?" I asked, pressing my hands against the sides of my head.

"Lord Cyrus and the king want to meet with you this morning, remember? He sent me in to make sure you get ready according to his expectations."

"Yes, that's right. I've been desperately trying to purge that from my memory," I said sarcastically.

Akilah laughed as she hopped over to the side of my bed and gently took my arm. I allowed her to pull me onto my feet again, ignoring the urge to bury myself under the blankets and fall back asleep. She bounded over to my closet and slid it open. "What would you like to wear today?"

She reached into the layers of dresses and pulled out one in particular, holding it out so I could inspect it. It was a dramatic royal blue color, with frills that mimicked ocean waves. It was beautiful, flashy, and expensive, definitely something a princess would wear. In fact, if I were to wear it, I was sure to be the center of everyone's attention.

So, it wasn't an option.

"No. Can I pick something else?"

She grimaced. "Seriously? Do you know how much I would give to wear this dress? Why are you so against flashy clothes?"

Akilah didn't know I was Malopathic, even after knowing me for years, because I couldn't determine how she would react if I told her. We both thought of one another as friends, but I hadn't analyzed exactly how she felt about the emotion stones and the guidelines. She always wore at least one of the stones, just like the rules stated. If I told her, she would probably do what everyone else would do: scream and tell the guards, who would ask the king to arrange my immediate execution.

I bit my lip and brushed my hand over the soft blankets of my bed. Akilah still held the dress out to me hopefully, her eyes begging me to wear it. I sighed. "You were specifically ordered to get me to wear fancy things, right"

"Yes," Akilah answered immediately. "It's part of my job; now, please wear it."

Admitting defeat and a little annoyed, I yanked the dress from her fingers. After I had finished putting it on, with Akilah helping me tie up the back, I twirled around for her to inspect me. The material felt comfy and light, like being wrapped in a cloud. I rubbed my hands against the fabric, touching the smooth, delicate folds.

Akilah quietly clapped. "You look stunning! Do you want me to do your hair?"

Wanting to get this over, I shuffled into the room where my grooming accessories lay, although I rarely used them. Akilah trailed behind me and gently pushed me in front of the mirror before I could change my mind.

She snatched a jewel-encrusted brush and expertly led it through my hair. In an instant, she tied up my hair into a bun. It was simple but elegant and kept the hair out of my eyes. Then she set it in place with two crisscrossing pins that sparkled with diamonds.

"Do you want to wear a necklace or earrings or something?" Then she clapped her hands and exclaimed, "Wait! You have a pearl necklace that you like. How about you wear that? The color would match well with your blue dress."

"Yes, I *did* have a necklace that I liked. However, it was maliciously destroyed about . . ." I thought for a moment before continuing, "I don't know, eight hours ago?"

"Oh. What happened?"

"Cyrus got mad at me; that's what happened."

Akilah cocked her head to the side, confused. "Really? Wasn't he wearing a ruby? He usually does."

"I suspect he *wanted* to get mad at me."

"Really? Who would *want* to be mad at someone?"

You don't understand. I shrugged. "He'll probably say something about it when he meets with me."

When he meets with me, I repeated in my thoughts. *He still hasn't explained the reason behind the requested meeting. Is it going to be very important? Meeting with the king isn't a very normal thing for me. It's too formal. Just . . . try to get through it.*

"Well, if you don't have the pearl necklace, do you want to wear something else? Maybe earrings?"

"No earrings, please," I winced, recalling the day when I thought piercing them was a good idea. "I think I'm ready."

Her eyes swept over me. "You're right. You look like a princess for the first time in your life. Now, go out there and make sure your family doesn't kill you." Her tone of voice meant for it to be a joke, but it was more realistic than she could have known.

"I'll try." I made a beeline for my bedroom door. When I reached toward the necklace stand beside the door, my hand paused. My skin brushed against the cold metal chain as I felt the texture of the metal links. With trembling fingers, I fastened the chain around my neck. My eyes grazed over the hanging jewels: an emerald, sapphire, ruby, and onyx. They were innocent looking and beautiful, yet they had the power to strip someone of what made a person human. I would have to bury my emotions deep inside and pretend they never existed.

I let all of my muscles relax as my breathing became slow and even. The familiar coolness rolled over me like fog settling into a valley. In my head, I repeated the words that were so embedded I would never forget them: *Nobody cares. Nobody pays attention. You are invisible.*

Exhaling, I pushed against the smooth surface of the door and stepped into the hallway.

Both Cyrus and the king wore stone faces as I shuffled into the meeting room. I forced my expression to be passive and empty like theirs. I selected a seat near the door but not so far away as to draw suspicion. I rested my hands underneath the table so they couldn't glimpse my clenching fists. Then I spoke in the most neutral tone I could muster: "You asked to see me, Father?"

"Yes, I did." He nodded his head. "Lord Cyrus and I have something important to discuss with you."

Right to the point. Typical of him, I thought. My father, Kadar, had ruled throughout the entire war, which had taken quite a toll on him. Trying to seek peace with a more established kingdom was quite a discouraging task, one that many diplomats had sworn off years ago. Any flimsy negotiation usually just fell to pieces afterward. Meanwhile, the war continued to drag on as both kingdoms competed for resources the other needed. Our kingdom had access to many mines filled with metals and precious stones, but Tanum was surrounded by the bountiful Northern Forest, land that we desperately needed access to. It was a recipe for a fight that would never end.

Kadar's life had been long and stressful. Even with the help of stones muting his emotions, the worry lines etched onto his face were pronounced, as if drawn with a pencil. Having the war last his entire reign, he had gained a reputation of being direct and straightforward, not wasting any precious time.

Cyrus abruptly started talking, dragging me out of my whirlwind of thoughts. "I'm grateful that you fulfilled all of my expectations with your appearance." He leaned forward to continue. "Syona, as you know, throughout your entire life, you've been mostly detached from the events around you. You're completely oblivious to the rules and customs of our kingdom, and you don't interact with any political affairs. Frankly, you don't act like a princess. I've also accessed your daily schedule, and you have been given no political or diplomatic experience. You have no knowledge concerning the structure of our government or justice system. Clearly, you are not educated, experienced, or qualified for any of the responsibilities you could have."

I dug my fingernails into my arm, the sharp pain distracting me. I desperately tried not to let my anger reflect on my appearance. *Is this it? A lecture on how I could better fulfill my role as a princess? Does this have any importance?*

I voiced my opinion, barely managing to keep the neutral, slightly apathetic tone that all people talked in when the stones nullified every emotion. "Excuse me for interrupting, but what is the purpose of this conversation? Surely you called me here to talk about something other than how I could do better as the princess of Ashlon."

"Fine. In summary, Syona, despite all of these faults that add up to your overall incompetence . . ."

A twinge of annoyance fired up inside of me. *What did he say? Overall incompetence?*

"You are the only one left."

I paused for a few seconds, choosing my words carefully. "What do you mean by *the only one left?*"

"The only *heir* left. We got the news last night. Your brother, Prince Davin, was in an accident while hunting in the Southern Forest. The details are sketchy, but it was sunset and very dark. Apparently, one of the other noblemen accidentally shot him with an arrow when they mistook him for a doe. They tried to save him, but he died shortly after."

"What?" I cleared my throat and tried again. "Could you please repeat that?"

Cyrus placed his hands on the table and glanced over at his brother before proceeding. "Prince Davin is dead. Which means . . . you are the sole heir to the kingdom of Ashlon."

I felt tears at the back of my eyes, and I strained to rein them in. I was going to lose it. Hot tears were going to spill down my face in plain view, right in front of the king and Cyrus. There couldn't have been a more sure-fire way to get myself executed.

Davin is dead . . . my brother, my protector, Davin? I refused to believe it. Complicated emotions churned violently inside of me, not only because of Davin's death but also because of the knowledge that I was now crown princess. I would be the center of everyone's focus, not to mention that I would have to consistently wear the stones and follow the emotion guidelines to the letter. I wouldn't last a day, not in those conditions. The cold air in the room suddenly pressed down on me, making me feel vulnerable and exposed.

Say something. I pleaded with myself. *Say something, anything! Just open your mouth and break the silence.*

"What will my new responsibilities include?" I managed to choke out.

Cyrus stared straight at me, his direct eye contact making the situation a thousand times worse. "Naturally, political lessons and diplomatic protocols will be immediately added to your learning curriculum. You also need hands-on experience, so you will be accompanying your father to all of the diplomatic meetings and court cases. Also, I will be asking Akilah to get rid of all of your plain and unadorned dresses. You are soon to be the crown heir. Act like it."

"Would you mind telling me when all of these changes will be implemented?" I whispered.

"In one week," he immediately answered. "When we announce Davin's death and your official recognition as the crown heir."

"Is there anything else?" My throat was completely dry.

The king shook his head. "No. You are dismissed."

"Thank you." I brushed my cold, tingling fingers against the back of the chair as I unsteadily rose. Before my expression could break, I quickly spun around and walked as steadily as I could toward the door.

"We expect great things from you, Syona," the king called out. "Don't disappoint us."

I didn't respond. I didn't even turn around. I grasped the doorknob, my sweaty fingers slipping against the metal a couple of times until I could twist it. I exited the room as fast as I could.

I found myself in a shadowy, deserted hallway. I frantically surveyed my surroundings to ensure the emptiness was real; there was no soul in sight. I resumed my heavy breathing, my mind reeling from the news. My thoughts sped down a river, plunged over a waterfall, and splashed into a pool of future scenarios, drowning in the unknown.

Davin is dead. I am now the heir of Ashlon.

My brain unearthed the teaching Mareena had offered over the years, lessons on remaining emotionless and invisible. I had formed them into a familiar refrain: *Nobody cares. Nobody pays attention. You are invisible.*

But then a fresh realization arose: *Not anymore.*

The tears were back, threatening to spill down my cheeks and drip onto the marble. I pressed my back against the wall, sliding into the shadows. Nobody could see me. Now I could display my true feelings.

Wait. No, Syona, emotion is not allowed in the kingdom of Ashlon.

I ignored those thoughts as I sank to the cold stone floor, wrapped my hands around my face, and sobbed.

FOUR

A week of sapphires. A week of sapphires was all the recognition my brother received. No funeral. Very few people did funerals, and most considered them a waste of time and productivity. Wearing sapphires was a much better way to get over any grief—if you were sad about someone's death in the first place.

I cried in my room for the entire week as it was the only safe place to do so. There, I could safely manifest my emotions and eventually dispose of them.

The kingdom of Ashlon took Davin's death well. The people hadn't been worried. They had known the entire time that if something unfortunate were to happen to him, I would be there to take his place. Life passed by in a blur, but I didn't care anymore. I let them do whatever they wanted to me.

"Syona?" a muffled voice asked through my door, a voice I recognized as Akilah's.

I jolted awake, not realizing I had fallen asleep on my bed. My tears had wet the blankets near my head, so I immediately folded some loose fabric over the wet spots to hide them. It was late, several hours after the special celebratory dinner where I had recited some pre-written oaths and read a bunch of legal documents that I could hardly understand. It had been a draining day, and I somewhat recalled stumbling to my bed and passing out shortly afterward.

"Syona? Are you asleep?" she continued.

"I was," I mumbled into the blankets.

"I just wanted to check on you to see if you're okay. You haven't been yourself for the past few weeks." She paused, knocking on the door. "Can I come in?"

"No," I grumbled.

"You've been rather isolated, though. Are you sure you don't want some company?" she persisted.

It was useless trying to shoo her away, so I gave up. I dragged myself off the bed and moved to open the door. Akilah stepped into my room and looked at me with an unsure smile. "Do you . . . need anything?"

"No. I think I'm just going to go outside." I snatched one of the blankets off of my bed and flung it around my shoulders, letting it drag on the floor behind me.

"*Outside?* Outside where?" she asked.

"Out of the palace," I replied, choosing to be vague. "Anywhere other than here."

"You're going out into the kingdom? Really?"

I shrugged, wrapping the blanket tightly around me. "Why not? It shouldn't be upsetting. I'm just going for a walk."

"But you're going out at night! Unsupervised! Anything could happen! Aren't you worried you'll get hurt?" Akilah exclaimed.

I snorted. "Not really. I don't think anybody would dare do something to me. The common people have good relations with the royal family because we supply and regulate the trade of emotion stones. Anyone who isn't stupid would think twice before laying a finger on me, and nobody will know I'm the princess anyway."

Akilah stubbornly continued, "I just think that—"

"Is there a problem here?" a commanding voice rang out.

I recognized the voice immediately: Gerrand, Officer Raynott, whatever I had to call him. Of course it was him. The captain of the guard had assigned him to me personally, partially because he had lived in the palace for his entire life and also because we knew each other when we were younger. We saw each other every day of our lives, treating ourselves to the occasional conversation. He was always nice to me and could have been a friend, or something more, under different circumstances.

There was a problem, though—six problems, to be exact, now dangled on a silver chain around his neck in plain view. A year ago, Gerrand had turned eighteen and received his love-sucking stone; the friendly interactions had stopped. To make it worse, he was a guard now. Guards were required to wear all six stones. It was much safer if they didn't struggle with tricky moral decisions when fighting, everyone reasoned.

I pivoted around and came face to face with Gerrand. My eyes examined every detail of his expression, though I didn't want to. His hand was already on his knife, anticipating the time when he would have to protect someone. The worst thing about him was his eyes. His beautiful caramel-colored eyes had no life inside them anymore. Everything about him was without feeling and inhuman. I hated it. I wanted to know what he was really like, but that wasn't going to happen anytime soon.

Akilah immediately faced him. "Yes! There's a problem. The princess wants to go outside the palace at night. On a walk! It's not a very smart decision." She turned to me sheepishly and added, "If you don't mind me saying so."

"If you want to go so badly, it would be my duty to accompany you," Gerrand replied. "You should have more than one escort, though. If you could—"

My teeth clenched tightly, but I snapped my eyes shut and tried to regulate my breathing. "No. Only you, if I must have someone following me around."

"Wait! Before you go . . ." Akilah shot into my room and returned a few seconds later with a black cloak. "At least wear this. It'll keep you warm, and you'll be less noticeable."

I sighed in defeat. I let the blanket fall to the floor as I wrapped the cloak around me instead, fastening it in the front. I stole a glance at Akilah, who looked pleased with herself, and I couldn't help but roll my eyes. "Don't expect me to be back anytime soon."

"Fair enough," she muttered under her breath.

I took off down the hallway with Gerrand in tow behind me.

———

The crisp air enveloped me as soon as I stepped outside. By the moonlight, I could observe my breath pluming from my mouth. I wrapped the cloak around me and admitted to myself that it *did* help combat the freezing temperature.

As I paced down the streets, I tried to recall the layout of the palace city, which my tutor had taught me only a day before. Homes of nobility and guards surrounded the main palace in a circle. Beyond that, a large stone wall bordered the city. Outside of the wall was farmland and other small towns and villages where most of the commoners lived. The organization was practical, everything important was placed in the center of the kingdom.

Though the sun had set hours before, people still lingered in the streets. Nobody paid me any notice as I passed by. I aimlessly wandered around the buildings with my thoughts as scattered as my sense of direction. I just wanted to clear my head and momentarily forget about everything that had happened. I kept breathing in the crisp air, hoping it would clear my head. I despised being the center of attention, but the only way to fix that was to have Davin back. I wanted to fade into the background again.

Because I was lost in my thoughts, I didn't notice the building in front of me until I slammed into it. I stumbled backward, almost falling to the cobblestones. Gerrand instantly appeared at my side, grabbing my hand and pulling me back to a vertical position. I gingerly rubbed my aching forehead. *How embarrassing. At least I don't have to worry about Gerrand judging me.*

"Are you okay?" His question wasn't based on concern. It was instinctive. Making sure the princess was in perfect condition at all times was obligatory, and it sliced my heart to pieces.

I wanted to snap something back in reply, but I bit my lip and mumbled, "I'm fine."

"Just checking," he replied in an even tone. Several of his stones flashed in the darkness—something that happened when someone felt emotion strongly—but they flickered so quickly that I couldn't decipher which ones.

I swiveled my head upward to observe the open night sky. No clouds were in sight, giving the moon full range over the darkness and lighting up my field of vision like a white sun. It shone like a silver disk, brilliant and illuminating in the darkness. An army of bright, twinkling stars flanked the metallic orb, carpeting over the night sky like a blanket. It was the most stunning thing in the world and the biggest reason why I liked to walk in the dark. The glimmering stars kept me company. I felt as if I could reach out my hand and brush against the velvety darkness, losing myself in it forever.

Before I could talk myself out of it, I reached upward toward the stars and splayed my fingers outward, drinking in the moonlight. I closed my eyes and tried to forget myself. For a few precious seconds, I sought refuge in the pristine night sky.

Gerrand's gaze flicked upward, staring at the sky with me. He seemed confused as to why I reached upward, but in his current state, he wouldn't be able to comprehend anything even remotely sentimental.

He cleared his throat. "Princess? We should probably return to the palace. It's already been an hour, and I don't want to worry anyone."

I sighed, retreating from the dome of stars above me. "I agree."

I scurried back toward the palace, relying on my horrid sense of direction. My shoes didn't noisily scrape across the stones like everyone else's. I was completely silent. I relished the feeling any time I could slip through a crowd unnoticed or pass right under the gazes of my family completely undetected.

I discreetly glanced at Gerrand, who plainly strolled among the crowd. He mingled with others like any normal person would do, whereas I stuck to the sides of buildings and crept among the shadows. He was a people person. I was not. He had always involved himself in other people's lives and tried to help, but after he received the stones, those simple actions turned to obligation instead of kindness.

We could go back to that. He could care about me again, not just because of his position or duty. If he didn't always wear the stones, I'm sure we'd be able to express ourselves. If I'm really thinking unrealistically *. . . maybe we could even develop a relationship again.*

But he won't. He can't.

Not if he's required to wear that cursed necklace.

CHAPTER
FIVE

Akilah greeted me the next morning by bursting in and flinging herself onto my mattress. Good thing I was already out of bed and standing on the other side of the room. "I still can't believe this is what you sleep on every night." She swept her hand over the silky blankets, curling her fingers into the fabric. "It's amazing!"

Then, she suddenly bolted upright, startling me. "So. What are you doing today?"

I snatched a brush off my desk and frantically started combing through my hair. I attacked the tangles, wincing as the bristles of the brush hit the knots, struggling but failing to get them out. I would have to try something else. I broke away from the mirror and faced Akilah behind me. "The king is having another, probably unsuccessful, round of negotiations with the king of Tanum. He's actually coming to the palace again. I'm supposed to sit in the back and watch them argue and intimidate each other over how many guards they bring . . . as if somehow that'll make me learn something about politics."

"If the negotiations are almost always unsuccessful, why do they keep doing them?" Akilah asked.

"I think both kings are using them as an excuse to continue the peace. We haven't had any actual fighting in almost two years. Anyway, the meeting is going to start in . . . I don't know. I lost track of time. Soon."

"Ooh. How exciting."

My fingers closed around the handle of a comb with stiffer bristles. "Are you being sarcastic?"

"I haven't decided yet."

I chuckled to myself as I ran the comb through my hair again, determined to get the knots out. After hacking at the tangles for a few more minutes, I finally managed to get rid of most of them. I weaved my fingers through the brown strands, checking to see if it was truly tangle free before I raced back to my bed.

"How do I look?" I asked, flipping my hair over my shoulders so she could inspect it.

"Like a princess," Akilah answered, leaping off the bed. "What are you going to wear? I think you should wear this." She picked up an emerald-colored dress. The fabric was entirely green except for golden, diagonal slashes on the forearms of the sleeves. The light green and gold matched well together, so after thinking for a moment, I took it from her hands.

Akilah shook her head. "I don't get it. Why do you always wear dresses with sleeves?"

"I don't know. Without them, I feel . . ." *Exposed. Vulnerable. Defenseless.* "Cold. I get cold really easily."

She laughed. "Well, the winter months are starting soon. Here . . ." She pulled the dress, which dangled limply from my fingertips, away from me. "Let me help you get ready. Are you sure you don't want to wear any earrings today?"

I earned double takes from people wandering in the corridors, but I moved too quickly for them to dare stop and force me into a conversation. Those stares were well deserved, though. I wore a much brighter color than I ever had before and earrings for the first time in maybe a year. Akilah hadn't let me leave without them. She had selected a pair of golden, leaf-shaped ones, which had condemned me, along with my green dress, to look like some kind of nature advocate.

I slid across the smooth stone, following the crowd to the throne room where the meeting would take place. The wooden doors were already open to let everyone invited come inside. Taking a few seconds to compose myself, I tried to record which stones I was wearing as knowing the specific emotions I had to bury made it a little easier to keep my thoughts straight. I had a ruby, for anger. Though I wasn't participating, the king required all the attendees of diplomatic meetings to wear one. I had onyx for fear and a sapphire to eradicate sadness. Since they stole negative emotions, I could handle faking their effects. I was in a pretty good mood today.

I slowly walked underneath the stone archway into the throne room. The room was covered in marble, and the white color reflected light from every angle. A golden chandelier hung from the ceiling, glowing with warm light that contrasted with the white light flooding in from the windows. The wooden throne was located near the back of the room, polished and a darker color to offset the white.

The room held over a dozen people already. I picked out the king and Cyrus conversing with a person I didn't recognize. Gerrand's father, Aidyn, stood beside them, eavesdropping on what they were saying. A few ambassadors from our kingdom were scattered throughout the room, but I couldn't name them. Guards from both kingdoms lined themselves against the wall and at the door. A few other nobles looked familiar to me, but the rest were strangers. They must have arrived from the kingdom of Tanum.

I inched closer to the king and Cyrus, peering at the man they were conversing with. Who was so important as to demand the attention of the king and his closest advisor? I noticed that he *did* stand out from everyone else. He carried himself taller. The man didn't wear any expensive jewelry, but he exhibited an air of authority and power that was extremely familiar to me. He didn't wear a crown or anything obvious to indicate his standing, which threw me off, but he was definitely Raymon Westbay, the king of Tanum.

I tried to shuffle closer to the wall, scanning for a spot where I could stand and quietly listen. My instincts still screamed at me to not draw attention to myself. However, as soon as I attempted to move, all three men glanced over at me. Any self-confidence I had gained immediately wilted under the combined pressure of their gazes. I felt myself shrinking backward, yearning to press myself against the wall and stay there.

Kadar instantly pointed me out before I could escape back to anonymity. "Let me introduce you to my only child, Syona. She's the princess of Ashlon and my crown heir."

I almost winced at the words *only child.* The memory of Davin's death was still fresh in my mind, but I managed an awkward curtsy. *Can you stop staring at me, please? I would appreciate it.*

King Raymon strolled over to me and bowed deeply. "Your Royal Highness, I believe we haven't had the chance to make one another's acquaintance."

I cracked a smile. I certainly liked his friendly and open attitude. The people from the kingdom of Tanum didn't use the emotion stones as we did. They behaved like normal human beings, showing their feelings and expressing themselves freely. The king's face was not a maze of wrinkles and lines like my father's. He seemed relaxed and easygoing, and I suddenly felt awkward next to him with my rigid, anxious outlook on life. Now that he was closer to me, I noticed that he *did* wear jewelry—a simple chain necklace without any attachments. As far as I could tell, it served no purpose, but it was simple, and I liked that. He was royalty, but he had the sense not to flaunt it like everybody else did.

As he mimicked my smile, I clasped my hands in front of me and bowed my head slightly. "Thank you. You are most kind."

Kadar continued speaking, addressing everybody in the room. "The princess is here to observe our proceedings to become familiar with the political affairs between our two kingdoms since she will manage these negotiations when the throne passes down to her."

A bolt of lightning flashed down my spine, freezing me to the floor. I had been so absorbed in the present moment, trying to survive until the next day, I had completely forgotten that if I *did* escape execution, I would be ruling the kingdom of Ashlon *as queen*. I panicked inside. Davin was supposed to do that, not me. He was the perfect prince and would have molded easily into his position. He was supposed to become king. I should have remained a shadow, unnoticed and unseen.

"As I said, she will only be observing," he repeated, shooting a glance at me. His voice was calm, but it was meant to be a threat. "I promise she will not interfere with anything we're doing today."

I pressed myself against the wall into the largest shadow I could find, and everyone's gazes mercifully left me a second later. I relaxed. This was where I was supposed to be, passively studying and not involving myself in anything.

After the meeting officially got started, I discovered it was a complete waste of time. Nobody argued, of course, because of the rubies. The absence of anger disturbed me because of the importance of the meeting, but none of the talking helped. King Raymon wanted to share our mines filled with ore, and King Kadar wanted access to the rivers and lakes of the Northern Territory. None of the ambassadors or officials could agree on common ground. Many legal documents were sourced and read, but it didn't help much. It wasn't negotiating as much as it was making childish remarks over why each kingdom deserved the land more.

After about an hour, they had accomplished absolutely nothing except another round of empty promises of a peaceful solution. As the meeting dissolved, the diplomats from Tanum spoke in tense voices instead of shouting. Kadar announced that another negotiation would take place in a month, and the people from Tanum agreed.

I almost slid down to the floor, but I decided against it. The entire ordeal had worn me out. I had attempted to pay attention to their style of speaking, their arguments—although they weren't actually arguing—and the conducts and laws they had referenced. I filed all of that information into my brain and prayed I would remember it.

As final words were exchanged and the visitors streamed out of the throne room, King Raymon suddenly paused in the doorway and stared at me. "How old are you?"

"I'm . . . seventeen. I'll be eighteen in about four months," I choked out.

He nodded and strolled out into the hallway with the last of the officials trailing behind him.

All of my muscles relaxed, and this time, I really did slide down to the floor. I was done. I had no more responsibilities for the rest of the day. I wanted to rest there forever, but Cyrus slithered over to me. "A princess should not be *lying on the floor*."

I hastily climbed back to my feet. "I apologize. May I go now?"

He held my attention for a few more seconds before nodding. "Yes. You are dismissed, but there's one more thing you need to know. We are having a special celebratory dinner tomorrow. Everyone important is expected to be there, especially you."

The words had hardly left his mouth before I dashed out into the hallway. I didn't care that I had another responsibility added to my pile. I would probably stress and worry about it tonight, but for now, I would be okay. For a few hours, I would be free.

I immediately retreated to my room. It was sunny, and I always had plenty of space. The light brown walls soothed my emotions, and I could spend hours there with my thoughts. I could freely express myself because nobody could come in without my permission.

I pressed my fingers against the wooden door and gently pushed it open to see Akilah sitting cross-legged in the center of my bed.

I placed my hands on my hips. "What are you doing?"

Her voice sounded quiet but playful, "I let myself in."

I shot her a disappointed look, and she threw her hands up in defense. "What? Wouldn't you let me inside your room anyway? I'm your personal servant, which means I have a free range of anything inside your room as long as I have a reason to be here."

"Fine. What reason do you have to be in here?"

Akilah reached behind her back and produced a small cream-colored box, the size of her hand. The box had been marked with a flower petal design, which added a touch of elegance to its appearance. "I found this on your bed."

"Did you open it?"

She raised her eyebrows, her mouth falling open in overexaggerated shock. "What? No! I would never do such a thing! Never!"

I chuckled to myself as I sat down next to her. I took the box from her hands, flipping it over. "Do you know who it's from?"

She shrugged. "How should I know? No note was attached."

I gently opened the lid of the box. Nestled among velvet was a white pearl necklace glowing against the contrast of the red color. I gingerly lifted it out of the box and inspected it. The pearls were small, expertly strung, opaque and shining in the light.

Akilah gasped. "Oh, wow. Someone gave you a pearl necklace. Do you know how expensive those are? Who do you think it was? Are they replacing the one that Lord Cyrus destroyed?"

My hands brushed over the smooth pearls, and that's when I realized something. They weren't new. They were worn, a little misshapen as if touched many times before. "They aren't replacing the one that Cyrus destroyed. This *is* the one Cyrus destroyed." I studied it again, lifting it to my eye level. "This is *my* necklace."

Akilah tilted her head. "It is? That's even sweeter! To repair that necklace, someone would have to gather every individual pearl and then string it together for you again, and they were scattered all over the hallway. That must have taken forever."

"I suppose." I shrugged, staring down at the empty box. "But there isn't a note attached, so I have no clue who gave it to me."

I passed the box to Akilah and stood up, traversing the room to take off my earrings. I didn't want to wear them anymore. I paused in front of the mirror, squinting hard against the semi-darkness.

"Syona?"

I glanced over at her. "Yes?"

"I found something," she announced, her eyes twinkling.

"Did you?" I dropped the necklace on the counter. Pacing back to the bed, I took the box from her again, peering at what she wanted me to see. She had peeled away the bit of velvet that the necklace had been lying on, revealing a folded piece of paper. I slid the folded note out from underneath the velvet and unfolded it.

Words were scrawled across the page, messy but readable:

I believe this is yours. It seems to be your favorite necklace, so I took the liberty of repairing it for you. The jeweler did a good job, but if it's not up to your standards, I can find a better one.

—Officer Raynott

"Hmm . . . That's nice of him to do something like that," Akilah remarked.

I scoffed at her. "Do you really think so? It's a formality. He felt obligated to do that for me."

She shrugged. "Maybe, but it was a cool gesture. Maybe he likes you somehow."

I winced. *I would like that. I would like that more than anything in the world, but it can't happen.*

"Have you forgotten that he's a guard?" I snapped back. "He has his amber stone, and he's required to wear it at all times. It is biologically impossible for him to love me. Do you understand?"

She laid down, sprawling herself across the bed. "Okay. I guess it would be somewhat impossible for him to actually like you. He's a guard, too, so it would be bad, but it was still kind of him to—"

I exhaled angrily. "Why must you talk about this? Why are you suggesting the possibility of someone liking me? Don't you think emotion is a curse? Doesn't everyone in this kingdom think emotion is a curse? Love is dangerous. Sadness is a burden. Anger causes conflict. Fear is for the weak. Don't you believe that propaganda? Isn't that why people wear these stones?"

I continued ranting as I paced along my room in front of Akilah. "Especially the amber stones, those cursed amber stones. Love: the most dangerous one of all." When I said those words, my voice became high and mocking. "It's ridiculous! Can't we develop relationships with one another? That's impossible if nobody can love. So, no. Gerrand does not like me. He will never like me, and our connection will never be anything but formal. Now, shut up about it."

Akilah sat silently, her mouth agape. Her expression didn't portray sadness as a normal person would feel at that moment. Maybe it was anger or shock? I immediately looked down, frightened that I had exposed my secret. Seeing my neck bare, I breathed a quiet sigh of relief. I had remembered to take my necklace off when I came into my room. I hadn't completely given myself away. At least not yet.

"Is that really how you feel?" Akilah questioned, her voice woven with tension. "That we should have emotions? I mean, I know that you bend the emotion guidelines all the time and that you don't take it seriously, but I didn't think you didn't believe in them."

I blanched. *Had I doomed myself? Was Akilah going to find me out? What would she do?*

Her brightened demeanor dropped ever so slightly. "Are you a—"

"Stop talking now," I snapped, interrupting her. "I'm just a princess who's used to being invisible and spreads unpopular opinions all over the place." I studied Akilah's face, shaking my head. "Now, get out . . . please."

Akilah leaped spritely off the bed and fled straight out of my room, refusing to make eye contact with me.

I sat back down on my bed and tried to unclench my fists. Bursts of anger shot through me. I felt annoyance at myself for letting my emotions loose again and because I had snapped at Akilah, one of my only friends. Even though she would never hold anything against me, I still regretted yelling at her. The stress of this world became painfully apparent once more. I was trapped. This palace was a cage built especially for me, and it had harmed me so many times I could hardly feel anything anymore.

My eyes closed. I tried but failed to hold back my tears.

CHAPTER
SIX

I got ready for dinner by myself. Akilah had been avoiding me the entire day, which was weird for her. Usually, when a person got in a fight, they just wore a ruby for a while until they got over it. *Does Akilah even own a ruby? She's supposed to have one, but I've never seen her wear it.*

Getting ready was an ingrained routine. I brushed my hair, leaving it down for the time being. I wanted to wear my usual colors, red and black. Unfortunately, all my regular dresses of that color were too plain for Cyrus's liking, so he had pruned away most of them. One of the new dresses was scarlet colored with swaths of orange fabric layered into the red like fire. It was a little dramatic, but it would have to do.

Shuffling out my bedroom door, I snatched my black shawl off of a hook and slung it over myself. I didn't care if someone would reprimand me for it. I felt exposed, and I wanted to put a few layers between myself and my family. I also hastily grabbed my necklace of emotion stones, meaning to fasten it on when I arrived at the dining hall. I didn't know what we were celebrating exactly, but I was sure that they would announce it when everyone arrived.

The king had sent me the guest list a couple of hours beforehand, and I ran through it in my head a couple of times to memorize it. The usual people would attend: the royal family, the court of nobles, a couple of ambassadors who I would probably recognize, and half a dozen other guards. Gerrand, thankfully, was not one of them. Everything was too awkward with him.

The extravagance of the dining hall greeted me when I arrived. Stained glass windows flooded the room with familiar light. A long wooden table stretched to the very end of the hall, accompanied by several adorned chairs. A sparkling chandelier hung from the center of the high ceiling, and the light reflected off the dangling crystals like a shining miniature sun.

As I entered, many of the people in the room approached me and greeted me with proper titles like *Crowned Princess Syona* and *Your Royal Highness*. My response was always a passive nod or a curtsy. After that, they would usually leave me alone and return to the person they were originally conversing with.

Everyone waited for another couple of minutes, not wanting to appear improper by sitting down before the king arrived. I could tell that some of the guests were starting to get restless. Some stole glances at their assigned seat but then resumed their conversation so they wouldn't appear impatient or rude. I, too, played with the folds of my dress and studied the room to amuse myself.

Then, ten minutes after the event was supposed to start, Kadar suddenly appeared at the door. Everyone simultaneously turned to face him, conversation withering away. King Kadar appeared more official than normal. He wore his crown, something he hadn't done in months, a solid gold object inlaid with precious stones. Mostly made of onyx and rubies, it glittered sharply in the light. He also wore a silky black cape that dragged on the ground; it was fastened by the same brooch Davin used to wear.

He clapped his hands, shattering the stiff silence. "I apologize for the delay, everyone. My advisors insisted that I should be outfitted traditionally for this celebration, considering how ceremonious this event is. You may all be seated."

I slid into the nearest chair, not bothering to check if they had assigned it to someone else. I watched as the king strode into the room, with Cyrus and Mareena trailing behind him. My eyes immediately flicked to everyone's neck. Kadar wore all of the stones except a crystal, which was typical of him. Cyrus's necklace had the usual: sadness, love, and anger. I rested in my seat a little easier, knowing that he couldn't experience anger and that nothing dramatic would happen. His dark eyes were blank slates, normal.

Mareena looked particularly nice that evening. She wore a light lavender dress with flecks of white, which mimicked snowflakes, scattered on the sleeves and the hem of the dress. She had woven her brown hair into an intricate braid without the help of a servant. She did everything herself, and I admired her for that.

Her eyes immediately picked me out from the crowded room. She sent me a small smile, then refocused her attention on the king. A smile, no finger tapping, so she wasn't afraid to show happiness. I glanced down at her neck and saw a single sapphire threaded onto a silver chain, only one stone. As the king's sister-in-law, she wasn't technically royalty or bound by the same rules I was. She could get away with wearing only one stone to important gatherings—nothing like the burden I had to carry daily.

Like usual, she sat beside me at the table but kept her mouth shut. We had to wait until everyone finished their official announcements. Then, we could freely speak to one another. That's how the king set up all formal dinners. I entertained myself by subtly playing with the tablecloth and trying in vain to calm down. I would have to behave myself and keep my composure as best I could.

The king traversed the room and sat down at the head of the table, capturing everyone's attention. Nobody made a sound, waiting for him to state the motive behind this celebration. He pounced right into protocol, not wasting another second of his precious time. "Thank you for coming. I have checked that everyone on the guest list is, in fact, present, and we can start with the official announcements and reports."

I tried to calm myself by breathing. It wasn't such a big deal. I had gone to these formal dinners before, and usually they weren't much of a problem.

"First of all, I want to assure you that our negotiations with the kingdom of Tanum are going well. They have not encroached on any of our mines, and they have not invaded our territory. Of course, as long as we keep having scheduled negotiations with King Raymon, the cease-fire will continue. We are trying our hardest to end this fighting with diplomacy instead of violence."

Mareena and I, the only ones present who had access to the emotion of fear, breathed discreet sighs of relief.

The king continued, "After the food is served, Officer Hazen will explain the motive behind this celebration." He gestured to a man who stood in the back of the room. I briefly wondered what he was going to announce before my mind drifted to other thoughts.

A small handful of servants carried platters of steaming food out of the kitchen and into the dining area. The smell was intoxicating, but I didn't feel hungry. I was a bundle of nerves. Mareena probably read my expression because she sent me another encouraging smile. The servants set down the platters of food and quickly disappeared back into the corridors to the kitchen.

The food, as always, was highly decorated and visually pleasing. The servants set an entire roasted chicken in the center of the table. Plates of fruit and vegetables had been arranged in colorful geometric designs. The little farmland that we had acquired from our area of the peninsula was mostly infertile, the soil stripped of its nutrients, so food from plants was hard to come by. Meals were mostly meat and animal products. This one was no different.

After they had laid the food out, Officer Hazen pushed away from the wall and positioned himself beside the king. Most of the people seated at the table were probably hungry, but they couldn't eat until all of the announcements were given. This was an honored tradition but one I had long thought of as impractical.

"Hello, everyone. I am Officer Hazen of the Ashlon Royal Guard. Most of you have probably not seen me before, but I direct all of the officers at the palace. We are in charge of the defense of the kingdom and indirectly responsible for carrying out all public sentences.

"A few moments ago, our beloved king referenced the war with the kingdom of Tanum, but I am here to discuss the more hidden war, the war that started almost thirty years ago as well, the more discrete war that has been fought within our people. It's the battle we don't often speak of: the war against the Malopaths."

The breath caught in my throat. My blood froze inside of me. I clenched my teeth and tried to calm my expression, but my thoughts raged. My hands shook, but I kept them under the table so nobody would see them. I became painfully aware of my heartbeat drumming in my ears, a steady accompaniment to the humming from the stones.

My eyes flickered to Mareena, who, honestly, I couldn't read. I studied her neutral expression, searching for clues that weren't there. She lazily glanced at Officer Hazen, just like everybody else seated at the table, and managed an even, apathetic expression. She was master of her emotions, and I envied her. Having more experience, she didn't struggle as I did.

I ended up squeezing my eyes shut, praying he would finish speaking soon and hoping I wouldn't lose control of my emotions in front of everyone important.

Officer Hazen's voice became distant, and I tried to refocus on what he was saying: "Malopaths are a plague on society. They are a danger to the people and the kingdom of Ashlon. Uncontrolled emotions are menacing, and they should be feared."

Most Malopaths are just lucky to be alive. They hide, never knowing if they'll live another day. You can't kill someone for that. You're the monsters, I thought angrily.

I reached across the table and clutched the glass in front of me, hoping that touching something would help my nerves. It was already filled with water, so I shakily lifted the glass off of the table and tilted it to my mouth.

"I am overjoyed to report that the Malopathic population is at an all-time low. I estimate that there are less than fifty left, with hundreds more in our prisons awaiting immediate execution tomorrow."

I choked on my water, almost spitting it all over the table. The droplets spilled all over the front of my dress. I hurriedly placed the glass back on the table and took some deep breaths. I snatched up my napkin, trying to wipe some of the water off of the fabric, mumbling a quiet, "Sorry."

Cyrus immediately pounced on the opportunity. "Syona, are you alright?" He asked with fake concern. "Why did you react that way to the happy news?" I followed his gaze down to my neck where five glittering stones were dangling on a silver chain—stones that were supposed to mute my emotions.

"She choked on her water," Mareena piped up, defending me. "That's all. It's not that weird."

"But it was in response to—"

"Officer Hazen, please continue your announcement," Mareena sternly ordered. She didn't dare glance my way.

The guard looked a little flustered, confused by the commotion. He rocked on his heels, wringing his hands together. "As I was saying . . ."

Cyrus had the weirdest expression on his face. I honestly couldn't tell what he thought. Was he figuring me out? He was probably smart enough to. He had always been suspicious of my true nature. I cringed, wanting to shrink away and become invisible.

"Excuse me," he said, standing without waiting for any response. He slunk behind the seated guests, keeping his vision fixed on the door and giving no clue as to his abrupt exit.

His pace slowed as he approached my seat, mere inches away from me. His dark eyes grazed over me, reflecting a piercing quality that would be impossible to portray without emotion. I could have sworn that his eyes were filled with anger.

That kept my attention for only a moment before I noticed a sheeny glint reflecting off of something he held in his hand. What was it? A blade of some sort? *Why would he be carrying that?*

His next few movements were so catlike, so subtle. He stepped close enough to be only a few inches away from me; then he flicked his hand carrying the blade, carefully keeping it under the table to obscure his actions.

He dragged the knife across the back of my hand.

CHAPTER
SEVEN

I started screaming, the sound of my frantic voice piercing my ears. It was an instinctive reaction, but one that betrayed all of the churning emotions inside of me, especially the fear that was supposed to be nullified by the onyx stone around my neck. I jumped out of my seat and stumbled backward, hitting the wall as I stared at my hand in shock.

Everyone seated at the table slowly turned their heads toward the source of the screaming, studying me with passive expressions. A few exhibited mild interest, but most were bored. *Statues. I'm the only living thing in a room full of statues,* my thoughts flashed. *Isn't anyone even remotely worried? Doesn't anyone care?* My vision blurred as I sank to the floor, gingerly clutching my hand. *What have we allowed the stones to do to us?*

The muscles in my fingers were limp. I couldn't move them if I tried, and I didn't think I wanted to. Searing waves of pain raced across my skin. The cut slashed from my knuckles to my wrist and bled profusely. I didn't know how deep the cut was, but it hurt like someone had heated a blade until scalding hot and then pressed it across my skin. My blood pounded in my ears and rushed through me, a sharp contrast to the frozen room around me.

Mareena moved first, darting out of her seat to my side. She snatched at my necklace and snapped the chain, scattering the jewels across the carpet. *She's probably trying to make sure I have an excuse for showing my emotions. That'll work from this point onward, yes, but they have evidence against me now. I screamed a few moments ago while still wearing the stones. Everyone heard it. There's no getting over that.* I could hardly contemplate the trouble I had gotten myself into.

She pulled out a handkerchief and pressed it against my hand to staunch the bleeding. "I'm here for you, okay? Just breathe. Breathe," she whispered. Then she twisted her head, glaring at Cyrus. Her voice leapt in volume as she spat, "What was *that for*, you cursed—"

"Silence, Mareena, I recommend that you wear a ruby to palace gatherings like the rest of us." Kadar's voice rang out through the room. Though neutral toned as ever, it commanded respect. "What happened here?"

I studied Cyrus who stood frozen next to me. My line of sight dropped down to his hand. He indeed carried a knife tainted with blood. His blank expression gave nothing away. Anger sliced through me, and I tried to choke out a few accusing words. "Cyrus cut . . ."

"Let me rephrase myself," the king interrupted again, facing his brother. "*Why* did this happen?"

Cyrus gilded forward and immediately responded, his words wrapped in silk. "My knife wasn't as clean as it could have been. I found it undesirable to use for eating." He held the blade in front of him for everyone to inspect. "I was walking to the kitchen to switch it out for a different one when I lost my footing for a moment and just happened to harm the princess."

Liar, I thought, *you deliberately flicked the knife and dragged it across my hand. You did it on purpose.*

"Why didn't you just alert the servants and let them switch it out for you?" Kadar asked.

"I didn't want to bother them, and they had all left after the announcements started. I thought it would be more efficient if I just did it myself."

The king's gaze lingered on his brother for a few more seconds before he glanced at Officer Hazen, still standing beside him. "Go get her a pain stone and try to find someone with medical expertise."

My stomach twisted. *No. Please don't give me a crystal. I'll be better without it.*

Mareena swore under her breath and clutched me tighter. My heart thrashed around so rapidly I thought it would explode. Black spots danced in my vision, and the room started spinning.

As I cringed again from pain, I observed the seated guests. They still stared with remarkably unconcerned expressions, which irritated me further because I was just seconds away from hyperventilating.

Officer Hazen burst into the room with a crystal strung onto a silver chain dangling from his hand. He promptly dropped it around my neck and rushed out the door again. Besides the quiet humming that accompanied the cacophony of sounds already around me, the stone did absolutely nothing. My hand still throbbed like the knife was stabbing it over and over again. *This is it. Everything has led up to this moment. This is what Mareena has been preparing you for. This is the real thing, the day when you're actually tested. You must pretend the stones work on you. This is a challenge you cannot fail.*

Mareena gave me a reassuring squeeze. Her previously spoken words trailed through my mind, almost as if she projected them into my thoughts. I had heard these words a thousand times throughout my stress-riddled life: *Focus. Control. You are like ice. Cool. Composed. Nothing can crack you.*

I forced air out of my nose and tried to relax my tense muscles. My tendons were like taut wires being relentlessly stretched to pieces. I hastily threw chains around my inner emotions and pressed my mouth into a thin line. *You do not feel pain anymore. This stone works. Act like it works because your life depends on it.* My hand kept screaming in protest, contradicting my thoughts.

The king glanced at me. "Is everything alright now?"

It took everything I had, but I made my muscles visibly relax. "Yes. I'm completely fine."

He again faced Cyrus who was still planted next to me. "You're saying this was entirely accidental?"

Cyrus nodded, never dropping his emotionless mask. His voice sounded calm and controlled. "Of course. Why would anyone even suggest the idea of intention? I assure you; I have never had any ill will against your daughter. I wear rubies like everyone else. Any anger I have against her, if it existed in the first place, vanished under the weight of the stone. What motive could I possibly have for harming her?" He slinked toward me and knelt on the carpet, dropping to make eye contact as he crooned, "Please accept my sincerest apologies, Princess. I hope I can make this up to you."

His acting was unparalleled. Flawless. It could have convinced anyone—but not me. I stared into his eyes, trying to discern his intentions. *Why did you cut me? Why do it in front of everyone?* My hand throbbed again, and I tried to stamp out the pain before it could manifest on my face.

Cyrus acted like a hawk, perched above its prey and counting the seconds until he could swoop down for the kill. He scrutinized me: my expression, my body language. His eyes raked over me, searching for something, but what?

The tiniest smile tugged at the corner of his mouth then vanished.

A feeling of dread washed over me. *Oh. He's studying me for any signs of pain or emotion. He's testing me to see if I'm Malopathic. That's why he cut me in front of everyone. He hoped I would show signs of pain while wearing a crystal.*

I stared into his black eyes, cold and filled with malice. The anger he felt toward me was apparent now, creeping into his expression. My eyes flicked toward his necklace where the ruby hung, glittering in the light. *I severely doubt you're Malopathic like me, so that's probably fake. a normal one that's not enchanted. I don't know how you can get one of those, but if someone could, it would be you.* I glanced back up at his face. *My, you thought of everything. Wearing a ruby is the perfect cover. Nobody would suspect you of cutting me on purpose if you can't feel anger.*

"I have a suggestion. How about I take Princess Syona with me to get help? It would be more efficient than bringing someone back here. Would that be okay with you?" Cyrus asked the king. The question was innocent, but I knew exactly what he would do. *Please don't let him. Please don't leave me with him alone.*

Kadar glanced over at me, surveying the two of us. "You're suggesting that you take Syona to a doctor yourself?"

"Yes. It would be faster, and I wouldn't mind doing it. It would be my way of making it up to her," he reasoned.

The king nodded. "That seems fine. Make sure she gets the proper care she needs."

"Thank you." Cyrus whipped toward me and latched onto my wrist. He half dragged me toward the hallway, going as fast as he could without drawing suspicion. He yanked me into a nook in the corridor obscured by a swathe of curtain and blanketed in shadow. My heart rate leapt, and lightning shot through my veins. I tried to pull away, but he gripped me more tightly.

As Cyrus's eyes burrowed into me, they became darker. Despite all of the fear coursing inside me, I managed to muster up the courage to form words. "You can take off the ruby now. I know it's fake." My voice dropped below a whisper. "What do you want with me?"

"You know what I want with you." His grip slid lower, toward my injured hand. His fingertips brushed against the edge of the wound, and pain bit at my skin. It stole my breath away.

Suddenly, Mareena appeared, darting over and ripping Cyrus's hand away. "What are you doing?"

"I'm just testing something," he answered innocently, his voice smooth and sweet once more.

"Testing what?"

"You know exactly what I'm testing." His eyes narrowed ever so slightly. "In fact, you might already know she has it, or you may have it yourself. I'm the king's advisor. I can do whatever I please."

"You may be her uncle or a lord or the king's personal advisor, but you cannot physically harm her," Mareena protested.

"Shut up," he snapped. "I can do whatever I please when you're not around, and I *outrank* you. So . . . you are dismissed. Go."

The minute of silence that ensued was painstaking.

Then, Mareena did something I never would have expected. She glanced at Cyrus, then at me. Her expression was so pained that I wanted to comfort her. After a moment's hesitation, she stepped backward and took off down the hallway, leaving me alone with a monster of a person.

With my protector gone, he pounced on me. "You screamed when I cut you. Everyone heard it. You can't deny it."

Breathe. Just breathe. I was prepared for the interrogation. I already had composed responses in my head to combat the barrage of questions. "Screaming is a perfectly natural response to feeling sudden pain."

"No, people scream when they feel pain because they're *frightened*—something you could not have felt as you were wearing an onyx stone," he shot back at me. "You also had an—how do I put this—*interesting* response when Officer Hazen told us about the Malopaths."

"You can't accuse and condemn someone for being Malopathic on hunches and theories. There has to be physical, irrefutable evidence. You don't have irrefutable evidence."

"We do, and when has that ever stopped anyone? Those people don't deserve trials. They're dangerous. People have been imprisoned and executed on accusations less than these."

"You can't do anything to me. I'm the princess. You can't execute royalty."

I could tell he was enjoying this. "Yes, you can. You absolutely can."

I threw out my hands in defense. "If you're so mad at me, then why don't you just wear a ruby?" *That's what everyone does instead of sorting through the argument and actually solving the problem, of course. It's lazy and unsympathetic but efficient in this case.*

He exhaled hard, moving closer to me. "Anger may cause conflict, but it can be a *very* useful weapon. Why would I *ever* want to get rid of it?" A bit of a smile broke through his dark expression. "I love *hating* you."

I held eye contact with him for a few more seconds before I couldn't stand it anymore. I peered at my hand, which reminded me of another problem.

"I have to go," I protested. "I need someone to fix the *accident* you caused." I managed to pull my wrist out of his grip. I spun away from him and strode down the hallway as quickly as possible. Even though I could no longer see him, I could feel his cold stare on the back of my neck.

He knows. He most certainly knows. He just has to prove it, either by making me confess or throwing me into a situation identical to this one. I clutched my injured hand to my chest. *He's willing to do some pretty reckless things to prove it.*

I guess I'll have to be a bit more careful from now on.

The halls of the palace were eerily silent. A few of the candles were still lit, probably for my benefit. Everyone knew I stayed up ridiculously late sometimes, especially after a rough day like this one. I always needed time to analyze events.

I had wrapped up in a blanket because the hallways were too cold for my liking. The palace was always cold at night, and the freezing temperatures hampered the productivity I could gain in going to bed a few hours later than everyone else. The thickness of the blanket worked effectively and kept the cold from penetrating my skin. But in a way, I felt like I wanted to be cold, my hand especially. It felt like I had laid it into a bed of hot coals. They had stitched it so that it no longer bled, but it still hurt. The stupid pain stone they were making me wear—that they were requiring me to wear for at least another day—didn't do any good.

After a few minutes of pure indecisiveness, I decided to walk in the direction of Mareena's room. I needed a safe place, and the hallway was not a safe place. Besides, I desperately wanted to talk to her in private, to talk about something I had wondered about for almost a decade, ever since Mareena first told me what I was and what my life would be like because of it.

I paused in front of her door and gently knocked, hoping she would be awake or at least awake enough to let me inside her room. The door suddenly yanked open, startling me. Mareena stood inside the doorway, fully dressed with all of her candles lit.

I exhaled with relief. Of course she was still up hours after midnight like me. We were both constantly paranoid, but she not only had herself to take care of but also a teenage princess, a Malopath who was almost impossible to protect. The fact that she slept at all surprised me.

"Well?" she whispered with one eyebrow raised. "Are you going to come in or not?"

I let out a tense laugh, but I hurried inside. Mareena pressed her hand against the door and closed it immediately. Her movements were slow and weary as she staggered to her bed and collapsed into the blankets, sinking into them like she would stay there forever.

"Why did you leave when Cyrus asked you to?" I immediately questioned.

"I *do* have to follow his orders, and I thought it would be too suspicious if I constantly defended you. I'm sorry for that." She paused. "Did he do anything to you?"

"No." *Just an interrogation and threats that will keep me up at night.* "He didn't do anything to me besides what he did in the dining hall."

She absently stared up at the ceiling, still not making eye contact with me. "What . . . a stressful . . . day."

I smiled, sliding into a chair next to her. The effects of constant anxiety were plainly visible on her face. I saw overwhelming exhaustion marked by the deep creases beside her eyes and across her forehead.

"I'm sorry," I managed to say.

She chuckled, pushing herself into a sitting position. "You don't have to apologize. It's all part of the job, but it's getting a lot harder to hide what you are. Who knew Cyrus would be cunning enough—and reckless enough—to actually cut you in front of everyone? He was able to make it look like an accident too. We'll have to be more wary of him now. He'll do anything to expose you." A few seconds of silence followed, and she asked, "Why didn't you just clench your fingers into a fist after you were cut? That's the signal for fear. You could have expressed your emotions *that* way."

"Oh, *seriously?*" I scoffed at her. "The scream was an instinctive response! Do you know what it would have taken for me to move my fingers? Are you *kidding?*"

"Yes, yes. I'm kidding," she assured me, laughing a little.

I leaned forward. "Someone should worry about you, though. How can I guarantee *your* safety?"

Mareena's smile was tired. "I'll be fine. I'm just a simple lady at court, not even related to the king by blood. Nobody pays attention to me. Unlike you, that'll never change."

I closed my eyes and settled back into the chair. "Thank you. Thank you for helping me."

"Malopaths have to stick together, especially in the palace."

We sat in silence for a couple of minutes before I spoke again. "Does anyone know where Malopaths come from in the first place?"

Mareena shrugged. "It's not like you can just ask anyone. No research has been done to answer that question. As soon as they discover a Malopath, they kill them. No questions asked."

I leaned forward again. "I'm already aware of that, but this is a serious question. Nobody knows where we come from or why the stones don't work on us?"

"I haven't put much thought into it," Mareena admitted. "But based on recent events, I think I should."

I dove right into the realm of possibility; it's where my mind is happiest. I twisted through different scenarios and started fitting theoretical puzzle pieces together. "Could it have been something we were exposed to when we were younger?" I suggested.

She shook her head. "I took care of you your entire childhood. I promise you weren't exposed to anything the entire palace hasn't already been near too."

"But we're royalty. Is there anything we do that's different from others when a baby's born?"

"I highly doubt that relates to anything. In twenty-five years, there hasn't been a single Malopath of royal or noble blood besides us. It's unheard of. Most Malopaths appear in cities farther away from the capital."

"Was it something magical?"

Mareena raised an eyebrow. "You believe in magic? That doesn't actually exist, you know."

"I'm just spouting out ideas, no matter how implausible they are," I said in my defense.

"Well, you'd better come up with more ideas. Malopaths are discovered all over the kingdom all the time." She smiled. "So, my little scientist, what's the correlation between all of these people?"

I paused for a few moments. "Maybe . . . maybe it's hereditary."

Mareena stared at me. "What?"

"It's a possibility that being Malopathic is something that's passed down through families. It's not a bad guess. Even newborns can be Malopaths. You told me yourself. You noticed it moments after I was born, so it can't be coming from an external source. It's something you're born with."

She faced away from me, rubbing her forehead, her face creased with skepticism.

"Just think about it for a few seconds." I threw my hands out to get her attention. "We're family. You're my aunt. You're Malopathic. I'm Malopathic. Maybe, somehow, since you and my mom were sisters, something was passed down."

"But Ionda wasn't Malopathic. I'm certain of that."

"I . . . I don't know, but I don't think it's a coincidence that two Malopaths are so closely related. It makes more sense than anything else we've come up with so far." I frowned. "Why do you look so doubtful? Isn't it a compelling theory?"

"It *is* a compelling theory," she eventually responded. "The problem is that it might just be true. The trait doesn't show up often. Your mother wasn't a Malopath, and your brother wasn't either. You're possibly right, but we still don't know how this trait got into the royal family in the first place."

"Your parents." Everything suddenly clicked in my head, tumbling into place. "We didn't know about the stones back then, so there's no way you could have known if they were Malopathic, but was there anything different about them? Their origin? Ancestry? Anything?"

She shook her head. "I never knew my parents. They died when we were very young. Your mother and I were adopted into another family."

"What? How come you never told me this? Do you know how they died?"

"I didn't tell you because I didn't think it was important. You never asked. No, I don't know how they died. All the information I have about them is hazy and full of holes. Our adoptive parents discouraged us asking about our biological parents, so we didn't. We were only a few years old. I don't remember anything."

"We need to find that out, then! That might be the answer!"

Mareena placed her hands on her hips. "Are you trying to make something out of nothing?"

I laughed. "At this point, I'd be willing to accept any possible leads or anything that could shed some light on this mess."

The conversation simmered down, both of us drifting off into our own thoughts. Now that we were alone, I took the opportunity to unfasten the crystal necklace Offer Hazen had given me. I gathered the chain and gently laid it onto Mareena's mattress. As soon as the crystal left my skin, the insufferable humming stopped.

Mareena studied my actions. "Why are you taking off the necklace? You're required to wear it, and everyone thinks you're in pain without it."

I grimaced. "Nobody's around except the two of us, and that stupid humming noise bothers me."

She was hesitant when she responded. "What humming noise?"

I waved my hand dismissively. "You know, that humming noise we hear whenever we wear the stones. It kind of sounds like a beehive, a buzzing noise, a vibration. It's the really quiet background sound that drives me insane . . . You know, *that* humming noise."

Mareena shook her head. "I've been wearing the stones for over two decades, and I've never heard anything like that. Ever."

I threw my hands up in exasperation. "*Great,* so you're telling me that I'm even weird for a *Malopath?* How does that even work? I might as well tell Kadar my true nature right now and arrange for my own execution because this is *ridiculous.*"

"There aren't very many of us! We certainly don't go around talking to each other about our experience either. Maybe hearing that noise is a normal thing for Malopaths, and I'm the one who's different," she suggested.

"It doesn't matter anyway. Do you know how much the people hate us? The royals call us Malopaths, which means a *bad feeler.*"

"It's not that . . ." Mareena tried to say.

"A *bad feeler.*" I sighed, resting back into the chair. "What hope is there for us? We're either executed or forced to live a life of danger and misery."

Mareena hesitated for a few seconds. "What can I do to make you feel better?"

I thought for a few seconds. "Apparently, this humming noise that I hear makes me different from all the other Malopaths, or maybe the noise is normal and you're the different one. We don't know anything about this noise, so could we discuss some theories?"

"You are, without a doubt, the weirdest girl I've ever met. Normally, I would let you talk, but we've stayed up for too long. You need to go to sleep."

"Seriously?"

"Yes. Human beings need sleep to function, and you are not getting enough of it."

I chuckled. "Really? You're ending this conversation that abruptly and on that note?"

"Yes," she immediately replied. "Now go to bed, Highness."

Mareena only used my proper title when she was trying to be serious with me. Taking the hint, I leaped out of the chair and darted out of the room, carrying the blanket with me. I sped down the hallway, trying to keep my steps quiet in the insufferably echoey corridors.

There's something different about me, different from the people around me and possibly even different from other Malopaths. I'm not only cursed but double cursed.

So help me, I will find out why I'm so unlike others.

Or I'll get myself killed trying.

EIGHT

The night passed, and Akilah came to my room in the morning. I decided the best thing to do was to get the apology over with. I hopped onto my bed and forced myself to open my mouth. "Um . . . Akilah?"

It took a while for her to answer, but I knew she would. She was obligated to. "Yes, Your Highness?"

She used my royal title. Great. This was an awkward, tangled up mess of emotions that I didn't care to experience. "Can you come here, please?"

I heard an overly dramatic sigh as she moved to stand before me. Akilah looked the same as always: white dress, braided hair. Her eyes drifted away to avoid eye contact.

"What would you like me to do for you, Princess?" she asked in a bored tone of voice.

"I . . . would like for you to accept an apology?" I hated the way it came out like a question, but it did. I couldn't take it back.

My response obviously startled her. She grew as stiff as the palace walls. "Do you think this is how normal people act?"

Her question threw me, just as mine had thrown her. *Have I done something wrong? Did I offend her again?* I was usually a terrible judge of other people's feelings, and she gave me the impression that I had messed up again. I thought that I had passable social graces, but I may have over-estimated myself. "No . . . Yessssss?"

She smirked. "I accept your lame apology, Princess. I was beginning to think you would avoid me forever."

That got a reaction out of me. "What? Do you think *I'm* the one avoiding *you?* Has everyone in the palace gone insane?"

She tapped her chin playfully. "Last time I checked, no . . . except Lord Cyrus, maybe. He's been more brooding and mysterious since you cut your hand a few days ago. Am I imagining that?"

I exhaled wearily. "Probably not."

"Good, then at least *I'm* not going crazy."

I laughed. "Do you mean what you said? That you accept the 'lame' apology I gave you?"

She threw her arms down, huffing. "Yes, Syona. For goodness' sake. You don't have to be so poetic about it. We're fine. Everything's fine. I don't care what happened before."

"Do everyday people forgive so easily?"

Akilah shook her head. "A little. Arguments can end in seconds with the help of the right stones. So, what do you want to talk about?"

"I . . . umm." The sudden change of emotion startled me. *You're just letting it go? I yelled at you. Can't you feel angry or sad for just a few seconds? You can't really appreciate happiness unless you feel sadness. There has to be a spectrum of emotion, and you're just cutting out the lower half.* "Don't you have chores to do?"

"Nope! Finished them already. Really. My list of responsibilities is awfully short, which is beneficial for both of us. I get to annoy you all day, and you don't turn out anti-social."

"You act like such a fifteen-year-old," I remarked sourly.

"And you're such a seventeen-year-old sometimes," she shot back. "No. Wait. Remind me. How old are you again? Because your mental maturity speaks otherwise."

My voice was like icicles. "That's funny."

"Come on, Syona. Is there anything we can gossip about?"

"You act like an endlessly energetic little sister who never shuts up."

"I'm okay with playing that stereotype," came her instant reply. She glanced down at the sleeve of my dress. "How's your hand?"

I rubbed my forehead, exhausted. "Akilah, can you please leave me alone? I have . . . things to attend to."

"Oh? What stuff do you have to do exactly?" she responded, without natural disappointment.

"Nothing at the moment, but in about half an hour, I have a tutoring lesson on the boring political aspects of this kingdom, as well as a skill test on negotiation and diplomacy, which is the worst. I'm not a talker. Davin was the talker. I was the one who sat in the back and observed what people were doing. That's all anyone expected of me, and I was very, very good at it."

I dropped the tangent. "Afterward, I have a meeting with my uncle." I shuddered even mentioning Cyrus. "He wants to judge how much I have progressed in politics, negotiation, and diplomacy, and he will most certainly be disappointed in me—even though I've worked as hard as I possibly could for over a month. He'll lecture me on how I'm such a disappointment and how I don't act like an actual princess." *And interrogate me again and try to make me confess.* "Then, everyone will let me go, and I'll be able to spend the rest of my evening in blissful invisibility."

"What are you going to do for the next half hour?"

I peeked out my window at the pink and golden colors of a beautiful sunrise. The colorful streaks were so pronounced that it almost looked like a painting. "I don't know."

"I know what you should do," Akilah announced in a cheery voice.

"No. Let me stop you right there. Any suggestion of yours will undoubtedly be a terrible idea," I said sarcastically.

"I was going to suggest that you go for a walk, to clear your head or whatever. You could get out of the palace and go experience something real."

"Maybe, but I think that would take more than half an hour."

"I know."

I whirled around to glare at her. "Is that what you're suggesting? Do you think I should skip all of my responsibilities? You're *certainly* a bad influence on me."

"Try it. You'll get back in time. Probably. It'll be a well-deserved break. You could ask someone to go with you—Officer Raynott, maybe. I don't know."

Gerrand? Maybe I could try. "Okay. I'll do that."

I was out the door before I even realized it, pacing down the corridors and searching for the one person I wasn't sure I wanted to see. I immediately spotted him down the hallway, standing at perfect attention outside of a room entrance, looking exactly as a guard should. His hand was pressed against the knife in the sheath strapped to his belt, his six stones glittering in the candlelight. A cold, stoic expression clouded his brown eyes. His face seemed chiseled from stone. Everything about his appearance screamed guard: emotionless, serious, loyal, with no time for any nonsense or relationships.

Not someone anyone could easily crack.

I immediately scolded myself for even remotely considering the possibility of a real relationship. I was done. This was a world where nobody welcomed or respected love. Sure, I got a little lonely sometimes, but I didn't need a significant other—especially when people looked down upon royals having any kind of unarranged relationships. *I'm not that desperate, right? Not yet anyhow. Sticking to conformity and loving no one and nothing might be the answer. If I become like everyone else, maybe that will allow me to fade into the background.*

I quickly swept my ruminations away as I approached him. I wasn't wearing a blanket or jacket this time, and I became aware of the cold air surrounding me, something that always happened when I got nervous. My teeth clenched. *Get through this. It's a formality. You've done this a thousand times before. Forget about it, Syona. Forget about everything: your emotional needs, your dreams, your thoughts, everything. Just focus on survival. Nothing else matters but that.*

I strolled up to him, my language formal and direct—like everyone expected it to be in a world without emotion. He faced me to politely acknowledge my presence, staring with hollow eyes. "Hello, Officer Raynott. I want to go on a walk throughout the kingdom, and I think you would be the best person suited for the responsibility of accompanying me."

He responded without even blinking. "It would be my honor, Princess."

—————

I didn't wear a cloak this time, and I seriously regretted it. Winter came crashing down on me as soon as I stepped outside. It beat me with its icy fists. My breath hung frozen in the air, even though the sun had already risen.

I despised the cold. It made me second guess the whole walk idea, but I clenched my teeth again and continued. No. I was not giving this up. I still had some time before I had to crawl back inside my cage. I would reap all of my advantages, even if that meant spending my time with someone who would never like me back.

"May I ask you something, Princess?"

I briefly glanced at him, trying to appear detached. "Yes?"

"Why do you wish me to accompany you on these walks?"

I like you, and I once knew you. I could've called you my friend. "You're conveniently posted in the hallway near my room."

Gerrand didn't respond to my comment while the two of us strolled farther away from the palace and passed the various buildings surrounding the courtyard. After a few seconds, the bustling crowd of the town swallowed us. I appreciated the mass of people. There was a sense of anonymity, even though the noise forced itself into my ears and lingered there, screaming for attention.

The people swarming me appeared content. I glimpsed that all of them wore jeweled necklaces, so that was probably a contributing factor. Most of them wore only one stone, the rest two stones, and a small percentage wore three stones—unlike the people at the palace who could string on all six.

How much does a single stone cost? It's apparent people want to wear them, but if people can only afford one, then how pricey is it? Cyrus once said that a single stone costs a person what they would make in a year. Why is it so expensive? Is it because the supply is running out? That would make sense, but how many are left? In fact, how many did we discover in the first place? Thousands? What's the population of this kingdom? Why haven't I been paying attention to anything I've been taught?

My thoughts were so rampant that I almost didn't notice two young children scampering up to me, a boy and a girl with smiles stretched across their faces. I assumed they were less than ten years old, for that's when everyone received their emerald stone. Both of them had the same shade of messy brown hair, and I could spot some similarities in their features, so I assumed they were siblings. Their sudden appearance startled me, and I couldn't help but stumble backward a few steps. Gerrand almost didn't react at all, simply stopping in the street and glancing down at the two of them.

The younger child, the boy, spoke first. He seemed to almost burst with excitement. "Are you Princess Syona?"

This situation surprised me so much that I just responded with the truth. "Yes."

He clapped his hands, his expression breaking into another smile. "I thought you were! This is so cool! I didn't think I would ever have a chance to meet you, and here you are!"

The joy conveyed in the tone of his voice jarred me. I wasn't used to anybody besides Akilah acting even remotely happy—or emotional for that matter. I tilted my head. Another thing he had said hadn't made any sense to me. "Why did you want to meet me?"

The older girl bowed her head slightly and spoke in a calmer voice. "You're the princess of this kingdom." She chuckled softly. "Everyone here loves and respects you."

"They . . . they do?" I stammered. I kept forgetting that this was my kingdom, a kingdom of people like these two children—children who happened to be observant and courageous enough to come up and *ask* me if I was the princess.

I'll someday be their queen, too, I thought with a slice of dread. *How am I supposed to lead these people? Why would I even want to lead people who would kill me if they knew what I was? No one deserves that.* I sighed. *I'll have to deal with it someday but not right now, not for a long while.*

I glanced over at Gerrand who continued to stare down at the children, stone faced as always. I couldn't possibly discern what he thought about the situation. *Does he think they're a threat and want them to leave? Why isn't he saying anything?*

The girl looked up at me again. "Well, I . . . I think we should get home now. Thanks for this and . . . sorry to have bothered you."

The two of them turned and were about to walk off into the crowd when Gerrand suddenly spoke: "Wait."

He knelt down in the street to be at eye level with the boy. He slowly reached his hand toward the child's face but must have decided against touching him because he pulled back a few seconds later. That seemed strange on its own, but then I noticed the stones around his neck had flashed, something that only happened when very strong emotion was felt. The emerald stone and the amber stone had lit up.

The boy spoke. "I know you too! You're the oldest son from one of the noble houses!"

His sister nodded at him. "Yep. The richest and most prestigious of all of them."

That caught my attention, and I turned to stare down at him. "You are? I thought you were the son of a minor noble."

He replied with only one word. "No."

I decided to ignore my astounding ignorance and push for more information. "Then why did you choose to become a guard? You could have managed the outer villages. You could have been an advisor to the king, or holed yourself up in a fancy house with servants. You could have been anything."

He stood back up. "I can't really remember. I think . . . I wanted to protect people. That's why."

Gerrand nodded to the children as he started pacing down the street again, leaving them behind. I came up alongside him, thinking about the information I'd just discovered. *He wanted to protect people because he cares about people or because he* cared *about people. But he doesn't anymore, not in the emotional sense. He's doing it out of obligation now. He probably cared about me too.*

I dragged myself out of my thoughts. "Where are we going now? Are we just wandering around?" I asked.

"You're the princess. It's your choice."

"Can we . . ." It was a stupid request but one I had been wanting to make forever. There was somewhere I had yearned to visit for almost my entire life. I loved spending time outside, and this would be an amazing opportunity if he agreed. "Can we go to the Southern Forest?"

An incredulous expression crossed his face. "The Southern Forest?"

"Yes?" I was a little unsure.

He shook his head. "Sorry. I'm not taking you there. It's too far from the palace, outside of the kingdom even. It's not a place for a princess. In fact, we should probably get back."

It was a vain hope to even ask. I nodded glumly. "Yes."

Gerrand pivoted around in the street, and I felt a twinge of panic. I wasn't about to end the conversation there. I had to say something more. "I . . . thank you for accompanying me."

He gave me a polite nod. "Yes, of course. Whenever you ask, I'd be glad to do it."

A formal response. The expected response. *I might as well give up now. Why haven't I already? There's no emotion inside him anyway.*

And yet . . .

I could have sworn that, as he turned away from me, his amber stone had flashed. Once, briefly, but I managed to notice it. It was something I could have missed if I hadn't paid attention. This golden flicker sent a flicker of hope through me.

Does that mean he likes me? Does he actually like me? If he weren't wearing the stones, would it be different?

Maybe I do have a chance.

CHAPTER
NINE

My mind was still stunned as we made it back to the palace. In the undercurrent of my thoughts, I congratulated myself, hoping and wishing that what I wanted could unfold right in front of me. Maybe there was the slimmest possibility that Gerrand would embrace his emotions as much as my condition forced me to, but I couldn't worry about that at that moment. My dominant thought as I raced down the palace hallways was this: *That walk definitely lasted more than half an hour.*

I sprinted, trying my hardest to keep my footing. I wound down the passageways, brushing my hand against the walls to keep my sense of direction. I almost let out a gasp of relief when I spied the ebony-colored door that led to Cyrus's private study. My mind started whirling, straining to remember all the things I knew about the political workings of the kingdom, knowing for certain that he would test me on that subject. I scanned my brain for any possible information. What I reaped wasn't enough to ease my nerves, but it would have to do for now.

My hand was inches from the brass doorknob when a sly voice rang out from behind me: "Are you late to something, Syona?"

All of my muscles stiffened, but I refused to face him, to grant him more control. You never wanted Cyrus to gain more power over you than he already had. The best plan I had composed so far was not to maintain eye contact with him. He might be discouraged from talking to me as long as I didn't turn around.

"Turn around," he ordered.

I silently pondered why the universe despised me so much as I turned on my heels to face my uncle. I studied his appearance, same as always: a black jacket layered over his expensive clothes and a gold chain around his neck, strung with an onyx, sapphire, emerald, and amber stones (but once again, no ruby). A sick feeling twisted in my stomach. *He's going to tear me to pieces.*

"I think we should start our evaluation meeting right away," he suggested, his voice like steel cords. "Don't you agree?"

It's not an evaluation anymore. It's a personal vendetta. "Yes. That would be an excellent idea."

I sensed the bitterness radiating off of him in waves as I crossed the threshold into the room. It was uncomfortably small, containing a single desk and a few candles, with papers scattered all over the tabletop.

"Sit down," he ordered, gesturing to a chair.

I obediently sat down. The request seemed innocent enough, but I heard the tiniest strain of venom in his voice that he hadn't bothered to mask. *I'm going to die. I might literally die.*

He suddenly snapped his fingers, the crisp sound tearing me from my thoughts. "You aren't wearing your necklace. You're required to. Do the emotion guidelines mean nothing to you, or are you just as scatterbrained as I thought you were?"

My eyes drifted down to my hands beneath the table, lying on my lap like limp snakes. I was carrying my necklace in my hand, intending to fasten it on my neck after I arrived, but he hadn't given me the chance to do it before pointing it out.

Stress twisted through me. "I was planning on putting it on after I sat down. I apologize."

Cyrus placed his hands down on the table, climbing to a standing position. His eyes pierced mine, like needles, like he was trying to peer through my soul and pry out all of my secrets and insecurities. "Syona," he shoved the entire force of his anger into that one word. "I am going to mention this only once, so pay close attention. I am going to make a deal with you. If you admit to me that you are Malopathic, I will forget that you broke any rules, and I'll leave this room without hurting you, emotionally or physically."

"If I were a Malopath, wouldn't the punishment be immediate death by execution?" I asked.

"If you do it now, without any trouble, then I'll make sure to lessen the sentence to life in prison," he responded dismissively, as if that was a suitable alternative.

"You wouldn't dare. I'm the last surviving heir to this kingdom. It would destroy the foundation of our kingdom and probably lead to revolution," I pointed out.

He casually flicked his hand away. "I'm sure I could convince my brother to change the law to make brothers and sisters eligible for that position. Kadar is a lot older than I am. He will die before me, and I will become king. Our kingdom will not collapse, and the royal line will stay intact. The problem has an easy solution." Cyrus slammed his hands down on the table. "Confession. Now."

A sudden accusation burst into my head. One that was pretty bold and outspoken, but before I could rein in my thoughts, I opened my mouth: "Is that what this is all about? Do you want to get me out of the way so you can become king?" My voice lowered to a tense whisper, barely audible. "How do I know you weren't the one responsible for Davin's death? You'd have the resources to do it."

It was a plausible theory, but I immediately regretted saying it. He slammed his hands down onto the wooden surface of the table again, producing a sharp, hollow sound that skewered my ears. I instantly wilted, wishing I could take those words back.

"You know *nothing*, Syona. Nothing! Nothing about how hard I've worked to make this kingdom a better place for all of its inhabitants. We are in the middle of a war, a war that has stretched on for three decades! You couldn't possibly know the extent of its effect. If we were unfortunate enough for you to ever become queen, our enemies would trample us under your ill-prepared and incompetent leadership."

Cyrus paused for a second to take a breath, shattering the rising tension in the room. Moments later he continued his rant: "You are a mockery to this family and everything that this kingdom was built on. You do anything to avoid attention, hiding in the shadows. You are grossly ignorant of the delicacies of diplomacy and decorum. You yourself—the princess—break rules and protocols. How could our kingdom possibly survive under your reign?"

All the air was sucked from the room. I felt shell-shocked and bewildered, hollow. I knew that Cyrus harbored a lot of grudges and complaints against me, but this was the first time he had voiced them aloud. All of them. At once.

Cyrus loomed over me, those black eyes burrowing into mine. The shadows across his face grew darker every second. "Your actions have been apathetic and irresponsible. For the past seventeen years, you have been a liability to your family and this kingdom. We don't have room for mistakes. The kingdom of Tanum is growing stronger every day, and unless we find a peaceful solution to this resource shortage and somehow unite the kingdoms, the negotiations are going to fail. The cease-fire will shatter, and the war will drag on to climax in our spectacular defeat. Tanum will take our mines and the Southern Forest and leave us with nothing. And all those subjects who look to us for protection will not even be able to subsist on what is left of our lands. These are the stakes we are fighting for—ultimately the lives of thousands of people."

He snapped again to get my attention. "Davin's death was tragic and sudden, but you must rise to take his place. Effectively. Act like the princess you were born to be. I could tolerate the first couple of months— an initiation to your new position—but now, if you break another rule, especially one that relates to the emotion edicts, I will tell the king that you are Malopathic. I'm his most trusted advisor. He *will* believe me. Do I make myself clear?"

The pile of threats overwhelmed me. "Why are you lecturing me on this? Now, specifically?"

He shot me an irritated look. "Because you are not living up to your position. Also . . ." He broke eye contact with me, sighing. "King Raymon of Tanum has requested to meet with you alone. Immediately."

⚜

A trail of advisors, officials, and nobles snaked behind me. Basically, anyone with a high enough position in the palace to not be sent away was behind me. I was already stressed, and their incoherent rambling drove me crazy.

"He's waiting in the library to meet with you. That's all he said," one of them rambled.

"Don't worry, Your Highness. Guards will be posted outside the doors. You'll be perfectly fine," another joined in.

"King Raymon? Why on earth is he here?"

"I don't know! He just showed up at the palace entrance half an hour ago! Without any advance warning or anything! Does anyone have an extra onyx stone?"

"Has anyone been told yet? The rest of the palace? The kingdom?"

"No. Of course not. The king has ordered this be kept a secret."

King Raymon—a man I had only met a few weeks ago, the most powerful man on the northern side of the peninsula, our enemy—wanted to have a private meeting with me.

No wonder I felt like throwing up.

I immediately got to the door before anyone could open it for me. I wanted to do this myself. My hand slipped on the doorknob a couple of times before I managed to get a hold of it. The turning squeak immediately silenced all the people chattering in the background.

One of the members of the crowd spoke: "Remember, Princess, he claims this meeting is for diplomatic purposes. He ordered his own guards to wait outside the palace, and he volunteered to be searched for any kind of weapon, but we found none, so he won't be able to hurt you. We have taken several other precautions just in case something happens."

Another person piped up, "Yeah, but it's so secluded! Anything could happen! Oh, dear, have we found any more onyx stones?!"

"Shut up. This will be a simple diplomatic conversation."

Their words faded away as I finally got the door to swing open on its hinges. The crowd abruptly scurried away, desperate to remove themselves from the line of sight of the person inside. I was alone.

My eyes zeroed in on the man seated at the library's wooden table. As before, he wasn't wearing a crown or a cape or anything that signified royalty. His only adornment was that simple silver-linked necklace I had noticed at our first encounter. He nearly had the appearance of a commoner, which made this entire situation weirder than it already was. King Raymon casually leaned against the back of his chair, with his arms folded behind his head. When I came into his sight, however, he immediately jolted upright and bowed deeply. "Hello, Princess Syona. It appears you received my request for a meeting."

I tried to curtsy, but my bones were made of wooden planks, awkward and stiff. Raymon gestured to the only other chair at the circular table. "Please, sit."

Hoping for a speedy conversation, I scurried across the room and promptly sat down. "Thank you." I suddenly realized I didn't know exactly how to address him. *Should I say King Raymon? Sire? Your Highness? Your Majesty?* I settled on the last one: "Your Majesty."

He smiled. "*King Raymon* will do just fine or just *Raymon*. For this meeting, I thought it would be in our best interests if you did not wear any emotion stones. I've always felt uncomfortable having a conversation with someone who cannot feel. I also want to get a glimpse of your natural reaction. Would you mind taking off your necklace for the duration of our time together?"

I swept my fingers over the stones of my necklace. *What an odd request.* My brain immediately began dissecting his possible motive. *Is he trying to disarm me, to make me comfortable while talking to him? Does he know about Malopaths and is testing me somehow? Is he going to blackmail me?*

I twisted in my seat to inspect the door behind me where I knew the guards were posted conveniently within listening range. Would they figure out that I was removing my necklace and breaking the law? Would it be an exception if the king of Tanum asked me to do it?

King Raymon chuckled. "Don't worry. I know you have codes in place that prohibit you from taking off the stones. You would probably get in trouble if they knew, but I won't tell anyone. It'll be our secret, okay? Actually, I'll gladly let you get away with never wearing the stones in my presence again."

The word *why* repeatedly buzzed in my head, but I unclasped the necklace and set it on the table beside me.

He nodded with approval. "Thank you. Let's get started." He placed his hands face down on the table and scooted his chair closer. "Now, I understand that your brother was Prince Davin?"

"Yes," I answered, not trusting myself to say anything else.

"I remember Davin: obedient, trusting, always did what was expected of him. I wouldn't be surprised if he never broke a rule in his life. Is that description accurate?"

"Yes."

He leaned closer to me. "Let's be honest. You're not like Davin. You're his complete opposite, and I don't think you would disagree."

"No, I wouldn't. I . . . I wasn't raised to be in his position. I wasn't expecting it, and I'm not used to it. I don't like being the center of attention," I admitted.

"You don't like being the center of attention, huh?" He repeated, musing over the words for a few seconds. "I'm sorry. That must be hard for the crown princess. What other mandatory responsibilities do you hate?"

Why are you asking me this? "I don't like all the lessons about politics. It's not that interesting to me. I have lessons on learning how to negotiate with people, which I also hate because I don't like talking to people very often. I like spending time by myself. I have to learn about our justice system and history, and all of this useless information is tedious for me."

Raymon smiled. "Anything else that you find difficult?"

I thought for a few more seconds. "I also have to attend every diplomatic meeting between you and Kadar, which always ends in disaster. You two never agree on everything, and the war is going to drag on endlessly if we can't solve this problem."

"Yes. I'm sure you've already noticed that, and it's true. We aren't getting anywhere with negotiations. Your father is a difficult man to work with." The king pointed at me with his finger. "What about you?"

"What *about* me?"

"As you are such an intelligent person, I would guess that your inquisitive brain has already come up with a few possible solutions." He leaned back in the chair. "Tell me. What do *you* propose could end this war?"

That was an interesting question. I hadn't thought about it very often because I was more concerned with my immediate survival than the safety of the kingdom, but I had a few ideas. "What if my solutions are idealistic?"

"Tell them to me anyway."

I mimicked his body language, leaning back into my chair as well. "We could have joint custody over the resources, our mines and your forest, giving both kingdoms free range over everything on the peninsula instead of taking it for ourselves."

"Go on."

"We could open trade between the kingdoms. It's an incredibly simple solution, and one that we could have implemented a while ago."

"And what's your opinion on these solutions?"

"They're simple," I responded, "and somewhat realistic and easy to do, but they can only be put into place after the war is over for good. Actually . . ." I leaned forward. "Sharing the resources is easy. We can sort *that* out. The real problem is uniting the kingdoms in the first place. Someone needs to find out a way to permanently end the fighting so we can rebuild relations and start trading again. You can never agree on anything during negotiations. The problem isn't coming up with a sharing solution, it's that our two kingdoms are at *war*."

The king stared ahead for a few seconds, contemplating my words. "Well, Princess Syona, it just so happens that we . . . *do* . . . have a way to restore the relationship between our kingdoms. An option that I hadn't seriously considered until now." He hesitated momentarily. "The reason I called you here today is that I wanted to hear your opinion on the subject, to see whether or not you think it's a good idea."

This stunned me. "I have input on this?"

He nodded. "Of course. After all, it directly involves you."

I leaned across the table, intrigued. "What's the idea?

"I'll be blunt with you. Syona, one of the easiest and most binding ways to unite our kingdoms is . . . by a marriage alliance."

Ice splashed into my veins. "What?"

"Presently, the only way to permanently unite the kingdom of Tanum and the kingdom of Ashlon is through a marriage alliance."

Wait. What? I've never considered that a possibility. Even my overactive imagination hadn't produced this scenario. *A marriage alliance? It makes sense, and I'm old enough but still. Now? After I've made some progress with Gerrand? All that for nothing.* I couldn't wrap my head around it. *I'm a princess, yes. The heir, yes. Alliances between kingdoms do fall under my responsibilities, yes, but . . . but.*

"Who? Who would I marry?" I managed to spit out.

"I have a son named Crevan. He's around your age, and I think the two of you would work perfectly. He's the crown prince, the heir of his kingdom, just like you. I talked to him a few days ago, and he's agreed to the proposal. What do you think?"

What did I think? What did I *think?*

I think this is awfully abrupt. I think getting engaged to a person I don't even know is highly unrealistic. Well, that's not entirely true. Arranged marriages happen all the time. I've just never mulled over the possibility that one could happen to me. It's not as if my opinion matters anyway. I have the illusion of choice, but this is really out of my control.

I phrased my words carefully: "I think it would be beneficial for both of our kingdoms."

King Raymon clapped his hands. "Splendid! I already talked to your father. He wants to end this conflict as swiftly and efficiently as possible, and he said it was an excellent idea. I'm glad you approve as well."

"If you don't mind me asking, are there any logistics I need to be aware of?"

"If you want the details, I'll be happy to tell you. I think it will be more comfortable for you if you meet Crevan before getting married . . . spend some time together, get an idea of what he's like, that sort of thing. Your father and I have decided that my family will stay at your palace in the months leading up to the wedding, to get to know everybody. We haven't quite worked out all the details yet, but we will soon enough. How does that sound?"

"That sounds good," I numbly replied.

"We'll announce it to your kingdom in a week, which is around the same time my family will arrive to stay at your palace. After that, the war will officially be over."

"Thank you."

"No, thank *you*, Syona." He breathed a sigh of relief. "You have no idea what this means for the people in my kingdom. You're playing a vital role in making a three-decade-long war come to a peaceful end. Thank you."

King Raymon jumped up out of his seat and sauntered toward the door, probably meaning to discuss the proposal with the king again. This left me planted in the center of the room, my mind analyzing and breaking down his words.

That was sudden, I thought. *A marriage alliance? We never considered that an option before. If it was a plausible solution, why didn't they marry off Davin? Doesn't King Raymon have daughters, too?*

I leaned against the table, a little faint. Either way, this was big, life-altering. I honestly didn't know what to think about it. My brain ran around in circles, searching in vain for answers that weren't there.

I can't tell if this is very good or very bad.

Either my world is about to end, or it's just beginning.

CHAPTER
TEN

Akilah stared me down, and from her expression, I could see the gears clicking inside her head. "So . . . let me get this straight. King Raymon just suggested ending the war with a marriage alliance?"

"Yes."

"A marriage alliance?" she repeated.

"Um, yes."

"Why didn't he suggest this sooner?"

I shrugged. "Maybe it never occurred to them before. I think this is the first time in the war that anyone has thought this was a possibility."

"Okay, but why not just start sharing the resources now? Isn't that what started the war?"

"Both kings agree that after three decades of fighting, the kingdoms have grown far apart, both culturally and socially. They need a way to unite the kingdoms and end the conflict before they can start negotiating specifics."

"Hence, the marriage alliance."

"Exactly."

"And you're getting married to . . . I can't remember." Her face scrunched up. "What's his name again?"

"Prince Crevan."

"Right. Prince Crevan. King Raymon has a son named Crevan, to whom you're getting married."

I nodded. "Right."

"When exactly?"

"That tiny yet significant detail has not been announced. Everyone's rushing into this, so a lot of the information has been left out. All I know is that the royal family from Tanum will be staying at the palace for the months leading up to the wedding. They're coming today, I think."

She studied my expression. "I can't decide whether to be terrified or ecstatic."

I laughed. "I advise you to choose quickly. I don't know exactly when all of the guests are going to arrive, but it'll be soon." I paced over to the set of doors that led to my balcony and creaked them open.

The melting pot of sound spilled into my room and washed over me. That roar, by itself, scared me away. I didn't even bother scanning the courtyard. I immediately slammed the doors shut and faced Akilah.

Her face stretched into an impatient expression. "Well? Did you look? How many people are outside?"

"Um . . ." My fingers slid across the cold glass. "No. I didn't look."

"You didn't *look?* At anything?"

My breath caught in my throat. "I just . . . need a few minutes, okay?"

"Seriously?" Akilah rolled her eyes. "You have got to be kidding me. It's not a big deal or anything. Well, actually, it *is* a big deal. It's a major deal. This entire thing is probably the biggest thing that could potentially happen to you. It's life-altering and scary. You can't afford to mess anything up. Really—"

"Stop. Talking. *Now.*"

She didn't even skip a beat. "Do you know why they're even implementing this idea in the first place? Because it seems a little weird and out of nowhere. How did it take thirty years for someone to come up with this idea?"

I threw my hands up in the air. "Oh, I don't know. How about you go to King Raymon and *ask him yourself.*"

She snapped her fingers. "Ooh. That's a good idea. You could totally do that. It would be a good conversation topic."

"I'm not *planning* on talking to him."

"Then, what *are* you going to do? Sit in the background and do nothing?"

"That's what I've done for most of my life, and I see no reason to stop now," I argued.

"Do I have to remind you that you're the princess? You're the focus of everyone. Now, before you decide against it, or I accidentally talk you out of it, please open the door and describe what's going on in the courtyard."

I pivoted back around and placed my hands against the smooth glass. My eyes closed, and I forced myself to exhale. *Nobody will care. Nobody will pay attention. You will be invisible.* I knew it wasn't true, but saying the words helped. *Everyone is gathered at the courtyard, so I'm willing to bet that not even one person will look in your direction. Everyone is too absorbed with what's going on below. Whatever it is.*

I tightened the muscles in my fingers as I banged the doors open. The intense noise enveloped me again, but I consciously chose to ignore it. I examined the scene below the balcony, trying to pick out what was going on.

An enormous crowd of people filled the entire courtyard in front of the palace, spreading across the stones like a draped blanket. They lined the streets, making way for something. I squinted and leaned over the railing to see more clearly. There were maybe a dozen horses trotting across the cobblestone streets. Their snowy color made them stick out like a campfire on a dark night. Maybe that was on purpose, to draw everyone's eyes to them. I had never seen white horses before. The only ones anyone bothered to breed in Ashlon were as black as coal.

Oh, shoot. I thought I would have another hour or two. Now? They're here right now? I backed away from the window ledge.

"Nope," Akilah called out, her voice muffled through the doors. "I can see what you're doing. I'm going to lock these doors until you stay out there for as long as I want you to."

"Must you make everything so difficult?" I whispered under my breath.

Scanning the scene below, I tried to recall everything I knew about the kingdom of Tanum. Scattered details from my political lessons started surfacing in my brain. They were the exact opposite of us. Their main focus was on agriculture and hunting. Ours was mining. They weren't as badly affected by the war as we were. They had more land, a higher population, and more power. The only thing that had kept us alive this long was our abundance of metal.

Now that they were a little closer to the palace, I was able to pick out the people riding the horses. They were undoubtedly the royal family and possibly some advisors or people that had a high position in their palace. I spotted Raymon right away as he was the only person I recognized and knew from before.

A few yards behind him was a triplet of horses that trotted so closely beside each other that the riders could have reached out and touched one another. They were all wearing dresses, so I assumed they were the queen and two princesses, but I couldn't remember any of their names. *Shoot.* That would be embarrassing because they, undoubtedly, knew my name—another great reason to stay in my room all day.

My eyes drifted over to one of the horses that wasn't clustered with the rest. Though moving just as fast and in the same direction, it was isolated from the others. I leaned out as far as I could without falling over the railing to get a better view.

I suddenly backed away again. I didn't need to risk my life trying to lean out of a balcony. I knew who the rider was. I knew exactly who he was: Prince Crevan, the mysterious heir to Tanum. I knew nothing about him. I didn't even know what he looked like. I certainly couldn't see from here.

And yet he's my future husband.

The more I mulled it over, the whole arrangement felt increasingly awkward and strange. I had known I would get married one day, for that was an unavoidable fate. I also knew it wouldn't be a marriage based on love and I probably wouldn't be able to choose my partner. But now I was *living* the experience. It was a lot different than I had ever imagined.

I clenched my teeth and squeezed my eyes shut. *Get a hold of yourself. This marriage is probably in name only, and you are a princess. You are the heir of Ashlon. You have a duty to this kingdom to fulfill, a duty to the people you will rule one day. That is . . . if you can survive without being executed.*

I whirled around. "Must I go down to the courtyard, or can I remain here?"

Akilah appeared unimpressed. "They're going to summon you anyway, so you might as well just go down now."

"Fine. What do you think I should wear?"

Akilah brightened up as if she had already decided. She darted over to my closet and selected a light green dress. Thick veins of darker green sprouted out from the hem of the dress and branched outward across the fabric, like a tree. It certainly looked nice, but the design perplexed me.

"Why are all of the designs plant themed?"

"Not all of them," Akilah protested. "Just some of them, but it looks good, okay? The seamstresses did an excellent job."

"Then the *seamstresses* spent too much time out in nature."

As Akilah started chuckling, a knock rang out from the door with an unfamiliar voice accompanying it. "Princess Syona? You have been officially summoned to the main hall. All the members of the royal family are expected to be there."

My heart leaped out of my chest. "May I bring someone?"

"The king has advised against it. He wants as few spectators as possible. It's supposed to be a secluded meeting."

I bit my lip and clenched my fists. All of my muscles tightened as stress and anxiety flooded through me.

Akilah probably sensed how I felt because she glided over and pried my hands open. "You'll do fine."

"I don't want to do this," the words started spilling out of me. "Not without someone like you, at least."

"Will you actually, literally, not be able to do it? Or do you just not want to do it without someone?" She shot back.

I sighed with annoyance. "Why must you always do that?"

"Do what?"

"Word something so tightly that I can't find any loopholes around it."

She smiled. "That's my specialty. Now, are you going to get out there and show the world that Princess Syona isn't a coward, or are you going to stay up here all day?"

I took a deep breath and focused on the cool air rushing in. "I'm going."

"Good girl."

After I changed into the green dress, I crossed the carpet into my main room, briefly surveying the surroundings before pacing over to the door. Akilah trailed after me. Turning to my necklaces, I plucked one from the stand and clutched it in my palm.

"How are you going to amuse yourself while I'm at the meeting?"

She shrugged. "They haven't given me any specific orders, so I guess I'll just do what I usually do."

"So . . . you're going to tidy up and stay here?"

"Exactly."

I swiveled around one last time. "I know what you're thinking . . . and no. I will *not* be wearing those weird little leaf earrings just because they match with my dress."

Akilah produced the earrings from behind her back, her face cracking into a mischievous grin. "Oh, well. It was worth a try."

CHAPTER
ELEVEN

I nervously fiddled with the fabric of my dress as I paced down the hallway. I refused a personal escort, knowing it would just draw more attention. It worked. I spotted only a few glances and double takes as I swept through the halls of the palace.

Good, I thought. *I don't need to get noticed any more than I already will be today.*

I ascended the staircase, focusing on the way my fingers slid across the banister. Its cool texture drew my attention to my hands. I allowed the lights from the chandeliers and the luster from the white marble to flood into my vision, chasing all of my thoughts away. The silver light radiated from the windows and pooled on the stone, painting everything with a metallic glow.

The palace hummed with more activity than usual. Hundreds of people crowded the hallways and stairwells, packed to fill every available space. The sound of chattering small talk echoed throughout the corridors. I slid along the walls and quietly slipped past the clumps of people: groups of gossiping maids, ambassadors talking with gentle words, and various servants catching up with friends. The lower social classes were too poor to own many stones, so they laced their conversations with bouts of laughter. The guards who lined the walls stood stiffly apart from one another, jewels glittering around their necks.

My eyes focused on the veins of black that trailed across the floor's marble as I wove in and around the crowd, feeling the heat of people's gazes. Finally, I reached the main hall, the largest area of the palace. People considered it our most beautiful space, with its high arched ceiling and stone chiseled columns rising out of the floor like trees. The glistening marble shined, crafting the illusion that it had snowed indoors.

I finally reached the bottom of the stairs, my progress impeded by the number of people who had smashed themselves into every available space. I laughed silently, trying to keep my face relaxed. *So much for a secluded greeting.* It seemed like every person in the palace was squished into the main hall.

Kadar, Cyrus, and Mareena stood on the marble, with a dozen palace guards perched behind them. They stood at perfect attention with rigid expressions on their faces. One was Officer Hazen, but I didn't recognize the others; nameless faces would help the entire interaction go more smoothly for me.

As I darted over to my family, I stole a glance at Kadar who stood stiffly with his hands clasped behind his back, surveying the surroundings with an expression of mild distaste. I guessed that he wasn't comfortable with so many spectators. *It's not like he kept it a secret, though.*

A handful of servants slowly opened the enormous wooden doors in front of us. The old metal hinges screeched in protest, but they still worked. The doors finally parted, slamming against the inner walls of the palace. The chilly air rolled across the floor of the palace and enveloped the crowd, causing everyone to shiver.

Standing at the entrance to the palace, in plain view, was the royal family. The king and prince were in the front, with the three ladies positioned behind them, appearing as regal and organized as ever. Behind them, I spied our servants leading the royals' white horses to the stables behind the palace.

King Raymon had again refused to wear any sort of crown, but that didn't make him any less intimidating. As soon as he stepped across the threshold and into the main hall, all of the scattered conversations immediately dissolved. His presence sucked the sound out of the palace. People were terrified of him. Why wouldn't they be? The man who had waged war against us for three decades stood directly in front of them, and we had been slowly losing the war until it was recently paused. I wondered why the spectators hadn't fled screaming from the room.

As the rest of the royal family followed, their guards and officials trailed after them. Even though we had more people and were in our kingdom, I could still sense waves of nervousness radiating off the people around me. It was a stalemate. Nobody wanted to be the first to speak. The stiff tension in the room was as tangible as the chilly air cloaked around us.

Of course, King Raymon was the first to break the silence. He clapped his hands, a sound similar to snapping icicles. "King Kadar! Thank you for your hospitality in giving me a few days to bring my family to your beloved kingdom. You have no idea what this means to me."

This first line of conversation seemed to bounce Kadar into "political" mode, and he finally started speaking: "I'm glad I was able to make this experience a little more enjoyable for you, King Raymon."

Raymon melted into a surprised expression and stepped forward, spreading his arms to appear harmless. He appeared remarkably calm for being in a foreign kingdom surrounded by their military support, but that was the carefree side of him that I couldn't help but like. "It *is* enjoyable. We are uniting our kingdoms after several decades of war. This is a time to celebrate." He dared to take another step forward. "I'm glad to see your family again." His gaze shifted, locking onto me. "Especially you, Princess. Would you like to introduce me to the lady next to you? I'm not sure I've seen her before."

I took in a quiet breath and transitioned into the conversation. "Certainly. This is my aunt, Lady Mareena, my mother's sister."

"Ah, yes. I've heard of you." He acknowledged her with a slight nod.

"I would like to introduce you to my family." The king waved the other four members of his family forward. Now that they were closer, I could pick out their facial features. All of the girls were copies of the same image, with blue eyes and silken blond hair. The two princesses looked far apart in age. The younger—probably close to Akilah's age—had faded eyes, washed of color. She shuffled timidly across the stone to join us. The older one—a few years older than me—stared at her surroundings with disdain. Her eyes were piercing, sharp as needles.

Their blond hair and blue eyes were typical of Tanum. I had never seen people from the kingdom of Tanum, besides Raymon and his advisors, but I knew what to expect, for the two kingdoms sported two very different races of people. Our kingdom had people with dark hair and eyes, brown and black with hardly any exceptions, with slightly darker skin. Everyone at the palace, and anyone I'd ever seen, had those same features. The people in the kingdom of Tanum, however, always had brightly colored eyes, like blue or green. They had varying shades of hair, but their eyes were always shards of vibrant glass.

King Raymon gestured to the queen with a flick of his wrist. "This is Queen Emerald, my wife."

The queen crossed the stone floor to fall alongside Raymon. She scrutinized the four of us, especially me. She spent an uncomfortable amount of time studying *me*. Her blue eyes inspected every aspect of my appearance. A cloud of stillness settled about her that I couldn't describe, but it was as though she had no thoughts or emotions.

"Hello," I managed to say.

Her voice was hardly above a whisper. "Princess Syona, is it not?"

"Yes."

"I deeply apologize for my intrusive actions. You just . . . puzzle me. We don't allow female heirs in my kingdom."

If the queen had worn an emotion stone necklace, she wouldn't have acted any differently. Her aura dripped with icicles, and she emanated a chilly discomfort.

The two princesses fell alongside their father, the older striding faster than the younger. She glued herself to Raymon's side and stared me down just as her mother had.

Raymon brushed his fingers along her sleeve to gesture to her. "This is my first child, Princess Ellison."

The younger princess arrived from the door to join the group, deliberately placing her small steps as if using stones to cross a riverbed. Her eyes quickly glanced in my direction but shifted down to the floor. She wore a floor-length, long-sleeved dress just like me, but hers was entirely sky blue and sewn with lace.

"This is Princess Everlee," Raymon introduced her. "She's the youngest of everyone."

The older, arrogant looking one is Ellison. The quiet one is Everlee. I think I can remember that.

I spotted another person sliding into view from behind Raymon, and I immediately shifted my gaze away from this figure. I didn't want to deal with him, not ever, but he ended up stepping into my line of sight anyway. Raymon faced toward him and smiled. "As you can probably guess, this is my only son, Prince Crevan."

He wasn't staring at me, not yet, but I was certainly staring at him. He was different from the rest of his family. Black hair, like his father, but that's where the similarities ended. He had green eyes instead of his father's sky-blue ones. The prince seemed quiet, but not in a timid way like Everlee. He seemed shy, maintaining eye contact with everyone but sticking close to his father. The smile he sent me was genuine but modest.

After a few seconds, he worked up the courage to approach me. "Princess Syona, what an honor to finally meet you."

I gave him a delicate curtsy. I knew how to speak politely and properly, probably the only thing I was good at when it came to being a princess. "You as well. Thank you."

Don't think about it too much, I ordered myself. *Don't make this awkward—or more awkward than it has to be. They don't expect you to like him. Get all of this over with, and then you can resume your semi-normal life again. You don't even have to spend time with him. You can make it a completely formal relationship.*

"Well, then." Raymon clapped his hands. "If we're going to be spending the next few months together, I think it'll be best if all of us get more acquainted."

Kadar nodded. "Yes, that's an excellent idea." He then lowered his voice to a whisper, "In fact, how about we dine together, just the nine of us? It can be as private as we wish." He waved around at the masses of people watching us. "You know, without the spectators. I can make the arrangements right away. I'll assign all of you to guest rooms, and I'll make sure all of your possessions are carried there immediately. We can have dinner at sunset."

"I think that's a beneficial idea," Queen Emerald suddenly piped up, which startled me. Her presence was veiled in shadow, easily forgotten.

"I'll see to it, then." With those words, a few guards broke off from the group and strode in the direction of the nearest staircase. The princesses, prince, king, and queen quickly followed them.

The mass of spectators, realizing the event was over, slowly dispersed. The various servants and officials resumed their jobs once more. After all, everyone had things to do. I didn't, though. Apparently, my only requirement for the time being was to sit through a boring dinner while the two kings discussed complicated political affairs. Though not an ideal way to spend my time, I reasoned I could probably suffer through it.

I started up to my room, where I knew Akilah would interrogate me about what had happened. I had already composed a detailed summary in my head when something snagged my attention.

Prince Crevan didn't trail after the rest of his family. He planted himself near the edge of the hallway, casually observing me from afar. His gaze was intense, like Cyrus's, but his grass-green eyes were bright with legitimate interest.

I purposely turned away from the eye contact, swiftly fleeing up the stairs and out of his line of sight. *You are in control of this situation. It can be whatever you want it to be. Don't deal with this right now. Don't let this blunder stop you from doing what you need to do. This marriage is for political reasons only.*

You are never going to make this relationship emotional.

Not now, not ever.

CHAPTER
TWELVE

I n the hour it took for the sun to set, the royal family from the kingdom of Tanum received a partial tour of the palace, with the promise of several more tours in the days to come. All of them delightfully agreed. If they were staying for several months, they would have to learn the workings of our palace. Of course, the guards didn't show them everything. A relationship of trust hadn't yet been forged and wouldn't be for a while. Even though the king had written the treaty, suspicion didn't fade easily.

The dining room Kadar selected was small and secluded. The walls were decorated with murals, and whoever painted them had splashed the walls with waterfalls and trees, mixing the bright blue and green into abstract swirls. The colorful strokes dripped down from the ceiling and pooled in a river of paint. I specifically chose a seat across from one of the waterfalls. Hopefully the peaceful image would distract me from the stiff awkwardness during dinner.

I scrolled through the ingrained rules in my head, a mental list I had composed to organize my thoughts: *Don't participate in the conversation. If you must speak, do so as little as possible. Watch but don't engage. Keep*

99

your arms under the table so you can move your hands without anyone seeing.
Keep your expression apathetic.

As I was rehearsing the rules, everyone else arrived. Cyrus entered the room and observed the table for a few moments before marching over to slide into the seat next to mine. I clenched my fists but didn't dare open my mouth. I stole a glance at what he wore: ruby, onyx, and amber. These were the three I would expect him to wear, but knowing him now, I assumed the ruby was an unenchanted one. I breathed out quietly. I just needed to get through a dinner, a simple dinner.

Abruptly, Mareena crossed through the doorway, with all the guests from Tanum trailing behind her. She hurried across the carpet and slid into the unoccupied seat to my left. She sent me a flash of an encouraging smile, then melted into a vacant expression, identical to the one I had assumed. I positioned my eyes to glance at her necklace, a single ruby. Because our present/former enemies were seated right across the table, the king had required all attendees to wear this stone.

Everyone else filed into the room, including a few guards, but that was it. It was mostly just them and us, which made me feel even more uncomfortable. Prince Crevan chose the seat directly across from me. He turned his head down and averted his eyes from anything but his empty plate.

What is he doing? His body language mimicked a flower with its stem broken. He was supposed to be the prince, a person comfortable at the center of the kingdom's universe, but it appeared he despised that role.

Kind of like me. I realized.

I immediately shook off the thought. *Nope, I am definitely not thinking about the similarities between us.* I took a deep breath and tried to clear my head, focusing on the scene around me and trying not to withdraw. I firmly tethered my mind to reality—sort of. I clenched my teeth and forcefully shoved everything out of my head.

The king suddenly rose from his chair, spreading his arms to address everyone in the room. "Thank you all for coming. It's an honor for us

to be here with you to celebrate our kingdom's first chance for peace."
He gestured toward King Raymon. "We express our gratitude to you for
being open-minded and giving us a diplomatic solution. I know that our
relations haven't been so helpful in the past, but we will all try and make
up for the lost time."

Raymon nodded. "Thank you for accepting my idea. I know it will
benefit both our kingdoms tremendously." He paused. "Shall we eat now?"

"Yes," Kadar agreed.

We ate for a few minutes in complete silence, the stiff tension dis-
solving the longer we went without exchanging words. Whenever someone spoke, there were many untold emotions to untangle, like invisible
strings stretched in the air that could be tugged and manipulated.

"It's winter here, right?" Raymon directed the question to no one in
particular.

Small talk? Are you kidding me? Who has time for small talk?

"Yes, it's winter," Cyrus answered.

"Has it snowed yet?" Raymon continued asking.

"No," Kadar replied. "It's just really cold, but thankfully it hasn't
snowed yet. All of our plants would start dying. What about you? Your
kingdom is farther north, so it should have snowed by now up there."

Raymon nodded. "Yes. It snowed—several times, actually. Winter
started more than a couple of months ago. The lakes are all frozen over,
and all the animals have disappeared. Winter up there lasts a lot longer,
and it's much harsher." He laughed. "Thankfully, I get to spend a few
months down here, where it's a little bit warmer."

"A few months?" Cyrus repeated. "Who's ruling your kingdom in
your absence?"

"I have a brother," a soft voice explained. I swiveled my head and
realized that the queen had spoken. I could still count on one hand the
number of sentences she had said since arriving here. Then, she lapsed
back into silence without elaboration.

This is the strangest dinner conversation I've ever listened to, I thought. *One half of the table isn't speaking at all, and the other half is speaking about snow.* I studied the two princesses. Ellison stared at her fingernails with a detached expression on her face. Everlee was staring off into space, and Crevan stared down at his lap. *I guess the conversation is to amuse the adults.*

Raymon resumed speaking. "I've noticed that all of you are wearing rubies. Is that a certain guideline you've set?"

"Yes, it is. I require everyone to wear at least one stone at all times, specifically a ruby when visitors from your kingdom are here. It makes things go smoothly," King Kadar replied.

"Wouldn't it be more natural if people were to express their feelings and opinions during negotiations instead of getting rid of them with the stones?" Raymon questioned.

The air went quiet. "What?" Cyrus said.

Raymon's question was interesting. That question was *very* interesting. Had I heard him correctly? Did he just argue against nullifying emotions? I shuffled forward in my seat so I could hear him better.

He waved his hand dismissively, cutting off that branch of conversation and my hopes of having a philosophical discussion. "Forget it. Do you use the stones often?"

"Of course," Kadar immediately responded. "Everyone does. They're very useful. It makes everything efficient and smooth. The kingdom has never been better." He hesitated for a few seconds. "We do have a problem that comes from wearing the stones, though."

Raymon tilted his head. "Oh? What's that?"

"Certain people—we've named them *Malopaths*— have a certain condition, or curse, that allows them to keep feeling emotions even when they're wearing the stones."

Raymon froze with his hands glued to the table, all of his muscles tense. I observed the tendons in his hands sticking out, his fingers splayed.

His mouth became tightly drawn, barely allowing him to speak. "What?" Crevan reacted too but not in such a physical way like his father. He just seemed to perk up suddenly.

Kadar didn't hesitate or drop his stoic demeanor for a moment. "There are people in my kingdom for whom the stones don't work, the Malopaths."

Raymon's brow furrowed. "I . . . do you know where they come from?"

"Of course not. We've searched for a connection between them all, but there's nothing we've discovered yet."

"Have you asked them? Do they know their origin?"

"No. We've never talked to them. Being a Malopath is punishable by swift and immediate execution."

Raymon and Crevan exchanged a glance with each other, the meaning of the gesture obscured.

Why is it such a big deal to you? Why would you care? I wondered. Both had the eager glint in their eyes that I got whenever I wanted to ask more questions, but Cyrus abruptly inserted himself into the conversation. "If we're on the topic of emotion stones, I'd like to ask a clarifying question, if you wouldn't mind."

"Not at all," Kadar assured him. "What is it?"

Just like that, Cyrus had effectively stolen the attention of all the people at the table. I wrapped my hand around my wrist and prayed it wouldn't be something of lasting consequence.

"Well, I just thought that since Syona's getting married and all . . ." He paused, glaring directly at me. A smile twitched across his face, which caused any hope I had to wither away immediately. "Perhaps it would be best if we were to reschedule the date of her Amber Ceremony to within the next couple of days."

No. You can't do that to me. You've already done enough damage. Every possible optimistic outcome for my life shattered into a thousand pieces like shards of glass from a broken mirror. I closed my mouth, fearful a gasp or a sob might burst from my throat.

Not love, the most precious and humane of all of the emotions, please do not take that. They would rob me of the privilege and gift to have compassion and care about others. To them, love was the most dangerous emotion of all. I thought I'd at least have another year before I'd have to pretend to have that feeling eradicated. They were stripping away my humanity in one violent jerk. I dug my nails into the skin of my arm, trying my hardest to stay calm. The spike of pain felt like piercing needles, but I didn't care. It helped me concentrate.

"Why are you doing that?"

My head shot up, and my thoughts flailed around for a few frantic seconds before I realized that Crevan had been the one who had spoken.

"What?" I replied.

He looked a little uncertain now. "Why . . . are you doing that?" the prince whispered to me.

"Doing what?" I snapped.

"With your arm? Underneath the table? What are you doing?"

I stared down at my hand, clutching the underside of my arm. Had he noticed my muscles tightening or my eyes flicking downward? Did Prince Crevan, across the table and appearing like he wasn't paying attention to anything, notice the slight shift of my hands? It seemed impossible.

Why are you so interested in me? I don't even know you! I thought.

"That's an excellent idea," Kadar agreed. "Syona? Would you comply with having your Amber Ceremony rescheduled to, let's say . . . tomorrow?"

I managed to choke out a response. "That would be fine."

"If you don't mind me asking," Raymon interjected, stammering a bit. "What exactly is an Amber Ceremony?"

"It's when someone has the privilege to receive an amber stone, a stone that wipes away love. Usually, the ceremony is held at eighteen years old. Naturally, some common people don't have that chance granted to them." Cyrus glanced at me again. "But we, being the royal family, always have the chance to receive the stones."

"Interesting," Raymon mused, exchanging another cryptic glance with Crevan.

The air of the room pressed down on me, a suffocating force. If I had to spend another minute in that room, I would surely lose control of myself. "May I be excused?"

Kadar didn't even bat an eye. "Yes, Syona, you are dismissed."

I darted out as quickly as possible without drawing suspicion. Cyrus turned to look at me as I exited the room. He probably had an amused expression on his face, but I didn't want to see it. I rushed past the unflinching guards and bolted down the hallway until no unwitting spectators could witness what I would do.

My fingers pressed against the stone of the wall. I desperately hoped I could replicate that coolness and douse my inflamed emotions. My thoughts thrashed around in my head, yearning to break free and be spoken aloud.

My stupid emotions, my cursed, cursed emotions! They're both wings that set me free and anchors that drag me down. I want them, and I despise them. They make me human, but they make me suffer so much that sometimes I wish I wasn't a Malopath. It's such a complicated relationship that I don't think I'll ever be able to sort it out.

I let out a hard exhale, and I pressed my head against the wall as hard as I could. I closed my eyes and wished so many unspoken things as I heard the gentle hum in my ears, a constant reminder that I would never be the same as anyone else.

I'm not going to cry. Not this time. I can't afford it.

But it feels like my life is crumbling to pieces.

CHAPTER
THIRTEEN

I t was late at night when the dinner party finally ended, but everyone had excused me long before. After wandering the palace for an hour, pondering how I could suffer through this impossible thing called life, I heard echoing voices, specifically Kadar and Raymon. They were chatting away, deep in conversation. Excusing myself to return to the upper floor of the palace, I ascended the stairs.

The hallways were eerily silent as I hurried down them. I was sure servants were escorting Prince Crevan, King Raymon, Emerald, Ellison, and Everlee to various guest rooms on the same floor, and I didn't bother confirming it. It was late. The sun had set hours ago. Any reasonable person would have already retired for the night but not me. I stayed up to worry about everything going on in my life. Such as, for instance, never being able to show love again after tomorrow.

Huh. Love. Such an idealized thing—for Malopaths at least. It's such a simple thing, too. Even the word is plain: four letters, one syllable, but it's an emotion that can rock the world and create and destroy kingdoms. It's the birth of all things good and bad. I sighed. *The meaning has been so distorted and the term so overused that nobody knows what it is anymore. Even I don't, and I'm a Malopath.*

I laughed to myself in the deserted corridor as I thought, *I'm not a very good Malopath, though. That's for sure. Half the time, all of my emotions are too inflated, and the other half, I wish the stones did work on me so I wouldn't have to deal with such a contradictory part of myself.*

Spying my room at the very end of the hallway and mulling over the possibility of going to bed at a semi-reasonable time, I sped up. Then I spotted something that made me stop dead in my tracks.

It was Gerrand, sweet, stupid Gerrand posted right outside my bedroom door. He stood as still and as straight as a statue. He had no expression, as usual. The weak candlelight painted shadows across his face. He didn't face me. I doubted he could pick me out in his peripheral vision, and even if he did, he wouldn't engage in a conversation without me speaking to him first.

I clenched my teeth. *Why do you always have to be around me, Gerrand? Gosh, Syona, you might as well start avoiding him like the plague because it hurts too much. The universe knows we can never become more than a guard and a princess.*

Not unless I make it otherwise.

My fingers curled into fists. I hated that thought. I hated the idea of being assertive and trying to take what I wanted as it rejected my entire life philosophy: *Stay secret and stay hidden. Don't go out of your way to get something you want. Stay invisible.* Just brushing against thoughts of being assertive made me want to scream.

Then, a few words pierced through my muddled thoughts like a sword slicing through plants in a forest. *Syona, if you want any closure, act now while you can still express love to people. This is your only chance. Take it.*

I took a deep breath and focused my sight on Gerrand. I walked up to him, not too fast, not too slow. I fingered my necklace of stones and gently unclasped the chain. I would need to show the full range of my emotions if this was going to work. Gerrand finally noticed me, and his head swiveled to meet my gaze.

"Hello, Princess. We were concerned when you did not immediately return from the royal dinner. I trust it went well?"

Just small talk. He wasn't interested in anything I had to say. I had to smash through the normal and get straight to the point: "Gerrand. I'm going to request of you something . . . odd."

If he felt any confusion from me addressing him informally, it didn't manifest on his expression. "What is it, Princess?"

Do it. Do it before you talk yourself out of it. "I'm going on a walk. I want you to accompany me."

This request alone was nothing new. I had already been on two separate walks with him since I had become crown princess. So, of course, he agreed immediately. "Of course, Your Highness. Whatever you wish."

"But there's one more thing I want to ask of you," I warned him.

"What is it?"

Oh, great. This is the hard part. "I want you to take off your necklace while walking with me."

He stopped and spun on his heels to stare at me. "What?"

"You don't have to explain it to me. I know that it's not following protocol. I know that it's highly inappropriate and you will probably be sent home if someone sees you, but I want this walk to be informal."

That tore him. Not on the outside, of course—his face was as cold as ever—but on the inside. I could sense him having a serious debate with himself. His position obligated him to follow the princess's orders, but what happened if an order broke one of the kingdom's most foundational guidelines?

"Please? I've known you for years. Since you've become a guard, I haven't had a single informal discussion with you. It'll be the first and last time." I hesitated. "Don't make me turn it into an order."

Slowly, carefully, he reached toward his neck and unfastened the necklace. "Fine, but only a little while. I am not getting caught without this on." His voice sounded clipped, hints of anger already filtering through.

"Thank you." With that response, I took off down the hallway with Gerrand reluctantly trailing behind me.

I got it. I got what I wanted. For real this time. I'll be able to see what he's really like, his real personality.

And maybe, just maybe, I'll get to know how he really feels about me.

———

The night air wasn't as chilly as I thought it would be, considering winter had finally begun. I didn't worry about freezing to death, but I *did* stress over the fact that I had done something highly illegal. Being out at night, without a necklace, with a guard I had deliberately ordered not to wear *his* necklace was a recipe for absolute disaster.

Let's hope I don't get caught, then, I thought.

I felt a small twinge of glee I couldn't suppress. I was breaking the rules. I wasn't bending them in an insignificant way like usual, but I was actually *breaking* them. I had approached Gerrand and just asked. That simple plan had *worked*, and it was a weird feeling for someone who had never once been assertive.

The two of us calmly strolled down the streets directly surrounding the palace—and only those. Gerrand had insisted on it since it was so late and dark outside, but he agreed to a walk at least. I studied his expression, glimpsing a certain emotion he was trying to mask. Was it annoyance that his princess had ordered him to do something illegal or confusion on suddenly having his emotions again? I didn't know for sure.

"Princess?" his voice sliced through the silence, startling me. "Why do you circumvent the rules so often?"

I gave him a simple answer. The rehearsed answer, before I accidentally told him the truth. "When I wasn't an heir, I could break the rules all the time. I guess that habit dragged over."

"But why did you break them in the first place?" came his immediate reply.

I shifted the conversation, hoping to distract him. "What about you? Why do you use every opportunity to stay around me?"

"It's my job to protect you."

His responses had loosened up. They were warmer, with more emotion and feeling. Intonation crept into his voice—a subtle but noticeable difference. I pushed on with the conversation.

"Are you sure it's not for any other reason?" I offered a direct question but a necessary one.

"Yes."

He won't give me the answers I want. He said that years ago, he wanted to become a guard to protect me and to protect people in general. I imagine that would bring someone a lot of happiness, but he can't feel happiness anymore. Maybe I can give that back to him.

In the limited light, I observed him press his hands against the sides of his head. Squeezing his eyes shut and grimacing. "Princess, I respectfully request permission to put my necklace on again."

"No," I said, panicking a little. "Not yet anyway. I'm conducting a science experiment."

"Oh, really?" His tone of voice was almost playful—almost. "A science experiment? Of what kind?"

The cold, bitter truth came out: "To see if the people in this kingdom, mainly you, really want their emotions taken away or if they're doing it because the royal family is telling them to."

He stiffened and paused on the street. "What?"

I faced him. "How long have you been a guard?"

"A year."

"Did you ever take your necklace off during that time?"

"No."

"And how do you feel now?"

"Like my brain is shredding itself to pieces." He closed his eyes again, but I snapped my fingers, reverting his attention to me.

"Gerrand, did you ever *want* to wear the stones?"

I noticed a tiny spot of reflection on his face, like a diamond shimmering in the moonlight. The reflection flowed down his face like a shimmering trail. Was he crying? "Well, I—"

"Because tomorrow, I'm going to wake up, put on a nice dress, and go to my very own Amber Ceremony. I'm going to say yes to the oath, receive the love stone, and never be able to . . . feel love again. You, however, you're not royalty. You have the choice, the privilege to feel compassion for other people, to care about them. That's what you *wanted*."

He huffed. "Why are you asking me this? We aren't *supposed* to have emotions. That's what *your father* ordered, and I don't see anything wrong with it. Besides, I'm still a guard. I'll always be one. I have to wear the stones. If I don't, then I'll lose my position and—"

I held my hand out. "Give it to me."

I heard him audibly growl, but he reached into his pocket and carefully laid the necklace of stones into my outstretched palm. I hooked open the clasp and gently unthreaded the amber stone, peering at it for a moment in the darkness. It looked plain and simple, like nothing special.

"Okay, Gerrand. At least promise me this. Don't wear the stones for a week. In fact, how about you just don't wear the amber stone for a week. That's all I'm asking of you."

"But—"

"Let me finish. You'd still have a necklace full of stones. Nobody would look closely or suspect anything. I can even give you a fake amber stone. During that week, pay attention to what you feel and experience. If you don't notice a difference, you can come back to me, get the stone, and resume your normal life." *And accuse me of being Malopathic if you haven't already figured it out.*

"I . . ."

"That's all I'm asking of you. One week without amber." I paused.

"No. That's breaking a lot of laws," he stubbornly insisted.

"Then let me compensate you. I won't ever bother you again. I'll let you do your job, and I won't ask you to do anything you don't want to. I . . . I can increase your pay, promote you, give you more release time . . . it doesn't matter. I can do anything you wish for that entire week. I can even make you the captain of the guard."

"They wouldn't allow me to. I've tried."

"Why not?"

"They said I was too reckless."

I snorted quietly. That didn't surprise me one bit. "I can get a normal gemstone." *It's slightly illegal and contraband, but I'm sure I can get it somewhere.* "Nobody will notice the difference. Please. I . . . I know you. We . . . we were friends."

He growled again but submitted. "*Fine.*"

I gently exhaled. Then, I bent down and placed the amber on the worn cobblestone street.

Gerrand flung his hands out, stopping me. "Wait. What are you doing?"

"I'm going to smash the stone. It'll signify that you're actually invested in this deal. It's a way to prove that you're going to go through with it."

"Yeah, but you're going to destroy it. I can't get a new one."

"I'm the princess. I can *get* you another one." *This is so illegal.*

Gerrand let out a sound that was part sigh and part grumble but didn't attempt to stop me. With him in partial agreement, I stamped my foot down as hard as I could. There was a satisfying *crack* beneath my heel as the stone smashed into pieces. A plume of a golden substance burst from the stone and into the air, the only thing that signified it wasn't normal amber. I felt drawn to the golden substance. The light sparked something inside of me, and I found myself reaching toward the plume as it dissipated.

As I watched the shards of amber scatter into the darkness, it reminded me of what would happen tomorrow. I would receive my amber stone and add another link to invisible chains.

I don't know what I'm going to do during the ceremony, but I know one thing for sure.

I'm in trouble.

FOURTEEN

W hen Akilah popped into my room the next morning, I was ready. I wanted to get up and get it over with as soon as possible. I had risen before sunrise, both to get ready and also to compose myself. I had to build an emotional wall that nobody could tear down. After about an hour, I thought I would be ready, but it was tough to know for certain. I would be forced to appear emotionless for almost an entire day in front of dozens of people, maybe a hundred. I had no idea how many people were attending my Amber Ceremony.

"Syona! Princess? It's time to get up." Her head appeared from behind the door. "You're going to be late for . . . oh."

"I'm ready." I wore the same outfit I had worn to Davin's Amber ceremony, but its appearance had been altered. Strips of black lace were sewn to the hem of the dress and the ends of the sleeves, granting it a bit of artistic grace, and a few more layers of silky fabric were stitched underneath the skirt so it would appear bigger. Even though the outfit had been remodeled, it felt poetic wearing the same dress.

Akilah scrutinized every inch of my appearance, obviously skeptical, before conceding. "Huh. I guess that makes my job easier."

"I woke up earlier."

"Nothing in this *world* can make you get up early," Akilah remarked. "What? Are you stressed about your Amber Ceremony?"

"Do you think I'm *not* stressed about my Amber Ceremony?" I shot back.

"What's there to be stressed about?" Akilah asked. "You go in, let the stupid official recite his pre-written speech, say yes to all of the questions, get your amber stone, and walk out. It sometimes takes less than half an hour. You'll have the rest of the day to do whatever you want. What's to stress over?"

I rubbed my face with my hand. *You really, really have no clue.*

She threw herself onto my bed, bouncing across the mattress. "You're lucky, though. You're royalty, and you have free access to all of the emotion stones. You're getting your amber stone today! Amber! Do you know how ridiculously expensive those are? I'll never be able to afford mine."

I spun around to face her. "You're a palace servant. You get the stones as part of your position. Three of them, if I recall: an emerald, a sapphire, and a ruby."

"That's correct."

"Then why do you only wear a sapphire? I know you're only required to wear one of them, but where are the others?"

"I, um, sold them."

What? She did what? Perfect rule follower Akilah did what? "I don't think you're supposed to do that."

"My . . . family needed the money, but it's okay! I kept the sapphire. I'm fine with all the other emotions. Just not . . . sadness."

I sensed some sort of history, like a painful memory, but before I could ask, she continued speaking. "Cheer up. I have one thing that's good about this situation."

"What is it?"

"All the guests from Tanum are attending your ceremony."

"*What?*" I shouted. "Are you *kidding?* I launched across the room to the mirror, inspecting my reflection. I straightened my hair and ran my hands over my face. "Is that supposed to make me feel better?"

"Um," Akilah muttered, obviously startled by my reaction. "Yessssssss? Maybe? What's wrong with them coming?"

"Everything!" I yelled a little frantically. "*Everything's* wrong with them coming! I've had enough of them already! They're already spending enough time with us, and now they've invited themselves to *my* Amber Ceremony? What is *up* with them?"

Akilah rolled her eyes. "Well, to be fair, you *are* marrying their crown prince."

"You're not helping."

"I heard that he's sitting in the front row, next to you."

I exhaled in exasperation, snapping my hands up in the air. "Is it possible for you to say something even *remotely* reassuring?"

She paused. "What qualifies as reassuring?"

"Any positive statement that has nothing to do with the kingdom of Tanum."

"You won't have to deal with the emotion of love after today?"

I barely managed to keep my fists from clenching. "Pick something else."

She thought for a moment. "You'll have free time for the rest of the day?"

"That's better." I spun on my heels and faced the door.

She shrugged. "Just get it over with. Besides, afterward, I was hoping I could try the stone on. You know, just to see what it feels like."

I rolled my eyes, sighing. "You know that sharing stones is illegal, right?"

"And when has *illegal* ever stopped you before?"

I chuckled, placing my hand on the doorknob. "Are you going to come with me?"

She cocked her head. "Can . . . I?"

"I think it's perfectly fine. Besides, I'll need someone to keep a crowd of people away from me."

Akilah clapped her hands together. "Yay! Thank you! I've never actually been to one of these. I've only been told what happens, but it seems cool. This is so amazing! Ha! Ha! I've never had the merits to—"

I slowly pushed the door open. "Akilah?"

"Yeah?" she squeaked back, delighted.

"I'm not exactly an expert at rules on these sorts of things, but I think talking is somewhat disrespectful. So, if you could avoid talking, at least for the *entire* time, that would be greatly appreciated."

―――

If someone approached me intending to initiate a conversation, I shot them down every time. I wanted to get there and get it over with. I didn't care if everybody thought I was an arrogant snob who disgraced tradition. I would burn out pretty quickly if I talked to every person I passed. I plastered on my apathetic mask and scurried as quickly as I could.

For the most part, people didn't flock to me like they had with Davin, but he had been friendly and outgoing, born for a stage. Me, however, I had already earned the reputation of being antisocial. I wove amongst the crowd, gaining a few glances from people. Akilah attached herself to me and acted like my shadow. To her credit, she didn't say a word as we arrived at the courtroom.

My thoughts composed a monologue worth of words, like they did whenever I wasn't conversing with people: *I am the girl made of glass who can shatter at any moment, the royal with a terrible secret, an insignificant girl in the background, the perfect princess. Quiet and subjective, I will continue being all of that if I need to. And I do, for this is the only way I've escaped death for the past seventeen years: not giving anyone a reason to be suspicious of me.*

I just hope it's enough.

I spotted Mareena, Cyrus, and Kadar stalking through the stream of people. The three eventually intercepted my path in the hallway.

"You're going to the ceremony, right?" Cyrus asked.

"Yes. What made you think otherwise?" I responded innocently.

"Akilah is right behind you."

"What's your point?"

He had a sly expression on his face. "She's not supposed to attend your ceremony."

You just want to cause as much pain in my life as possible. Is that it? "Why not?" I asked.

"She's your servant. It's improper."

"It's my Amber Ceremony. I can invite anyone I want."

"*Really?* Then if so, are you comfortable with having our guests from the kingdom of Tanum join us as well?"

I was grateful that I didn't hesitate when answering. "Yes."

"That's good because they're coming here now." Cyrus pointed somewhere behind me, and I turned to witness the royal family beelining straight toward us—all of them: Everlee, Ellison, Emerald, Crevan, and Raymon. The swarm of people parted slightly to let them pass.

Raymon approached us first. "Hello, Syona."

I repeated the greeting. "Hello."

King Raymon surveyed our group, briefly glancing at everyone. When his eyes grazed Akilah, however, he stopped cold. His gaze locked onto her, scrutinizing her features. His mouth fell open, and he tilted his head inquisitively. "Who is this?" He spoke after the slight hesitation.

His reaction jarred me, but I answered his question anyway. "This is . . ." *My servant? That seems too serious, even for someone who's not supposed to have emotions. My friend? That seems too sentimental for someone who's not supposed to have emotions either.* "This is Akilah," I finished, leaving a descriptor out entirely.

"Akilah," he echoed the name slowly, like he was treading on thin ice. "Do you have a last name?"

"Crossfield," she responded, sounding a bit confused. When Raymon heard the name, his eyes flashed. I was confused too. Why was Akilah, a teenage servant girl, significant to the king of Tanum?

He hesitated for a few more seconds. "Nice to meet you, Akilah Crossfield."

She nodded but uncharacteristically stayed silent.

King Raymon then turned to me. "Shall we go in?"

"Yes," I agreed.

We filed into the room along with everyone else. The room hadn't changed since Davin's ceremony. I noticed identical design, with stadium-style seating pushed up against the wall and red and black colors that looked like ash and fire. People occupied all of the seats except for the very front row, which I guessed was reserved for all of the royals. I rushed over to my assigned seat and sat straight down.

Everyone else took their time to settle down, but the noise gradually melted away. The guests from Tanum slid into their seats and stared straight ahead. None of them knew what was going to happen but tried to maintain an attentive appearance. Well, most of them did. Ellison stared at her nails again, and the Queen only concentrated on Raymon.

The official, whose name I still hadn't bothered to learn, suddenly strode into the room and raised his hands, silencing the audience. He nodded and pulled out a piece of paper with his pre-written speech. I had heard that Kadar changed the speech since the war was over. *Nice change of pace, I guess.*

"Hello, everyone. We are gathered here under . . . very interesting circumstances. The lady we are doing the ceremony for is not eighteen, yet it appears she wants to go ahead with it anyway. So, let's begin.

"Almost since the beginning of the war, the kingdom of Ashlon has been gifted with the ability to eliminate emotion. This has been a blessing of the highest measure. It has strengthened our people and given them the morale to persevere through decades of conflict."

I felt like a statue again, but I managed to direct my eyes to observe King Raymon. He stared straight ahead, just like the rest of his family, but something subtle changed in his expression. As the official recited the words, the edges of his mouth tugged upward. The small twitches and movements were hardly noticeable. Was he trying not to smile? What was particularly funny or interesting about the speech?

"We are at peace with the kingdom of Tanum, but our kingdom continues to have conflict every day. However, with the stones, there is hope. They have helped our society have the resilience to build and grow upon the ashes of conflict. There is no indecisiveness, no bias in making decisions. These stones have saved us."

Just like last time, the official produced a necklace with six glittering stones strung on the chain. He touched the amber stone, and it seemed to shine more brightly than the others as if taunting me. "The emotion of love, the most dangerous of all. Fortunately, our heir, Princess Syona, can erase that curse today. She will receive her amber stone. Please rise and show respect to Princess Syona of Ashlon."

I rose on shaky feet along with everyone else. It took a moment for me to realize that everyone expected *me* to walk forward. I took a few deep breaths, but I couldn't make my feet move. They molded to the floor like tree trunks. It was like roots had grown out of the bottom of my shoes and plunged into the marble floor, forcing with me to stay put.

My soul wilted. Everyone stared at me, expecting something, expecting me to be an example to them. I sensed people's gazes on the back of my neck, as if the stares had taken a physical form. Time froze; meaning disappeared. It was just me in battle with the rest of the world. I focused on keeping my head above water as everything else was bent on drowning me.

My thoughts seemed echoey and far away. *Move. Move.* It was a four-letter word, strung together in a specific sequence to convey meaning, but it meant nothing to me now, not in this situation. *Move, Syona. Walk. Go up there.* My mind stubbornly disobeyed.

My breathing slowed. *How long have I been standing? Five seconds? One? Ten?* Probably only five seconds had passed. Everything in my body screeched at me to bolt out of the room and retreat somewhere safe.

After a few eternities, I finally managed to shuffle up to the official, who held the stone out to me. The amber stone innocently dangled on the necklace, but it meant so much more to me than just a simple stone. It was another link to the chain, another bar in the jail cell, one more thing that prevented me from expressing my true self and forced me to construct a public version of myself to display: Syona Ashlon, the emotionless shadow.

I hardly know who I am anymore, I thought. *Is my identity what I truly am or how I appear to other people? It sure seems like the latter.*

And if I have to pretend that I don't have emotions, is that any different from not having them at all? What's the difference if I'm not able to enjoy them?

Through the fog of my thoughts, I still heard someone speaking: "Princess Syona, do you accept this stone willingly, swearing to refrain from using this emotion for as long as you shall live?"

I felt numb as I stood there, stewing over the question. I had to say yes. It was almost mandatory. It wasn't even a question at all, just words arranged on a page to make the event seem more ceremonial. The people who had written the speech decided to put it in as a question to create the illusion that the person acted of their own accord. In reality, there was no choice. The king expected everyone to agree.

"I do," I promised, selling my soul.

"Then we congratulate you, for you shall never endure the curse of love again." He gently lifted the necklace off my neck and threaded the amber onto the chain. Then, he dropped it over my head again, the stones brushing against my skin.

Nothing changed except for the mysterious buzzing noise, which grew considerably louder with the addition of an extra stone.

A few awkward seconds passed, but eventually the crowd of people dispersed. The audience filed out of their seats and out the door, apparently satisfied. Nobody shot me a single glance as the guests disappeared more quickly than I had thought they would. Obviously, everyone thought the activities they were doing before the ceremony were of greater importance than lingering, but I didn't mind. I treated this event with even less respect than the audience did.

After examining the amber stone, I glanced up to see that the Tanum royal family remained but showed a ridiculous amount of apathy. Crevan was staring at me, like usual. I didn't think he even blinked. He studied me like I was the only thing in the entire world.

What is up with him? He expressed the same behavior I had observed on the day we met. In fact, the prince hadn't stopped creepily studying me since arriving at the palace, and he had offered no explanation for his actions.

Maybe he wants me to say something first, I reasoned. *Maybe he's not very assertive and has no social skills, like me.* I chuckled to myself. *If that's the case, the two of us will get along terribly.*

I approached him, wishing to be as direct as possible. "Prince Crevan?"

His head shot straight up, and Raymon's did too. "Yes, Princess Syona?"

Keep your voice neutral. Scrape every bit of emotion out of your tone. Keep the act going for a little longer. Then you can retreat to your room and be as playful as you want to with Akilah.

"May I speak with you in a private location?"

"Whatever for?" he asked.

"I wish for you to . . ." *How am I supposed to word this? Explain why you've been constantly staring at me? Explain what you're feeling to make you act like this?* "Explain your behavior over the past couple of days."

He didn't hesitate. "That would be completely fine. What location do you have in mind?"

I tried not to hesitate either, leaping directly into a response: "Behind the palace there's a private garden I enjoy visiting. It's spacious and secluded. A high wall surrounds its perimeter, so it's perfectly safe. I thought we could take a short walk together and discuss some of the problems surrounding recent events."

"I haven't seen this garden, but it seems adequate. When do you propose we do this?"

"I don't have anything to do for the rest of the day. How about right now?"

He clapped his hands. "That would be excellent." The prince stood up and followed me out of the room. When I got to the door, I glanced back at Raymon who was giving his son a glare that could have melted the flesh off someone's bones.

FIFTEEN

I hadn't spent much time in the palace gardens since visiting as a child with Mareena. She would let me climb the trees lining the wall, and the wall itself, as long as I was young enough that such play wasn't considered improper. When I stepped outside, I appreciated the beauty of the landscape and felt nostalgic to stroll through a piece of my childhood.

A network of paved walkways stretched across the garden, plotted out in a grid-like shape. They snaked around the various plants and bushes, providing a space for people to walk without ruining the perfectly trimmed grass. The pathways flowed parallel with the main attraction of the garden: a stone fountain amongst a rectangular pool, which continually sprayed a stream of water and produced the only noise you ever heard there, a constant burble.

The patches of soil housed multitudes of bright flowers that sprung up from the ground. Bright, velvety petals reached out of the shadows to grasp the sun. Most of the flowers were roses, probably chosen because of their color: dark, scarlet red.

I stole a glance at Crevan who strolled calmly beside me observing his new surroundings. *Does he think I'm purposely intimidating him by taking him to a place with the color red? After all, that's the color of our kingdom. I don't know how anything is supposed to work anymore. If he does think that, this will be very awkward.*

If those were his thoughts, I couldn't tell. His expression didn't easily betray the emotions he experienced. His face was placid and expertly hid anything he might be thinking. It had been almost twenty minutes of walking, and neither of us had spoken a word. *Well, if this entire experience is going to be me walking around with a quiet, absent-minded prince, then it's an incredible waste of time. I have questions, and I don't want to wait for them to get answered. I guess I must say something to disrupt the silence and get him talking.*

"Are you . . . enjoying the garden?"

He nodded but offered no verbal response, which sent a flash of irritation through me. *Nope. That didn't work. Don't ask yes or no questions he can answer by simple gestures. I want actual words to come out of his stupid mouth! Please! Talk to me! I want to know what's been going through your head for the past couple of days.*

I tried again. "Do you have a garden in your palace too? What's it like?"

"Yes, but it's smaller than this one." He laughed to himself, startling me. I hadn't heard him laugh before. It was a pleasant sound, similar to the way Davin laughed. "In the wintertime, it gets so cold that all the plants will die, so it's horrible work to maintain. I applaud our gardeners because they have to keep the plants alive in a wintery climate. I'm sure they're not getting paid enough."

Good. He's talking. Not exactly the topic I want, but still. "Is it quite cold there?"

"Very. It always snows. If you live in my kingdom, you'd better like snow because we get way too much of it. The animals hibernate, the trees turn bare, the lakes all freeze over. It's pretty harsh. I think my father purposely suggested the idea of the marriage alliance in winter so he could get away from the blasted weather."

"What's your opinion on the weather at this moment?"

He glanced up at the sky, the cloudy, dreary, freezing sky. "It's a bit chilly but definitely not as bad as if I were home right now." He smiled again, and I wanted to mirror his expression, but my necklace wouldn't allow me. All I could do was stare blankly at him.

Crevan's face grew a little pained. "Can you, um, if you don't mind . . ."

"If I don't mind what?"

"If you don't mind taking off your necklace, I would very much like you to do that, please," he suddenly spat out. "I'm so sorry. I'm not used to this. It's like talking to a brick wall. If you wouldn't mind, I'd like for you to remove your stones while you're with me. I'm terribly sorry if that's disgraceful to your culture or something, but I absolutely can't stand talking to you while you're like this."

I was grateful for the request but puzzled at the same time. *That's the same thing your father asked of me earlier, which is innocent enough. But you haven't asked anyone else to take off their stones—just me. Why me?* I tried to file those questions away and focus on the task at hand. Slowly, I unclasped the necklace and bundled it up neatly in my palm. Crevan physically relaxed.

I tried to brighten up a bit as if suddenly gaining access to my emotions. "That was a lot of talking at once. You've hardly said anything to me during your entire visit. Where did all of those words come from?"

He chuckled. "I apologize. I wanted to wait to talk to you privately. My father would probably eavesdrop on every conversation we'd have in the palace."

"Why?"

The prince threw his hands up in defense. "I don't know! He's very interested in you."

"*Why?*" I questioned.

"I don't know. Maybe it's because you're marrying his *son*."

"Yes, but his *son* doesn't know how to carry on a conversation anyway." I said with a smile.

"Hey!" He laughed. "I just don't like talking to people that often. I'd rather be by myself and sit in the background. Does that make any sense to you?"

That made perfect sense, but I pretended I didn't understand. "No. You're the prince, for goodness' sake. You were born into a position of attention, and you'll never get out of it. Don't you have a lot of stuff to do? In fact, what's your life like? Just . . . in general."

He shrugged. "It's the same as yours, I guess."

"I bet this weird marriage alliance messed up all of it, right?"

"Yes. Absolutely. This is so strange! This has thrown my entire life out of rhythm. I mean, I'm the prince, but it's not like I have much control over my life. My father usually runs everything."

"Do you have any idea why he suggested this now?"

"He's been toying with the idea for a while, but I only got snippets of information. He wanted to get all of the facts straight before he suggested it to your family. Everyone wanted to end the war, but nobody knew how. I guess this is the quickest solution."

"What's your family like, exactly?" I asked, daring to press a little harder. "Princesses can't be heirs, right? How do your sisters feel about that rule?"

Crevan shrugged. "I don't talk to them that often. Everlee is young, and she doesn't ever say anything. Ellison is older than me, and she *would* be the heir if she could be, but I don't really know if she holds that against me or if she'd actually *want* to be the queen of our kingdom. She seems quite shallow; the only thing she cares about is her appearance and reputation. Political and diplomatic meetings bore her, so I don't think she's very interested in having my position."

I risked another specific question. "What about your mother? How do you feel about her?"

"Um, she's a little disconnected from the family. She isn't involved in any of our lives, especially my father's. She seems to hate my father for some reason, which doesn't make sense because she definitely agreed to marry him. She never spends time with him and doesn't speak to him at all. Something must have happened between them, but I guess I'll never know." He shrugged. "It took quite a bit of convincing for her to come here in the first place."

"Your mother's name is Emerald, right?"

"Yes. A while ago, someone decided to give all the girls in our family names that start with the letter *e*: Emerald, Ellison, Everlee."

I laughed alongside him. "Yeah. That's pretty weird."

"What about *your* family? It must be pretty weird too."

"Weird how?"

"None of you can feel emotion when you wear the stones. Your entire kingdom is like this, right? How does it feel not to feel anything? How do you function as a family?"

"We *don't* function as a family," I replied, avoiding the other two questions.

"But you don't know where the stones came from."

It wasn't a question. It was a statement, but I answered anyway. "No. We don't."

"Do you have any clue?"

"Ha! *Nobody* has any clue. We were digging in one of our mines when one of the walls collapsed, and we found a hidden chamber with chests inside. They held thousands of gemstones, even amber. All of them sparkled in the torchlight. It was like a miracle. We don't even know who made them or who put them there. It's not like you're supposed to find ancient treasure in a silver mine."

"That's strange."

I glanced upward at the late afternoon sun, feeling the warm rays of sunlight that brushed across my skin. The sun was a signal of how much time had passed: almost an hour.

I should be back at the palace by now. I turned to Crevan. "Maybe we should stop for today."

"Okay." His face didn't display any negative emotions, so I assumed that the agreement was genuine.

I stumbled over my words. "Um, thanks for talking with me."

"Yes. I enjoyed it," rang his cheerful response.

I observed him confidently stroll back to the palace as if he already knew the layout. He stepped across the gardens and located the entrance with ease. I found myself shaking my head in disbelief.

That boy is an enigma. I don't know what to think of him. The words from the conversation trailed through my head again, my mind recounting them and storing them away. *He seems friendly. Quiet. More of a passive communicator like me.*

I studied the necklace that curled inside my palm. *For one thing, he's not afraid to freely express his emotions—unlike everyone else who surrounds me and unlike me, who can't decide whether to embrace them or throw them away.*

Maybe our relationship won't be so disastrous after all.

⚬⚬⚬

As I hurried back to my room for some much-needed alone time, I ran into Akilah. Under normal circumstances, I wouldn't mind, but today had been exhausting. I wasn't in the mood to be interrogated by a hyperactive fifteen-year-old.

"There you are!" she squealed. "I saw you run off immediately after the ceremony, with Prince Crevan of all people. What's up with that?"

"I . . ." I stammered.

"Please tell me this isn't one of those times when you can't speak coherent words. At least tell me *something* about what happened. Please?"

"Maybe. I want to go to my room and—"

"Great. Let's go there." She latched onto my wrist and started yanking me down the hallway.

"Stop. Just slow down for a second." I ripped my arm out of her grip. "This day has been very draining."

"Oh, well . . ." Her eyes drifted down to my hand. "Hey, is that your necklace? You're not wearing it or anything! Isn't that—"

I made a frantic shushing noise that came out more like a hiss. "Stop it. I'll tell you about my day if you don't tell a soul about what I did, okay? Is that fair enough? Now, if you want to go to my room and talk, then let's do it." I took off down the hallway without waiting for a reply.

She looked a little flustered but trailed after me anyway.

As soon as we arrived at my room, she turned on me, seizing every second to talk. "So. What did you guys do?"

I selected simple words and simple explanations. "We walked through the gardens and talked. That's it."

Akilah wasn't satisfied by that response, so she pressed harder. "Come on. What did you actually talk about?"

"Just random stuff, like our families, the weather—he said it was so cold up north and that all of the lakes had already frozen over—the marriage alliance, that sort of boring nonsense."

"The marriage alliance doesn't seem like boring nonsense."

I waved my hand dismissively. "It only came up once, and we only spoke a few words about it. He seems to know about as much as I do. His father is hoarding all of the details for some reason." *It seems to me that Raymon's being very controlling, especially to Crevan, which is weird because he's been so relaxed and easygoing whenever he talks to me.* "I don't even know when the wedding is going to be."

She sighed. "I hope it's soon, though. Then we can get all of this nonsense behind us."

"Yes, that's what we talked about: the weather and the marriage alliance. That's it." I hoped those words would be the sum of our conversation.

No such luck. Akilah immediately pounced on another topic. "Did you get to know him? Is he an okay person?"

"I don't know quite yet, but he seems fine. He's friendly, a little shy, that sort of thing."

"Like you."

"Sure, but the difference is—"

A hollow tapping noise alerted me to someone at the door, promptly ending our conversation. The door swung open, revealing a person standing in the hallway. Because of her position in front of me, Akilah spotted the guest before I did.

"Oh, hi, Lady Mareena," Akilah said.

I sighed with relief. Out of all the people who could be at my doorway, I preferred her most of all. I turned around to greet her.

Mareena nodded. "Hello, Akilah, how are you?"

"I'm doing splendidly. Princess Syona just told me about her talk with Crevan. They went out into the garden and spent some time together."

Mareena raised one of her eyebrows. "Really? *Did* she now? How did that go?"

Akilah's eyes hooked on mine. "Good, I think, according to what she described."

She smiled. "That's fantastic, Akilah. Do you want to keep talking with her, or was your conversation finished?"

"I think our conversation was finished." She glanced at me again, and I nodded.

"Great. Would you mind if I speak to Syona in private then?"

"Not at all, no," Akilah promptly replied. She bowed her head and scurried right out of the room, a little more quickly than necessary.

After the door clicked behind her, Mareena chuckled to herself. "She's irritating sometimes, but she truly wants to make you happy."

I chuckled. "I guess. Why did you come here? Do you want to tell me something?"

"Let me see that necklace first." She stretched out her arm, palm up.

I opened my hand and carefully transferred the tangled necklace from my hand to hers. She stared at it for a while, intrigued. "The amber color fits well with the rest of the stones. I think it looks very pretty. You've had it for a couple of hours, right? How do you feel?"

The question confused me. "How do I *feel*? Really?"

"Answer the question, please. Use as many adjectives as you like."

"I feel suffocated, degraded, barred, powerless, constricted—"

"Okay, I think that's quite enough. Nice vocabulary though." She smirked at me then placed the necklace back into my hand.

"It's so hard! I hate it!" I pounded my fist against the mattress. "It's another emotion I have to pretend I can't feel. I can't show love to others anymore without danger of being punished. And how can I not experience love? Love is the most ingrained of all of our emotions. It's the feeling that comes most naturally to humans. At least, the feeling that *should* come most naturally to people. Right now, everyone thinks it's a liability."

"I know. It's very hard, and everyone expects so much of you— including me, I suppose. No matter how distant you think I am, I know exactly how you feel right now. I have *empathy* for you."

"Hey. Be careful about using any word ending in the suffix *pathy*," I jokingly said.

"Fine. I know what it's like to feel your humanity is being taken away from you, that you're being robbed of the privilege to experience life and all of its shortcomings, the emotional highs and lows, which are what makes life so fulfilling and enriching. But I do have one piece of advice for you."

"And what's that?"

She brushed one of her fingers against my nose. "Don't bottle up that side of yourself. I know it's slightly counterintuitive, but hear me out. The worst thing you can do is to pretend your emotions don't exist at all. That is not the right way to deal with this problem. If you do that, you're just as bad as everyone else. Cherish your emotions. You may not be able to show them but cherish them anyway. Take private moments by yourself to laugh, cry, get angry, and think of the people you love. Try to accept feelings are a part of who you are."

Mareena smiled and continued, "I know it's not going to be easy, considering that in public you've always swept your emotions under the rug and hidden that part of you. I know you sometimes don't like to express yourself anyway—public or private—but that's truly the only way to find balance and peace with yourself: accept your emotions."

Hmm. I guess that's sound advice. Advice that's hard to keep but I'll try to work on it anyway.

"What did you really come in here to tell me about?" I asked. "Or did you come to give me a motivational speech?"

She laughed quietly. "I don't know. Maybe I just wanted to spend time with you. We might not see each other as often once you're married, but I came here to inform you that your father and King Raymon have decided some of the more important details of the wedding. It will take place in the evening on the last day of the winter season."

"That's only a couple of months away."

"Is that bad? I thought it would be plenty of time for you to prepare."

"No, it's plenty of time. It's just . . ." I closed my eyes, covering them with my hands. "I feel so young. I'm only seventeen."

"Well, you'll be eighteen by the time the wedding takes place."

She was trying to be reassuring, but it didn't improve the situation. "It's not just that." I removed my hands from my face and stared down at them. "I don't feel ready. I don't feel mature enough to go through with all this. It's happening so fast."

Mareena lifted her hand off the blankets and rested it on my arm. The sudden touch startled me as she rarely showed physical affection. "Syona, you'll be ready. We'll both be ready. We're in unfamiliar territory, but we're in it together. Just one step at a time, I promise. Malopaths will always and forever stick together."

I stared into her soft brown eyes. "Thank you."

"Thank you for what?"

"For . . . being my mother, for taking care of me so well when others wouldn't. I am so grateful for you. I don't know what I would do without you."

She smiled, but layered within her smile were years of remorse and sorrow. Her eyes glistened. "Your mother was an amazing woman."

"I know."

Her voice was tender, fragile, like the thinnest branch on a tree. "I wish you could have met her."

"Me too."

Then, in that emotional moment, for the first time in my life, Mareena gently embraced me. I didn't fight it. I didn't even squeeze her back. I just sat there on my bed, soaking in the warmth of her skin and the steady rise and fall of her breathing.

Right then and there, it didn't matter that I was a Malopath. I couldn't have cared less that I was a princess arranged to marry a boy I hardly even knew or that tomorrow I would have to go out and face the world—alone this time.

Because there, in those few precious seconds, I finally felt safe.

CHAPTER
SIXTEEN

After a long, restless night, I decided I didn't want to engage with anyone for a while. I mulled over potential strategies on how to spend my day until I decided that I would take several books from the library and read. I didn't think anybody would question me for it. Only a week had passed since my Amber Ceremony, so I wouldn't have any lessons or responsibilities until tomorrow.

The king expected people in the palace to eat a formal breakfast in the morning, but I thought it best to sneak in and steal food without eating an actual meal. I was not in the mood to converse with anyone in the dining hall. I would creep in, snatch something to eat, and slink out. It was considered extremely improper, but I would risk it. Nobody would be in there besides the kitchen servants.

Checking that the hallways were empty, I quietly pushed open the double doors that I thought led into the kitchen. It was stationed right next to the dining hall so that various servants could relay food directly into the adjacent room. I heard a burst of noise as I opened the door. The sound included people shouting and the distinct sound of metal objects banging together. Strange but delicious smells assaulted my nose, but I couldn't tell what all of them were. I wasn't exactly an expert on foods or spices.

I studied the white counters and tables. Wooden cupboards filled with ingredients lined the walls, their overused doors hanging slackly on their hinges. Several brick ovens dotted the walls at eye level, but only two of them were the source of the strange but savory smells wafting through the air. People dressed in simple servant uniforms raced around everywhere, calling to one another and carrying various items in their hands. It was controlled chaos. *No wonder I've never been here before.*

When my eyes surveyed the scene in front of me, I saw something that made me think twice about executing this whole plan.

Ellison, of all people, was there in the kitchen. She was propped against the wall with her head angled toward the door as if expecting someone. Her blue eyes flashed with excitement, but it was more smug excitement than a happy emotion. Her straight blond hair was left down to fall across her shoulders. Just the sight of her made me want to shrink away and turn invisible. She hadn't said much to me, but the vibe she radiated explained it all. I had already noticed how she reacted to her environment and the people around her. Princess Ellison was an arrogant brat who was the center of her own universe.

Great, I thought bitterly. *Why are my hopes always dashed to pieces?*

"Oh, hello!" She exclaimed in a voice that dripped with honey. "If it isn't the cold princess."

"Cold princess?" I repeated. "What's that supposed to mean?"

"Your necklace," she said, pointing to the chain around my neck. "It makes you emotionless. Cold. Come on. How do you not get it?"

I stifled a sigh. "If you don't mind, I'd like to be called Syona."

"I was just having a little fun. There's no need to be upset. Oh, wait. You *can't* get upset, can you?"

I discreetly rolled my eyes. *Idiot. I'm not wearing a sapphire. Haven't you already learned that different stones correlate to specific emotions?*

"Would you like for me to take it off while we talk?" *And I hope that will only be for a few seconds longer.*

"Oh, no. Why would I ever want you to do that? I think you're quite entertaining with it on. Everyone in this palace is exactly the same. It's like talking to statues. I can't get a reaction out of anybody, which is funny and boring at the same time."

"Ellison, what exactly are you doing here?"

"Well, I've noticed you don't like people very much. It's kind of obvious. You take every opportunity you can not to speak to someone, but a person also needs to eat. I figured that instead of going into the dining hall where everyone else is, you would go in through the kitchen, and here you are! See how smart I am?"

"Let me rephrase myself. Why are you here to *begin* with?" I clarified.

"I want you to join us. Why else?"

I held up my hand. "Let me get this straight. You know how much I don't like socializing, so you went out of your way to catch me here so you could force me into conversation?"

"Yes," she answered bluntly. "But it's not that many people. Your family is actually eating somewhere else. My brother and my mother are still in their rooms, so it's just me, my younger sister, and my father. Three people. You think you can handle three people, or is that still too crazy for your sensitive mind?"

"I can handle it. I'm not a child."

"Aren't you, though? I'm older than you by a year, so you would be considered a child in *my* eyes." The princess prowled a little closer to me. "I'm still marvelously perplexed by the idea of you being the heir to this kingdom. It's awfully intriguing."

Marvelously perplexed? What book did she steal to learn those words?

"Why do you ask? Have you ever thought about it for your kingdom?" If I had to endure this conversation, I could get one thing out of it: information. I wanted to know about Crevan's family dynamic.

"Well, yes. I do admit I've mulled that idea over a couple of times, being the oldest. I would be the crown princess but, alas." A pained expression came over her face that was obviously fake. "The role fell upon my younger brother. The brother that you happen to be marrying in a little over a month. Oh! Does that mean we'll be sisters-in-law?"

"Do you know how he feels about the marriage?" I pressed.

She tapped her chin mockingly. "I don't know. I don't talk to him very much. He's been too busy attending political lessons and meetings." She paused. "What's it like?"

"What's what like?"

"Being the heir to a kingdom. What's it like?"

I clenched my teeth. I wanted to end this conversation. I had an entire day of nothing to do, and she was wasting my precious time. "It's as boring as you think it is. Now, if you'll excuse me, I would like to have the rest of the day to myself, please."

Ellison slapped her hand against the wall. "No. You're not leaving. Come and eat breakfast with my scared little sister and my overly energetic father. I'm sure you and Everlee will get along great. You have the exact same personality: dull, a wisp of a person."

"No thanks."

"Really. Come and eat with us. I mean it." She lowered her voice and added, "Or I'll make your life *miserable*."

More miserable than it already is? That'll take some serious effort. "Does it really matter?"

"Yes," she answered, flipping her hair across her shoulders.

She wants to control me. She thinks I'm timid and easily manipulated. Which . . . I am. There's no use in denying that, but I deserve some credit. I'm much smarter than her; that's for sure. I'm tired, though. I don't want to argue, so I'll let her have control. For now.

I exhaled. "Okay. Fine."

Her entire face lit up. "That's wonderful. I think servants have brought out the food already."

When I entered the room, Raymon, who sat at the head of the table, immediately smiled warmly, and I had to bite the inside of my cheek to prevent myself from smiling back. As much as I didn't want to admit, I liked him—a lot. His carefree, emotion-saturated attitude was everything I craved and everything the kingdom of Ashlon stood against. Though he had hounded me since arriving at the palace, I continued to like him.

"Why, hello, Syona! How good of you to join us! Please. Sit anywhere you would like."

"Thank you." I studied the dining table and the available seats before sliding into the one next to Everlee. She briefly glanced in my direction and then continued staring down at her lap.

"How are you today?" Raymon asked from across the table.

"I'm fine," I responded, deciding a simple answer was best.

"How does the amber stone work? Is it everything you wanted it to be?"

That wasn't a question I expected him to ask—now or ever—so I didn't have a pre-written response as I usually had for most questions. I experienced a moment of complete helplessness as my brain flailed around for a legitimate reply. Finally, I forced words out of my mouth: "Yes. I like it. It works great." There. Simple answers. That strategy was working so far.

"Isn't it just weird that everyone here thinks emotion is a curse?" Ellison suddenly interjected. "It's a little ridiculous. Everyone in this stupid kingdom is addicted to these stones. I haven't seen a single person without one."

"That's partially because Kadar made it a rule to wear them," I interjected.

Raymon tilted his head. "Kadar made it a rule that you can't go without wearing the stones?"

Here we go again. I like Raymon, but he drives me crazy. Why on earth is he so nosy? Maybe if I just give him the answer to the question, he'll stop talking to me. "Yes. It's a rule. You won't find a single person in the entirety of this kingdom without at least one stone. It's the most enforced law in our political system."

"Interesting," he mused.

At least that strain of the conversation is done and over with. I intentionally shifted the subject, turning to Everlee who sat slumped, hidden by her hair and staring down at the floor. "Is everything okay with you? You seem overly quiet."

Ellison gave a haughty scoff. "She doesn't talk very much. She's the youngest princess. Fourteen. *Fourteen!* She shouldn't have even been allowed to come here. Nobody gives her any attention, so she wouldn't have anyone to talk to anyway. Besides, she's already overshadowed by her older sister."

I wasn't completely sure, but I thought that Raymon rolled his eyes after Ellison made that remark.

With a sudden knock at one of the wooden doors, Gerrand's head abruptly came into view. His light brown eyes surveyed the room until they landed upon me. I reeled but not so much in shock. I was puzzled. *What on earth is he doing here?*

"I'm sorry for interrupting, but can I borrow Princess Syona for a moment?"

That could mean a few things: one, he had recognized the joy and usefulness of emotions and came to thank me for it; or two, he would angrily demand that I buy him another amber stone; or even three, he planned to demand a confession for being a Malopath. Not all of them were equally likely, but I didn't know which one would happen.

I got up from the table without waiting to be excused and rushed over to Gerrand. I grabbed the doorknob and, as quickly and quietly as I could, shut the door behind me. Then, I stole a few glances at the surrounding hallway to check that there were no potential eavesdroppers. What the two of us were doing could get us both either thrown in prison or executed on the spot. I hastily took off my necklace and shoved it in my pocket.

Gerrand stared me down and took a deep breath. "Hi."

"Hi?" I repeated. "You're starting out this vitally important conversation with the word *hi?*"

"How else do you want me to start it? *Hello? Salutations? Greetings? I need to talk to you about the walk we had about a week ago?* Nothing seems as efficient as *hi.*"

"Did . . . did the fake amber stone work okay?" I asked. I had snuck out of the palace at night a week earlier to buy it for him.

"Yes. It was fine."

"Okay . . . well?" I exhaled. "This is stupid. I shouldn't even be talking to you. You're obviously going to say something about how you want a new amber stone or something."

"Princess—"

Ignoring him, I interrupted: "I'm sorry for ever roping you into this. I was just so sure that—"

"Princess—"

"That you would, I mean, that you would learn—"

"Syona!" he harshly whispered. Even though he wasn't very loud, it was like a slap to the face. He had never said my name before—at least not without a royal title in front of it. It was more personal than I expected. "I did what you asked me to do."

My interest peaked. "Yes?"

"And . . ." He squeezed his eyes shut. "It's too complicated to discuss here. How about we go outside together and take a walk? You seem to like walks. Let's take a long walk around the palace, and I promise to explain everything to you while we're doing that, okay?"

I raised one of my eyebrows. "Okay."

He pointed down the hallway toward the door. "Shall we go, then? We have an entire day ahead of us."

"Yes. Sure. I don't mind."

Gerrand sauntered down the hallway toward the main entrance to the palace, and I rushed to keep up with him. As I trailed after him, my thoughts kept spiraling in circles, hope flooding my mind.

Maybe he'll do it.

Maybe. Maybe. Maybe.

CHAPTER
SEVENTEEN

The sun had risen, but it wasn't quite up in the sky, which meant fiery colors were still streaking across the clouds. It also meant that the light flooding around me provided no heat. The freezing air settled into every available space, like a thick blanket that discouraged anyone from going outside. I shivered violently. I hadn't expected it to be so cold, and my thin dress certainly didn't protect me against the bitter temperature.

Gerrand noticed it right away. "Are you alright? Do you want to go back inside?"

"I'm okay. I'll handle it. I've never been outside this early before; that's all."

He chuckled. "I have a few times, and it's quite peaceful, with not a lot of people roaming around. This weather means there'll be even fewer."

I glanced around at the surrounding buildings and streets. He was right. Nobody could be seen, which added to the stillness in the air. The scene before us might as well have been an image in a painting, unmoving and beautiful.

"The isolation is good, I guess," Gerrand remarked, a cloud of breath pluming from his mouth when he spoke.

"Why is it good? Is it so nobody will recognize me and draw in a crowd?"

"No. Of course not. It's so nobody will recognize *me*." He waved his hand at the empty space around us. "If people were outside right now, this entire courtyard would be filled with swooning girls."

I snorted loudly. "I'll try to contain my jealousy."

"What an *enormous* favor that would be! Are you sure you'll be able to manage it?"

"Oh, stop it." I flicked my arm to playfully push him away before I realized I had touched him. *Why did I touch him—and without even thinking?* "You know that nobody would recognize you. You're just a palace guard."

"A very high ranking, important palace guard," he protested. "But way to ruin the fun. I'm just joking around."

Gerrand being funny and playful? That's certainly a miracle. "Hmm . . . joking around. What is this *joking around?*"

"Great. Why did I agree to this again? Nobody likes a sarcastic princess."

I rolled my eyes. "Are you actually leading me somewhere?"

"Direct and to the point. I like it." He rubbed his hands together. "Yes, I am taking you somewhere specific."

"Oh? Are you going to bother to tell me where it is, or is that too much effort for you, being a guard who just stands around all day?"

"Ha! I thought you had no sense of humor. Yes. I *am* going to tell you where I'm leading you . . . as soon as we get there."

"You realize that doesn't make any sense, right?"

"Logical. Has anyone told you how logical you are?" Gerrand remarked.

I thought for a moment. "No, actually. Is that a good or a bad thing?"

He shrugged, a smile breaking across his face. "Let's just say I haven't decided yet."

I allowed myself a small laugh. "You're reminding me of Akilah."

"Akilah?"

"You haven't met her before? Um, she's young, energetic, talks a lot."

"Your servant? Yes, I've seen her once or twice. Are we that alike?"

"Very but she acts more like the annoying little sister I never had than a servant. She follows me everywhere."

"Oh," he tilted his head. "So, is *that* why you keep looking over your shoulder?"

I laughed again. I hadn't even meant to. It was just a reflex. I felt relaxed, and I wanted to spend more time with him. Gerrand brimmed with life. He helped me express the side of me that I never let out, emotional and human. As much as I didn't want to admit it, I craved that. I wanted it so badly, and here I was getting it. I never wanted it to end.

"Yes. That's exactly why I keep looking over my shoulder." I rolled my eyes again. "Your personalities are similar; that's all."

"Based on how you've described her, I'm not sure if that's a compliment or an insult. Which is it?"

I paused a few seconds to carefully craft my response. "I . . ." I cracked a smile. "I haven't decided yet."

Gerrand threw his hands up in exasperation. "Oh, *great!* What am I supposed to do now? How can I come up with another quirky yet lovable comeback to apply to this conversation?"

I scoffed at him. "You're certainly making a big deal out of this."

"Kidding. I'm kidding."

I couldn't help but smile, and he smiled back, glowing like sunshine. His personality mimicked sunshine, lighting up anybody who passed by. He radiated light, with a liveliness I had never experienced or witnessed before in such an unfeeling world. He made talking an art, like he had spent his lifetime mastering the skill. Even after wearing the stones for an entire year, emotion flooded out of him naturally, like it was never taken away in the first place.

At that moment, right then and there, I promised myself that I would never, ever let Gerrand wear the emotion stones again—regardless of his opinion, even if he wanted to, even if he begged me to. I would not let his personality slip away from me again, even if making that promise was unforgivably selfish of me.

When I finally glanced upward to study our surroundings, I realized a lot more time had passed than I would have liked. We had walked a large distance, almost to the edge of the city.

"Maybe, um, we should go back to the palace," I suggested.

"Aren't I the one who always tells you that?" he pointed out.

"Yes but shouldn't we?"

"Then I won't be able to show you the place I'm taking you to."

Gerrand approached the large stone wall; the border of the city, I presumed. If it weren't, I would've been surprised. It was at least thirty feet tall and several feet thick. I had to crane my neck straight upward to peer at the top.

"How are we going to get out? Shouldn't there be guards here?"

"No, there are not, actually."

I pointed to the set of large wooden doors in front of us. "Isn't this the main entrance?"

"No, this is not. This is a back entrance, a long-forgotten door," Gerrand explained with a smile.

"How did you happen to find that out?" I questioned.

"A lot of walking," he answered. "A *lot* of walking. But I like the southern part of the city, so that's where I hung out the most when I was younger."

Besides with me. "We're near the southern part of the city?" I pushed open the heavy doors. "There's nothing important in the south. Nobody lives in that area."

"Well, actually . . ." The doors finally opened, and at that point, I got a glimpse of the landscape surrounding the city. Gerrand pointed at something off in the distance, and I squinted. There, directly in the center of my field of view, was a large expanse of green trees stretching as far as I could see.

"You're taking me to the Southern Forest? Why?"

He grinned sheepishly. "I didn't allow you to go last time."

"Last time? When you still had the stones on?" I raised an eyebrow. "That was quite a while ago. Do you still remember that?"

"Of course I still remember it. I remember it like it was yesterday. I felt like I needed to make it up to you."

"Aww. That's awfully sentimental of you."

He smiled. "Shall we go?"

I peered again at the Southern Forest laid before us and tried to recall any information about it. It held the only source of wood the kingdom could rely on. The trees grew dense and gnarled. Not many hunters risked scouting out the terrain, knowing how dangerous it could be. It was the exact opposite of the Northern Forest, a spacious wooded area that teemed with life, right next to the kingdom of Tanum.

I shook off all of these facts. I wasn't here to be a scientist. I was here because Gerrand tried to do something kind for me, and we'd be able to enjoy it together.

I mirrored his smile, grateful that I didn't have to mask my emotions. "Yes. Let's go."

⸻

As soon as we stepped into the forest, foliage blanketed us in silence. Except for the occasional solitary bird chirping and the noise of crunching leaves, I heard nothing. The trees clumped together, making it difficult to maneuver, but I didn't care. I was in nature, outdoors somewhere, and it brought me joy despite the bark and twisted shrubbery continually reaching out to snag my dress.

The crisp air stung my nose, but I craved the smell of pine and dirt that accompanied it. I purposely brushed my hands over the roughest trees and rubbed the flaking bark between my fingers, getting dirt all over my skin and underneath my nails. The soft ground gave way under each step, sometimes crunching when my shoes crushed an unfortunate leaf. Dappled sunlight shone on the surrounding bushes like someone had flicked golden paint across the leaves.

Gerrand led me to an area of the forest where the trees grew farther apart. He sat down on a fallen log, and I found a patch of grass that wasn't so dirt covered to sit on.

"How do you like it?"

I swept my hand across the blades of grass. "It's amazing."

"I'm glad to hear it, but you don't seem like the type of princess who likes being outdoors."

"How many princesses have you met in your life, Gerrand?"

"Three and two of them would scream if they had so much as a speck of dirt on their dress. You, however, you're literally sitting on the ground right now. The fabric is going to get all dirty."

"I have plenty of dresses. It doesn't matter if I get a little dirt on it. Um, to answer your previous statement, I've always liked the outdoors. I used to go outside all the time when I was younger. Mareena would take me to the gardens or just anywhere. In fact . . ." I pointed to the closest tree, gnarled with twisting branches. "If I were to challenge you in a race to climb that tree, you'd lose."

"Really? You can climb trees?"

"Yes. I can climb trees and scale walls; I can go anywhere that has crevices and footholds. I did it a lot when I was younger but not so much now."

"Why do you like going outside more than being in the palace?"

"It's a nice change of pace," I exhaled with satisfaction. "I get sick and tired of staring at stone walls all day, especially white stone. They should redesign the palace, or everyone is going to go blind from the reflected light."

I paused for a second, deciding to go with the truth or part of the truth. "Also, being outside makes me feel . . ." *Like I don't have to wear the emotion stones; like nobody is watching me and I can finally feel alone; like I have enough space to breathe; like nobody is judging or expecting something from me.* I summed up all of those flashing thoughts in one word: "Free. It lets me feel free."

"Yeah. I get it." Gerrand brushed his hand over the log he sat on. "It's annoying when everyone's expecting something from you."

"Yes, definitely." I studied the trees clustered around us. "What are we going to do here? Are we going to . . . talk?"

He nodded. "That's what I thought, yes. Is there anything wrong with going to a place you've always wanted to see and just talking?"

"No. This is perfect. Thank you."

The forest went silent again. At that moment, I was painfully aware that nobody was around us. There were no animals nearby, no stray hunter, no other living thing except for Gerrand and me. Alone. Together. In a forest. The quieter the trees went, the more I could feel something in the air. Some specific emotion stretched between us, but I couldn't decipher it.

Say something. Say something now. I don't care what it is. Just break the silence. "You . . . you said back at the palace that you would explain to me what you've . . . felt over the past week without wearing the amber stone."

The mood clouding around him immediately shifted to a more serious tone. "Yes. I did say that."

I was intrigued. "And?"

"And . . . needless to say, it was one of the most confusing times of my entire life."

"Please tell the truth. I don't care what you say."

He plunged in. "I felt a lot more vulnerable and exposed. That first day was a terrible shock. It was like being thrown into ice-cold water. After over a year of feeling numb and . . . *secure*. That feeling you get when you wear the stones? It's like nothing can touch you. When your father says that emotion is a weakness, I completely agree. That numbing feeling is like you have no weaknesses. You've felt it, right?"

No. I haven't. I'll never feel it. I stayed silent, not knowing where the conversation was headed.

"I almost didn't make it through the first day. I know that I had promised you a week, but I didn't care at the time. I hated it. I wanted that part of myself gone again. It was honestly too much for me to handle. I must have searched for you for nearly an hour. I was planning on going up to you and demanding that I get a new amber stone—possibly giving you a lecture on how the emotion guidelines are important, that it *is* a privilege to get rid of that weak, fragile side."

"Then . . ." I prompted.

"But then . . ." He paused for a second, shifting his weight on the log. "I'm sorry. That was a lot more than I planned on saying. Where was I?"

"You were planning on getting a new amber stone?"

"Right. Yes. I was planning on doing that, but then I saw you at the end of the hallway. You were standing there, watching the people zip past you. The expression on your face was a look of quiet determination, like the world was trying to overwhelm you, but you didn't care. You were getting up and facing it anyway. It . . ." He broke eye contact with me and took a breath. "It made me feel something. It was a feeling I hadn't felt in a long time, but I felt it. It was beautiful and terrifying, but I craved it. I found myself wanting to feel it again and again. It made me feel weak and confused, just like what everyone says emotions will do, but it was light. It was like feeling liquid light, and I never wanted to stop feeling that again."

There was a brief moment of silence, both of us letting the rustling of the leaves fill in the sound of our conversation. "You felt it when you saw me?" It was an awkward question to ask but a necessary one.

"Yes, Syona. I felt it when I saw you."

I looked up into his smiling face, at his soft brown eyes that were full of eagerness and wonder. *I did it. I finally did it. I showed Gerrand that even though emotions are sometimes confusing and a pain to have, they're still an essential part of being human. I did it. I have another person on my side now.*

"Thank you for giving my way of thinking a chance."

He mirrored my expression. "No. Thank *you*. You've opened my perspective. You helped awaken a side of me that I thought was lost. *Thank you.*"

"Can I ask you a weird question?"

"Go ahead."

"Why do you like me, Gerrand?"

He leaned down and put his hand on my arm. Even through my sleeve, I could feel the warmth of his skin. Unlike before, I didn't flinch at his touch or think about how weird it was. My mind, for once, stayed silent.

"You're smarter than anyone I've ever met. You're beautiful. You're not afraid to express your opinion or break the rules, even if it's too quiet for anyone to notice. I love how your brain works, and you weren't afraid to show me your way of thinking. It was bold of you to do that for me."

Bold? Nobody's ever called me bold before. The only reason I express my opinions and break the rules is because I'm Malopathic, not because I'm willing to stand up for myself. Frankly, I try to avoid that. Should I tell him? I thought. *Can I trust him enough to do that?*

"I need to tell you something."

"What's that?" He leaned off the log a little closer to me.

"I . . ."

Our faces were mere inches apart. We were so close that I could feel his hot breath on my skin, pulled by some attraction that I hated and loved. My eyes widened slightly, and all of my buried thoughts came flooding toward me. *You shouldn't be doing this. Are you seriously mulling over the idea of kissing Gerrand? You do realize you're supposed to marry another boy, right? He's a boy you hardly know, yes, and it's more of a formality than anything, yes, but he's a prince. The marriage is for a good purpose. You can't afford to like another person—much less a guard.*

You shouldn't do this.

You shouldn't do this. Stop. Stop. Stop. Pull away now.

I obeyed my thoughts and broke away from him, thankful he couldn't witness my face flashing red. "I think we should get back to the kingdom," I stammered awkwardly.

If Gerrand felt annoyed, he didn't manifest it. I knew that he wanted to feel those emotions now, and I did too. Both of us badly wanted it, but my thoughts were so tangled that I couldn't discern what I needed to do. He stood up off of the log and held out his hand to me. I carefully took it, and he lifted me off the ground. "I think that's a good idea."

"Then let's go."

We started trekking through the forest again, Gerrand leading the way. With me in the back, I had plenty of time to wallow in my muddled pool of thoughts. It was like a mess of twisting vines that I couldn't break free of.

My thoughts were rampant and flinging themselves all over the place. One sentence molded into another in a vicious cycle: *Why did you do that, Syona? You got caught up in the moment. Do you even know if he wanted to kiss you? What were you doing? I can't be sure of anything. Can I? What's Gerrand thinking? I wish I knew.*

But one thought became clearer than the others: *Are we ever going to work this out?*

An answer came: *Yes, Syona. You are going to work this out. The answer is pretty clear. In around a month, you are going to marry Prince Crevan of Tanum. You will become a princess of that kingdom. Your two kingdoms will be allied, and the war will finally be over. There will be peace. That is the right choice. That is your only choice.*

If you care about your reputation or your people, nothing will ever become of you and Gerrand.

EIGHTEEN

When I came in for breakfast the next morning, I made a conscious decision to avoid the people from Tanum. I didn't want to deal with Raymon's nosy attitude, Everlee being a wallflower, or Ellison being a stingy brat. Sure, their personalities were pretty colorful. It was a little surprising that they hadn't torn each other apart by now, but I still wanted a bit of a break from the three of them.

When I arrived at the second dining hall that morning, I collided with both Kadar and Cyrus. They were calmly seated at the table, already eating food that servants had set out for them. They glanced up immediately when I came in, and I inferred that I would undergo a miniature interrogation before leaving the room. I probably wouldn't be scolded, though. Cyrus wouldn't do anything to me with the king right next to him.

"Hello, Syona," Cyrus said.

"Hello," I repeated in the same monotone voice.

"How have you been for the last couple of weeks?" he questioned me.

"Fine. How about you?"

"Fine as well."

The conversation was meaningless and instinctive, but it was necessary to diffuse any tension between the three of us so the actual communication could begin as soon as possible.

"You have a few things to attend to today."

"Do I? When?"

"A test about society and social classes in a few minutes."

So, the lessons had started up again. That made sense. It had been a week since my Amber Ceremony. Naturally, they wanted me to do as much work as possible. The lessons weren't exactly fun, but I could handle them.

"Where is it?" It was a legitimate question, one that I could safely ask.

"In the library with your private tutor."

"Is that all?"

"That is all."

I decided to ask another question, in hopes that I wouldn't get assigned more things to do. "Have you made any arrangements for the wedding yet?"

Kadar replied this time. "Not yet, but we will probably discuss it more the closer we get to the event."

"Thank you."

"Now go, or you will be late. You can have breakfast afterward."

I nodded and backed away slowly. *Huh. That was probably the least dramatic conversation I've had with Cyrus in a while. Maybe I should have the king around me more often.*

As I darted into the hallway, I smacked directly into Crevan. I collided with him so hard that I was knocked onto the floor, sliding across the marble. All of my breath went whooshing out of my lungs. It felt like I had run into a wall.

"Are you alright?" He mumbled to me. He reached his hand down, offering to help me up.

I reached out my hand so he could pull me to my feet. "Were you spying on me?"

"Yes, I was. I'm sorry."

His immediate answer jarred me. I hadn't expected him to tell the truth or any version of it. *I* would have made something up. "Why?"

"I wanted to see what you were up to, and it appears that you have some lesson in a few minutes, right?"

"Yes," I confirmed tentatively, not knowing his intentions.

He shuffled his feet on the floor. "Would it be alright if I joined you?"

"Joined me?" I repeated, struggling to keep my voice even. "In the lesson? You realize that I'll be taking a test, right?"

He nodded.

"A test that involves the kingdom of Ashlon."

"Yes. I've studied your history, society, and culture ever since I got here."

I reached up to the back of my neck and undid the necklace, tucking it into the pocket of my silky jacket. "How much spying have you done, exactly?"

"I'm not spying. I wouldn't call it spying."

"Then what would you call it?"

He thought for a moment. "Sneakily observing my environment."

I rewarded him with a laugh, and his face broke into a smile. I liked his smile. It wasn't very noticeable, but plenty of emotion was behind it. He was quiet but charismatic, like a warm hearth, and reflected a gentle kindness that wasn't obvious at first glance.

"Okay, then. How much of 'sneakily observing your environment' have you done?" I asked.

"It's *all* I've done. I've been to every room in the palace and wandered all over the kingdom. I've studied records, documents, history books, everything. I know everything about the kingdom of Ashlon."

"Oh?" I put a skeptical expression on my face. "So, you're perfectly qualified to take my test."

"Yes."

"I don't believe you. Do you really know everything? That's either impressive or creepy."

His expression broke into a smile. "Do you care to make a wager then? Let's turn it into a contest. Whoever answers the most questions correctly and the fastest wins."

I folded my arms. "What are the stakes?"

"You win, I do whatever you want me to until the wedding. I can stop sneaking around. I can avoid you. We don't even have to talk to each other—anything to make this less awkward for you. And I know that you think this is awkward. Don't try to deny it. We're a seventeen and eighteen-year-old getting married solely because of political gain, and we didn't know each other. It couldn't get more awkward than this. You can make me do anything to make this event as comfortable as possible for you."

That's a nice gesture. "Fine. What happens if *you* win?"

The prince suddenly fell silent, thinking for a few seconds before answering. "You have to do an activity with me tomorrow, just the two of us. I decide what we do, how long it is, and what we talk about. Is that fair?"

Hmm. Uncomfortable but not the end of the world. That's not nearly as bad as I thought it would be. I'm going to win anyway. I don't need to worry. Crevan's cocky and is clearly overestimating his abilities. "That's fair. I accept those terms."

"Okay then." He nodded. "Let's go."

‹‒⊏〣⊐‒›

I hadn't visited Evander in a while, so it would be nice to see my tutor's familiar face during the lesson. It was the same private library I always went to. It looked exactly the same, right down to the arrangement of the books on the shelves and the table in the center of the room.

Evander was sitting at the table completely engrossed in his book, so we definitely startled him upon entering.

His entire body jerked, like a tug on puppet strings. He slammed the book down on the table and whirled toward us, but his face immediately relaxed when he saw me. "Hello, Princess Syona! How are you? Ready for your test?"

"Yes, I am. Is okay if one person joins us today?"

"Sure. Who is it?" Evander asked.

Crevan stepped out into view, and my tutor's eyes widened slightly. "Prince Crevan. *You* wish to join us today?"

"Yes," Crevan confirmed.

"You see, we made a bet," I informed him.

He slid the book out of reach to give me his full attention. "Really? What are the terms?"

"The prince seems to think that he knows more about the kingdom of Ashlon than I do."

He laughed. "We can easily test that. Please, sit down."

The two of us slid out the chairs and sat down next to each other. Evander reached out and yanked a book from the shelf. He placed it on the tabletop and flipped through several pages before settling on one spot. "Alright. I'm going to ask you a series of questions that will test your knowledge. How do you want this to play out?"

"Whoever answers the most questions correctly and in the fastest time wins," Crevan immediately replied.

I shot him a glare. Even though that was exactly what I had in mind as well, I hadn't wanted him to say it, as if he had control over the situation.

"Good. Let's begin."

Crevan placed his hands down on the table and leaned forward in his seat. He appeared attentive and alert, ready to play. He seemed so sure of himself, like he had already won.

"Why is this kingdom named the kingdom of Ashlon?" My tutor asked us.

Crevan slammed his hand on the table, making me almost leap out of my seat. "The original nation, making up this entire peninsula, was named Tanum. When your ancestors broke off from our kingdom and established their own, they decided to name it after the family name of their first king, Ashlon, to separate themselves as much as possible from the central kingdom."

His response was lightning, calculated. I hadn't stood a chance against him. My brain hadn't even produced an answer, let alone said one out loud, and it didn't help that Crevan was now talking twice as fast as I could. "Wait a moment. The kingdom of Ashlon is a break off from the kingdom of Tanum?"

Crevan peered at me, confused. "Um, yes. Did you not know that?"

"No, Crevan. I did *not* know that." *How did I not know that?* "Would you mind explaining that small aspect of history?"

"Really? We're having a lesson in the middle of a test? That kind of undermines the purpose of—"

"Just answer it," I snapped.

"Fine," Crevan relented. "You know how there are two races of people, separated into two kingdoms? You guys have brown eyes—"

"Yes. I know. Please continue."

"There was originally just one kingdom, with the two races of people intermixed. There was a class system. Your race was of lower status than ours, with fewer rights, so you broke off and established your own kingdom. Simple, okay? It happened, like, a hundred years ago. Nothing really important."

"It certainly *seems* important," I protested.

"Important enough for the princess to know off the top of her head? Because—"

"Are we done here? We need to continue." Evander glanced back and forth between the two of us. "Are you keeping score? Because that's already one point for him. How many questions do you want me to ask?"

"Twenty," Crevan answered instantly. "If that's okay with you, that is."

I shrugged. At that point, honestly, I didn't care as long as we got done with this task as quickly as possible. My confidence was waning drastically based on how quickly Crevan responded.

"Next question: why can females rule in this kingdom?"

Again, a snake-strike answer: "When you establish your kingdom, you make up your own rules." He specifically turned to look at me. "Your race of people, already tired of being degraded and oppressed by us, decided that everyone would be treated as equals, which means you don't have the same gender restrictions as we do in our kingdom."

I realized at that moment that I might have seriously underestimated Crevan and his ability to absorb information.

My tutor smiled. "Syona? Are you actually trying, or is this a trick to get out of participating?"

"What? No, I just didn't—"

"Nobody really talks about it, and it happened over a hundred years ago, okay?" Crevan snapped.

"I'm trying," I promised. "Crevan is just faster than I am." *And he knows more than I do.*

Evander sighed. "Fine. Here's a question that I'm just asking you, to make sure you're actually remembering things. How many people live in this kingdom?"

"Around twenty thousand people, with three distinct social classes," I answered. "Nobility, middle, and lower. It's extremely rigid. Classes are determined by the number of stones you can afford to wear. The privilege of wearing three or four stones is for nobility, and the royal family, guards, and other palace workers distribute the stones to the people when they pay for them."

"Wait. You asked that only for her." Crevan paused us. "Are we going to count that question in her favor, then?"

"Yes, now stop talking," I shot.

"Next question," my tutor ordered. "What is the main resource and money system of this kingdom?"

"Silver," both of us answered in perfect synchrony. *Easy question. Any idiot with half a brain would be able to answer that correctly.*

My tutor continued, "What are the hunting regulations for the Southern Forest?"

Crevan immediately spoke: "Only nobility and the royal family can hunt in the forest. If any commoner wants to do it, they have to pay an extra fee. Even then, people can only hunt certain seasons, in the winter and fall."

I bolted upright, a streak of annoyance shooting through me. "There is absolutely no way that you would know such an obscure fact about a kingdom that you didn't grow up in and know the information off the top of your head. It's impossible. Are you looking at the book he's reading? Is that why you stand up every time?"

He frowned. "I'm not cheating if that's what you're accusing me of."

"I *am* accusing you of cheating." I gathered up the pages of the book and slammed it shut. "Tell me. What else do you know about the kingdom of Ashlon?"

He took a breath and leveled his gaze with me. "I know that Osion is the name of the advisor who oversees all of the stone ceremonies, and I get the impression that you've never actually learned his name before. You just don't care. The head of the royal guard is named Officer Hazen, but there's another officer named Gerrand who's a close second. He's your personal guard, I believe. You know his first name because you knew each other as children. Your mother Ionda died in childbirth, but she has a sister, Mareena, who played a big part in raising you. You have a servant named Akilah, who you probably treat more like a friend than anything. You had a brother named Davin, who was the role model you tried and failed to live up to. You're an outdoor person who likes to take walks all around the kingdom, and you don't like sleeping." He paused, folding his arms. "How's *that* for not knowing anything?"

I didn't speak. I was just too shocked. Crevan, after being here for only a few weeks, knew more about the kingdom than I had known throughout my entire life. Even worse, he knew more about *me* than anyone else. He had cracked my outer shell. My secrets spilled all over the floor for anyone to pass by and read.

"How do you know all of this?"

"I observe. I think. I listen," he responded, staring directly at me. "Just. Like. You. Except there's a major difference between us. You don't want to accept it. You withdraw from your environment instead of studying it. There's a lot you would know if you just focused on what's going on around you. I notice the tiny bits of evidence around me and draw conclusions from them. It's as simple as that. You could do it too, if you weren't so cowardly." He paused. "I think this lesson is over. I won our bet. This time I don't think you'll argue with me. We'll do the activity in the morning, just you and me." He smiled. "I'm looking forward to it already."

With those ominous words, he whirled out of the room, not bothering to shut the door.

"What did you agree to do, exactly?" my tutor asked.

I sighed. "I agreed to do an activity with him. He decides all the details."

Evander started gathering up the books and storing them back on the shelves. "That's not too bad."

I wasn't so sure. Crevan was nice enough on the surface, but he definitely had an angry side, a complicated version of him that I couldn't make out. He liked his secrets. He wouldn't let me pry very deep.

Is this all a ruse? Does he just want me to be alone with him so he can interrogate me or accuse me of things? He seems to know a lot of stuff about me already, based solely on what I do and how I act.

If those things are so obvious, has he already inferred that I'm Malopathic.

CHAPTER
NINETEEN

When I slowly woke up, I immediately noticed it was significantly colder than it had been the evening before. Even through my thick blankets, I could feel cold air seeping through the fabric. I gathered up the silk around me and flipped over in my bed, trying to nestle into the warmth, hating winter even more than usual.

A ray of sunlight hit my face, and I squinted against the sudden change in brightness. I pulled out my hand from under the warm blanket to block the rays of light from my face. The air enveloped my skin and immediately sucked the warmth out, as if I were sticking my hand in snow. Outside of the window, the landscape was painted completely white. *Oh, no. It's . . .*

Akilah abruptly burst into the room in a whirlwind, rushing over to my bedside. "Snowing! It's snowing! It's the first snow! Syona! Princess! It snowed!"

Please. Can't you be anything other than happy for just a few minutes? "I can tell," I deadpanned.

Completely ignoring my negative attitude, Akilah started humming. She leaped to the center of my room and started prancing around on the carpet. I exhaled wearily, tossing the blankets to one side.

"Why do you enjoy snow so much?" I huffed. "I don't get it."

"It makes everything just so bright and happy! Look outside! I love the color white. It's so magical."

"Magical," I repeated. "Nobody uses that word anymore. Magic doesn't exist.

Akilah shot me an odd look. "You realize that the emotion stones are enchanted, right? They're not normal gemstones. *Something* magical happened to them."

That was an excellent point, but I chose to ignore it. "We only *assume* they're enchanted. There may be some other scientific explanation we haven't yet discovered. Besides, I meant the aspects of magic having to do with casting spells."

"But I've read books about magic."

"Were they history books? They're stories. Fiction. Not real."

"Whatever, I'm still happy it snowed!" She bounded over to the window and undid the latch.

"Let me stop you right there. You can fawn over the white freezing stuff on the ground as much as you like, but the only thing that will get me legitimately mad at you is if you open the window."

Her hands shot back from the glass as if it were covered in thorns. "Yep. Okay." She turned back toward me. "Do you have anything specific planned today?"

"Unfortunately, yes," I admitted. "I promised Crevan that I'd do a recreational activity with him. I don't know what, though. He said that he'd work out all the details."

She tilted her head inquisitively. "Okay, so like, a date or something?"

"What? No! It's nothing like a date!" I protested. "Those only exist in the kingdom of Tanum anyway. Nobody goes on outings and dates in the kingdom of Ashlon now that everyone has amber stones. This is because I lost a bet. I didn't agree to do this."

"Why did he ask you?"

"I don't know. I really don't know. The one thing I know for sure is that our relationship is . . . complicated. I can't tell if he even likes me. He tolerates my presence at least. I like him. I enjoy being around him but . . ." I sighed. "Half the time, he's kind and funny. The other half of the time, he treats me like I'm the princess he's going to be marrying in a month because of an alliance."

"But that's good, right?"

I rubbed my forehead in exasperation. "It's awkward and frustrating."

"What are you doing, though? Where are you supposed to meet him?" Akilah asked.

"I have no clue. He didn't even tell me."

I heard a small knock at the door. Though so quiet it was hardly noticeable, I had anticipated it. I lunged for the door, almost certain I would catch Crevan off guard.

Nobody was there. It was an empty doorway. I swiveled my head back and forth, but the deserted hallway stared back at me. Somehow Crevan had disappeared. I grumbled. *He probably knows every inch of the palace by now.* Out of the corner of my eye, I glimpsed something stuck to the face of the door. I ripped the note off the door and slammed it behind me. "Unbelievable."

"What?" Akilah cried. "Oh, he left you a note."

Sighing, I carefully unfolded the paper and read. His writing was neat, scrolling across the page in perfect lines. *The opposite of Gerrand's, I suppose.*

Syona,

Meet me outside in the front courtyard in half an hour. I'm sure that's more than enough time for you to get ready for the day.

Wear a coat. It's cold.

"He didn't bother to sign it," Akilah remarked.

"He didn't *need* to sign it. I know who it's from. He knew I would know who it's from." I gritted my teeth. "Stupid prince. I knew he would make me go outside."

"So, your entire relationship with him now is based on outwitting and predicting the future moves of the other person?" she questioned.

"Come to think of it, that's exactly what it's turning out to be. Can you please help me get ready? I don't want to be late."

The thick, wet snowflakes swirled around everywhere, so visibility was at its minimum. The cold flakes seemed to be attracted to my hair, and even though I was wearing a cloak with a hood, the few strands that weren't covered by fabric were immediately sacrificed to the snow.

I searched for Crevan, my vision blurry. Throughout the entire court-yard, there was only one disruption in the curtain of white: a figure that stood among the stones with a blue cloak flapping in the wind, trying to get free.

Crevan immediately spotted me. "Hello, Syona! I'm so glad you could make it! You're on time!"

"Don't treat it like a miracle," I snapped, rolling my eyes. "I can be punctual when I wish to be." I scanned the snow, my eyes making out every individual flake. "How on earth are we going to do anything in this weather?"

"Oh, come on. This is nothing. I would beg for this mild weather back home, and cut me some slack. I may know a lot, but I didn't know it would snow."

"You, without a doubt, are the most arrogant person I know."

He smiled. "One of my best qualities. Shall we go?"

"Yes, but you still haven't told me what we're doing," I protested.

"Hmm. You probably can't see them because of the snow and because we painted all the equipment white to match."

"Them?"

"Yep." He patted something next to him, and the white background shifted. I heard the scraping of hooves against the stone. Over the howling wind I could make out the sound of heavy, wet breathing. "Them. This is Sugar and Cane."

"Horses? Are we going to be riding on horses? You have got to be kidding me."

"Nope. I'm not kidding. Besides, we're going to be riding among trees, so the snow won't fall on us," he explained.

"Wait. The horses are *named* Sugar and Cane? Like a sugar cane? I'm not associating myself with a creature so stupidly named," I said jokingly. "Besides, I've never ridden a horse before. Ever."

"Don't worry." Crevan produced a pair of reigns from behind his back. "I can teach you. It's really easy. We'll just be riding around for a few hours—nothing serious. Are you okay with it?"

I hesitated but caved. "Yes. I'm okay with it, as long as I don't fall off or anything."

Crevan stroked the first one's muzzle. "They're really gentle. As for the ridiculous names, you can blame Everlee. Since nobody takes her seriously that often, we decided to do her a favor and keep the names. Do you need help getting on, or do you know what to do?"

I couldn't possibly ask Crevan for help. That would be suicide, and it would make him flaunt his intelligence even more. I'd never done it before, but I'd seen other people get on a horse. I was smart enough to figure it out.

I walked up to the side of the horse named Sugar. I inspected the whitish saddle strapped tightly to its back, discerning how I would get on. I wrapped my hands around the straps and hoisted myself up, straining, then I promptly lost my grip and fell back to the ground.

"Do you need—" Crevan started.

"No."

"I mean, I know what happened to your hand, so . . ."

"It's healed. That's not the problem."

"Do you need he—"

"No, I do not." I kept interrupting him.

"I was just going to suggest standing inside the stirrups to hoist yourself up. You know what those are, right? They're th—"

"I know what they're called," I snapped back. I refused to let him get in a single sentence.

I managed to get one leg up and over the saddle, and soon after, the rest of me followed. I shifted my weight and tried to make myself as comfortable as possible. The leather was soft and expensive, which would make the ride easier, but it still felt unwieldy. I gathered up the reins in my hand and faced forward, trying to get my bearings. It was an interesting experience. I had to take a second to process the fact that I was on an animal, a living creature. The horse exhaled, contracting its sides. I couldn't resist the urge to reach out and smooth down its fur.

"You should have told me to wear a specific dress for this. I'm going to get stuff all over this one," I tried complaining.

"You're not, and you don't care about your dresses," Crevan immediately shot back.

"Where are we going anyway?" I questioned him.

"I thought that we could go to the Southern Forest. It's the only wooded spot close to here."

I stiffened. The Southern Forest? *He wants me to go with him to the Southern Forest? But that's the place Gerrand and I went together. Where we . . . kind of . . . almost . . . kissed. It has sentimental value. I don't want to share that with Crevan as well.*

Plus, it's really secluded. Nobody else will be there.

He read my body language. "Is there a problem with that spot? We can go somewhere else if you'd like."

"No," I automatically responded. "You won the bet. You get to decide all of the details. The Southern Forest is just fine."

"Then let's go," Crevan said. "Jostle the reins a little to make the horse move and pull them in the direction you want to go."

"I know," I replied, even though I didn't.

Crevan flicked the reins with his wrist, and so did I. Our horses slowly trotted across the courtyard. South. Towards the forest.

And into the snowstorm.

It was the same forest. Nothing had changed from when I had spent time with Gerrand, aside from the wetness of the snow. There wasn't much of it, though. The canopy was so thick that all the leaves filtered it from falling on us, so Crevan had been right.

I hated that.

After already showing his knowledge of the back exit that Gerrand and I had used, he also seemed to know about the denseness of the forest. He immediately led the horses into a cleared area, expertly guiding the animals through wide paths so they wouldn't get snagged by the branches. His intelligence was both admirable and annoying. The fact that he knew all of this already was incredible.

We traveled in complete silence for a while, the lack of noise only accompanied by the occasional sound of the horses dragging their hooves through the leaves on the ground.

"Crevan?"

"Yes?"

"Why did you want me to do this?" I wondered aloud.

He shrugged. "I don't know. I just felt like I wanted to spend more time with you. I want us to get to know each other more."

"But we already talked when I invited you out into the garden."

"Should we talk just once and call it good?" He chuckled to himself. "Learning about someone is a process. It takes multiple conversations over a long period of time."

I took the perfect opportunity to poke fun at him. "Wow. You sound like you're talking from *experience*. Does the invisible prince actually have the social skills to maintain and develop a relationship? I'm . . . I'm so impressed!"

He shot back his own sarcastic comment: "You're just as invisible as I am. You realize that, right? Oh, I forgot. You're not very observant, so I guess you wouldn't know."

I cut off that branch of conversation before it turned into an all-out war. "What do you want to actually talk about?"

"Talk about?" he repeated.

"You said that you would choose what we talked about. What are we going to talk about—if shooting sarcastic comments and insulting each other doesn't work for you?"

"I'll tell you in a minute." The prince shifted around to inspect me. "You aren't wearing any stones, right?"

"Nope. Per your request."

He visibly relaxed. "Thanks. I'm sorry if it's disrespectful to your culture, but it's much easier talking to someone who acts like an actual human being."

I'm completely fine with that, although I'll never be able to tell you. The request is actually liberating, and I like that about you. It's just weird. I wish you would give me a better explanation than what you've given me so far.

"What are we going to talk about, though?"

He paused. "How do the people of your kingdom view the kingdom of Ashlon?"

At least that was a question I could answer. "Not many people have strong opinions anymore. A lot of that is because of the stones. Everyone's compliant, but some people are upset because we've been fighting for so long. Hopefully, this marriage will smooth that over. There's also a bit of jealousy because your kingdom is located among a lot of natural resources."

And fear, too, because you're more powerful than us—a fact my family refused to accept until now. My thoughts paused. *Maybe that's because we broke off from you. We had to start from scratch while your kingdom continued to prosper.* It was a plausible explanation I never knew existed.

"Okay. Thanks. I'm just trying to understand your kingdom better," he summarized.

"Answer this, then. How do *your* people think of this kingdom?"

He chuckled. "A little bit of the exact opposite, I'm afraid. They're very condescending, a little disrespectful sometimes. There's an apparent lack of seriousness."

I remembered Crevan's words during the test. "You said it happened a century ago, right?"

"What happened?"

"The break-off, when the kingdoms split apart," I clarified.

"Yes. It did."

"Could you explain why again? I never knew this until a day ago."

"There were two races in the original kingdom of Tanum," he started explaining. "Yours and mine. When you guys joined our kingdom, you were treated as second rate people and not given any rights, so your people revolted and traveled south, wanting to establish your kingdom where we couldn't subject you."

"Do you know why you mistreated us?"

"I don't know," he answered simply. "We'd been doing it for decades. I guess the reason was generally lost."

"Is there still prejudice against our race in your kingdom?"

"A bit but we're trying to abolish that. Most of my people generally recognize, if not respect, the fact that you're an actual kingdom. However, some people think—including my father—that our nations would be better off combined again."

That was news. "What?" I exclaimed. "Merge the kingdoms? Tell me your father isn't actually considering that! Raymon thinks that? Does he realize how absurd that idea is?"

"Well, he's not exactly . . . serious . . . about it. He's just . . . discussed it once or twice," he explained vaguely.

That didn't comfort me at all. "Merging the kingdoms? Nobody wants that! Kadar would never agree! Ever! How would that even work?"

Crevan stayed silent.

"Why? Why on earth would you want us back? It wouldn't be beneficial for either of us! How could my people possibly be useful to you?"

He didn't answer, but his shoulders tensed, and his face became tight-lipped.

I exhaled. "If you want to talk about something else, let's talk about something else," I said in hopes of breaking the weird tension between us.

"He meant merging the kingdoms in a more political sense, as allies, with the marriage alliance," Crevan explained.

"Fine. I guess that makes sense. I'm changing the subject now. Is it hard being the heir to your kingdom?"

Crevan revived immediately. He smiled; the change in expression was comforting. His smile reminded me of hot coals in a fire, a gentle warmth. "Right now, it doesn't seem as difficult as usual. I have a lot of responsibilities, though."

"You're in a neighboring kingdom, counting down the days to a wedding that we're planning for you. What tasks would you need to complete?"

"I meant there are a lot of expectations." He groaned dramatically. "My father wants me to be perfect. Do this; do that. 'You're growing up to rule a kingdom one day, so you'd better learn as much as you can and be an expert at negotiating,' that sort of thing."

"That's the same with me." *Except I never even thought about ruling the kingdom of Ashlon. Never. I don't think that crossed my thoughts naturally even once in my life. All I ever cared about was getting to the next day. I can't think about the future because I don't know if I'll be able to experience it. I worry about myself the most, which I guess is a little selfish of me, but I don't think self-preservation is a bad thing.* "I don't get stressed out about it *that* much," I tried to reassure him.

He seemed to consider my comment for a moment before he suddenly leaned over and grabbed my left arm, jerking it palm up. I cried out in surprise, but before I could do anything about it, he pushed my sleeve upward to expose the underside skin, constantly red and raw from me scraping at it so often in trying to quickly control my thoughts and feelings.

"What about this?"

I hurriedly pulled down my sleeve again. "It's nothing. Don't worry about it."

He rolled his eyes. "Sure, it's nothing."

"Stop. You wouldn't get it anyway."

Crevan looked shocked. "Syona, I'm an heir to a kingdom too. It may be a different kingdom, but trust me. We're more alike than you might realize or care to admit. Both of us are continually drowning in a world we don't understand but a world we were born into. We both fight to keep our head above water every day, but we can't escape because our position and our birthright obligates it." His face suddenly grew somber. "I know what it's like to beg for a few simple hours of isolation while everyone's staring at you, to want to read but never have time. I know what it's like to want to do the things you love while your family forces you to do something else. Any heartache, any trouble you've ever been through, I will know what it's like. I'm sorry that life is so hard on you."

"It . . . is," I agreed, with a twinge of awe in my voice. "Thank you."

Crevan nodded and faced forward again, observing the trail ahead of him.

A new perspective was dawning on me as the pieces to this puzzle rearranged themselves in my mind. I now saw Crevan in a new light. He cared about me. He legitimately wanted the best for me, and we were astonishingly alike, too. Both of us were unwilling heirs to parallel kingdoms, destined to fill a position neither of us were interested in.

There's safety in common ground. We can both push through life together. Burdens are always easier if you share them with another person, especially a person who's sweet and sensitive and so very much like you.

Maybe it wouldn't hurt to spend more time with him from now on.

TWENTY

I t finally stopped snowing after a few hours. The freezing, wind-swept hallways kept me awake as I paced through them. Night had fallen—my favorite time of the day. Even though the temperature had plummeted and I could see my breath once more, nothing in the world could make me stop appreciating the time when the sun went down. When others went to sleep, I stayed awake to enjoy peace. The corridors of the palace were so deathly quiet you could hear a needle drop. To me, it felt like sinking into a soft mattress of silence. I could finally think clearly for the first time in the entire day.

It wasn't entirely quiet, though. I could hear the gentle whistling of the wind, echoing and echoing until you couldn't pinpoint the source. It was like a haunting song, low and somewhat sad. I strained my ears to try and pick out the melody, but it had faded.

The breeze blew the few remaining candles, making the flames dance wildly on the wicks and casting flickering shadows on the walls. I loved empty hallways: no tapping of shoes on the marble floor, no rustling of fabric as someone walked. The only sound was my red cloak brushing against my silk dress.

I wandered down the hallways, purposely getting lost. I could think best when I walked, so that's what I tended to do. I had a lot of time to kill, and exploring the palace was the easiest way to do it.

As I paced down one of the corridors, I stopped in my tracks, peering at a door that was different from all the others, trimmed with gold. The trimming design depicted oak leaves and acorns woven into lines that mimicked branches. An expensive decoration, one that was done to mark rooms that belonged to the royal family, like the pine cones and needles on mine. I recognized it immediately.

I rushed over to the door and swept my hands against the wood. *This . . . this is Davin's room. I've only seen it a few times, but I'm certain of it.* The realization sent a pang of hurt echoing inside my chest, which I tried to push away. His death had been several months ago, so I was supposed to be done grieving.

Slowly, I pushed open the door and peeked inside. A draft of freezing air wafted over me, and that alone made me hesitate to continue, but I pushed the door entirely open anyway. It was completely silent as it swung on its metal hinges. I had never actually been inside his room before, so I studied every detail. His canopy bed was tucked into the corner. There was a dresser, a closet, and a window, just like mine. A fine layer of dust coated the desk next to the bed, and the black sheets and blankets appeared completely untouched. Piles upon piles of books sat on the carpet next to the bed, arranged in neat stacks, not any of them disturbed.

The books made me smile. *He was the perfect prince, always studying, always dedicated to the kingdom he would rule one day.*

I dragged my shoes across the thin carpet as I shuffled to the center of the room. An absolute stillness overcame me, like time had stopped completely. The former crown prince had spent most of his time here. It was both comforting and nerve-racking. I had looked up to my brother, but I hadn't known him very well. During the seventeen years of my life, he'd never spent much time with me, always wrapped up in his political responsibilities.

Maybe I can make up for the lost time.

I decided against touching the books. They looked so neat and tidy, and I knew that I wouldn't be able to put them back where they were if I moved them out of order. Instead, I crouched down low to the carpet, peering under the bed to see if there was anything noteworthy. Lying among the shadows, I could make out the edge of a wooden box. The dimensions were wide and thin, so it fit perfectly underneath the bed. I scooted down and pushed my arms underneath, trying to reach it. My fingers caught the smooth corners, and I pulled it out into the light.

Crouching in front of the box, I undid the metal clasps and opened the wooden lid. I almost laughed out loud when I glimpsed what was inside. It was a bow: a honey-colored wooden bow with an expensive leather handle. I would probably find his quiver, still full of arrows, if I searched for it.

I felt a twinge of sadness and joy at the same time for discovering something so precious to him. It was like finding treasure. This bow *was* Davin, his most prized possession. He used it whenever he could. Gingerly, I removed the bow from the padding and held it out in front of me. I could imagine him notching an arrow, feeling the stretch of the string, and the kickback with the snapping release. The image was vivid in my thoughts, a ghost of my brother left behind.

He did like hunting, I thought. *He was born for the woods. He was born for everything about his position, and he embraced it. He seemed to thrive in it.*

Being heir wasn't meant for me. It was meant for Davin.

My fingers slid over the wooden surface, devoid of any splinters and perfectly sanded, as soft as silk. I wondered how much it had cost and who had crafted it, likely years ago. *He was an expert at the bow. It prac-*

tically molded to his hands. He would never miss. I don't think he missed a shot in years by the time he was killed.

"Ironic, wasn't it?"

My head shot up toward the sound of the voice. I was so startled that I almost dropped the bow, which would have damaged it and my heart too. Air flowed out of me in a sigh when I realized who it was. It was Gerrand, staked in the doorway with a somber smile on his face. A flickering candle rested in his cupped hands, which lit up a small section of the room. He paced over to the desk, set the candle on top of it, and then sat down on the bed.

I moved to join him, but then my attention reverted back to the bow in my hands. "Yes, it was." A hunting accident, Cyrus had told me. He was killed by one of his favorite pastimes, killed by a sport nobody could out skill him on. "Did you know him at all?"

Gerrand shrugged. "Everyone knew of him, certainly, but I didn't know him personally. I didn't get to see him much because I was posted in a different hallway. It was the hallway with *your* room, so I guess it worked out perfectly."

I smirked. "I guess it did, but what are you going to do now?"

"What do you mean?"

"How are you going to work out your position at the palace? You can't be a guard if you're breaking the rules about emotion stones."

He flicked his hand dismissively. "Nobody has caught me yet, so I'll just figure it out as I go."

I rolled my eyes. "I find your lack of a plan admirable and idiotic. I also can't tell if you're being courageous or just stupid."

"Courageous. I'm courageous. What about you? I can't tell if you're smart and logical or just uptight."

"I'm . . . trying not to be . . . uptight, I mean," I protested. *I have more people who care about me now than ever before. Akilah, Mareena, Crevan, you, all of you have been supporting me. I think Mareena would be proud of me, knowing I've finally built relationships with people while also avoiding execution.*

"Fine. I guess we both have our quirks." Gerrand glanced down at the bow I clutched protectively in my hands. "That's Davin's, right?"

"Yes." A flash of anger and puzzlement shot through me, and all of my unspoken thoughts spilled out: "I just don't get it! He was killed in a hunting accident? A *hunting accident!* Yes, that can happen, but it doesn't make any sense. Davin always hunted! He was probably the most careful person alive when it came to that sort of thing."

I kept on ranting. "And why now? Doesn't it seem like a coincidence that it was directly after his Amber Ceremony or directly before this marriage alliance? Does anyone know exactly how it happened? There wasn't a funeral, so did anyone see his body? Could . . . could he still be alive somewhere?"

Gerrand's voice was gentle but serious. "That doesn't seem very likely. You are just trying to make something you can puzzle and create theories over."

"I am not!" I snapped, more harshly than I intended, and his face immediately creased into a frown. I realized it was the first time I had seen him frown, but at the moment, I didn't care. "I'm just gathering evidence and thinking outside the box!" *Like Crevan said I should do.* "Is that a crime? Did or didn't anyone see Davin dead?"

He tapped his chin. "The guards . . . the guards who accompanied him to the forest. There were three of them. They were the only ones who could have seen what actually happened."

I exhaled. "That's a start. Do you know their names? Have you seen them before? Where are they?"

Gerrand squeezed his eyes shut. "I think all three of them resigned, so they could be anywhere in the kingdom now."

"What?" I exploded. "Why?"

He made a shushing noise. "Do you want to wake up everyone in the palace? It's past midnight. I don't know why they resigned. Yes, that's a little suspicious, but I trust the king. I trust your family, and I don't believe anyone in this kingdom would want Davin dead. We just have to trust that what they said is true, okay?"

I exhaled, trying to relax. "Fine. Why are you up this late anyway?"

"Everyone in the entire palace knows you stay up late, so I figured the best way to have a private conversation with you was to stay up as late as you do." He peered out the window at the twinkling night sky. "Although I didn't think it would be this late. I should have gone home hours ago. I'm so tired." He yawned. "Is this what you do every night? How do you still function?"

I wanted to smile back at him or at least laugh playfully, but I couldn't. Doubt was creeping in, mining away the solid foundation of the assurance that built up our relationship. I had to marry Crevan. That fact was set in stone, so I doubted I would even have the chance to be open *friends* with Gerrand. Relationships were nonexistent in the kingdom of Ashlon, not with half of everyone wearing an amber stone. Even the ones who couldn't afford the love-negating stone still avoided friendships and love to fit in socially.

On top of that, I had a nagging sense in the back of my mind that things could actually work out between Crevan and me. He would always show his emotions, and there was nothing that could change that. Even better, he seemed to be concerned whenever I wore the stones, so I could always act like myself around him. There was absolutely nothing that could stop Crevan and I from actually loving each other. Maybe it was already true.

Gerrand, however, Gerrand was unstable. We were both breaking the rules. I was a princess. I was supposed to wear all of the stones. He was a guard. *He* was supposed to wear all of the stones. We were risking everything by just talking to one another, and I still wasn't completely sure he was on my side. Who was I kidding? He was an Ashlon, a person who would always and forever not be completely comfortable with emotions, no matter how long he went without the stones. Risking so much and breaking so many rules, even by my standards, added unneeded stress to my life. I wouldn't have the security with Gerrand that Crevan would surely give me.

Even as all of these thoughts flashed through my mind, I glanced at Gerrand's face and his carefree smile, and I still couldn't decide. Logically, Crevan made sense. Crevan was the right choice. I would be happy with him. I would have the authenticity I wanted. But for some reason, my brain was going beyond logic for the first time in my life. Emotional tangles obscured facts and evidence. Even though the choice I should make was clear, I didn't have the heart to make it. It was both uncomfortable and soothing at the same time.

"I . . . should retire for the night." I stood up and strode briskly out of the room without turning back around. "Goodnight, Gerrand."

He could have interpreted the abrupt exit as me being rude, but he responded anyway. "Goodnight, Syona."

Once I was out in the hallway, I leaned against the stone wall and stared up at the ceiling, my thoughts spinning like a tornado.

Who should I choose: Gerrand or Crevan? Bright sunlight or a warm hearth? Energetic freedom or quiet charisma? Breaking the rules once again or staying inside them for once?

The guard I've known for my whole life, or the charming prince?

TWENTY ONE

Time had a habit of passing by in a never-ending blur, especially when something life-altering was about to happen, especially since I was both dreading and anticipating the wedding. I knew for a fact that even if I had to stay in the kingdom of Ashlon after I got married, the union would still shatter my normal life, although *normal* was a relative term. I hardly thought that being a Malopathic princess was normal. Somehow, miraculously, I had managed to keep my secret under wraps.

My thoughts drifted less and less in that direction and more to puzzling over how my life would change. Crevan was going to be my husband, and I had decided it was *not* the worst thing that could have happened to me. His family would become my family, and I would have Ellison and Everlee as sisters, which I had officially decided *was* the worst thing to happen to me. But I would have Crevan with me, so that would make it a little more bearable.

The days passed more quickly than I realized. It was only a couple of weeks until the wedding, which would take place on the last day of winter. I realized they had set that as the date because the last day of winter symbolized a new beginning, which is what they wanted the wedding to represent.

The wedding, I mused, *add that to the list of things that I should worry about, but I can't because I don't have the time or energy. I have to think about the bigger puzzle of loving both Gerrand and Crevan. I have to be with Crevan for the sake of both our kingdoms, but I can't deny I'm drawn to Gerrand.*

Honestly, I feel like my life is splitting apart all over again.

I perched on the edge of my bed, waiting for the day to be over, for all of this mess to be over. On cue, the door opened, and Akilah strolled inside to check if I was awake. She didn't need to. I had no lessons that day, but we were both completely silent as she tidied up my room and put things away.

The silence coming from her was extremely uncharacteristic. She was usually bright and cheery, especially in the mornings. "Akilah? Are you okay?"

"Hmm? Yeah," she absent-mindedly replied.

"Did you have any specific reason for coming in here? If you haven't noticed, I don't need to be up for anything yet."

"No. Just a habit." She folded up some clothes and slid them into a drawer.

A few seconds passed before I spoke again. "Akilah?"

"Yeah?"

I couldn't help but smile. "Happy birthday."

She dropped the dress that she was holding. "Thank you! What tipped you off, genius? Me not talking your ear off as soon as I came in?"

I folded my arms. "No! You didn't have to do that! I remembered, not like the last few times. Just . . . remind me how old you're turning."

"Sixteen. I'm sixteen."

"That's exciting."

Her face broke into a smile that was all sunshine. "Yeah, I know."

"Do you want me to do anything for you?"

"Nope." She beamed. "I just wanted you to say it. That's all. Thank you."

"You've already said *thank you* twice."

"Yes and I'll probably keep saying it for the entire day, just to annoy you."

The door suddenly swung open, and Crevan's head shot into view. "Syona, sorry for not knocking. I just wanted to tell you to . . ." He tilted his head inquisitively. "What were you guys talking about?"

"It's Akilah's birthday."

"Ah, yes. Akilah. Sixteen, right?" He faced her. "I don't think we've officially met before, but you probably already know who I am."

"Yeah, you're Prince Crevan."

He waved his hand. "You can do away with the prince title. Just call me Crevan."

Ha, I thought, *like me. No titles. We try to do away with the fact that we're royalty because we don't want the attention. Add that to the growing list of things we match up on.*

Akilah shook her head. "I'm sorry, but that's not in my job description."

His head swiveled to glance at me, questions written on his expression. "Is she joking or being serious? Because I honestly can't tell."

Akilah suddenly perked up. "I haven't—"

I cut her off with a flick of my hand. "If you say, 'I haven't decided yet,' I will forbid you from talking for the rest of the day, even though it's your birthday." I studied Crevan. "What did you come in here to do? If it's not more spying, that is."

He stood straighter and cleared his throat. "I'm here to inform you that our fathers have decided to plan the details of the wedding with us tomorrow—everything in one go, to get it over with."

"That certainly *sounds* like Kadar, being efficient and not wasting any precious time and resources. It'll probably last the entire day, right?"

"Um, yes," he admitted.

I sighed. "That's what I thought."

"You have today to do whatever you want, at least," Akilah reasoned. "And you're spending it with me, right?"

"Akilah, you'd follow me around all day regardless. You act like my shadow."

"What's everyone doing in here?" said a quiet voice from the doorway.

Everyone turned to see Everlee, of all people, stationed at the entrance to the room. She stood slightly slouched, head pointed down, eyes barely meeting the stares of the other people in the room. Everything about her, from her body language to the way she talked to the way she acted, screamed, "Don't pay attention to me!" She must have summoned up a lot of courage to get here.

"I came to inform Syona about something we have to do tomorrow. Syona is here because it's her room. This girl, Akilah, is here because it's her birthday, and she's Syona's servant," Crevan explained.

The young princess gracefully skimmed across the threshold and into the room. "It's her birthday?" she confirmed, her voice innocent and light.

"Yes," Akilah responded a little awkwardly. "Although you don't have to make such a big deal about it. I'm just a servant. Acknowledging my presence would have been good enough."

Everlee kept talking, "How old are you?"

I interrupted the question. "Why are you here, Everlee?"

She turned toward me. Her voice was high and sweet, like a child's, but her blue eyes looked piercing instead of faded like the last time I had seen her. It suggested a maturity and hidden intelligence that were beyond her years. "Oh, I wanted to get away from Ellison for a while. She drains me."

I was positive that everyone in the room silently agreed with her.

"Can I ask you something else?" I ventured.

"Yes."

"You look so timid all the time. You never talk. Why is that?"

"Well, I'm the youngest princess. I'm fourteen," she responded, waving her hand dismissively. "Nobody expects anything from me. Ellison and Crevan are much more important than me. Besides, everyone thinks I'm too young and inexperienced and easily malleable." Her tone of voice was as bright as ever, but there was a knife's edge in her words.

My interest peaked. "What do you do in the palace?"

"Oh, I don't really do anything. Nobody pays attention to me or gives me anything specific to do." She kept leaning against the wall, looking fragile and small.

And you say my family is weird, Crevan? It seems yours is just as strange. Sure, in my family, two people have died, two are Malopaths, and two have no emotions. However, in your family, you have one stingy brat, a wallflower, a carefree and extraverted king, a chilled queen, and a prince with uncanny observation skills. How does that combination even work?

"Why are there so many people here?" a familiar voice called out.

My teeth clenched as everyone turned to see who it was, but I already knew. It was Gerrand. Of course it was Gerrand. Everyone important I knew was ending up in my room.

Crevan ruffled his hand through his hair. He was confused, but he answered the question anyway. "Akilah is in here because it's her birthday. Syona is here because it's her room. I'm here because I needed to talk to Syona, and I have no idea why Everlee is here because this shouldn't interest her. How did *you* end up here?"

Gerrand shrugged. "I heard a lot of voices, and I wanted to check it out."

Oh, I'm absolutely certain he's lying. He came to my room because he wanted to talk with me.

"I know you. You're Gerrand, right?" Crevan asked, standing up.

"Yep, I'm Officer Raynott, palace guard and the princess's *personal* guard," Gerrand answered.

Oh, so you're still going to tell people that you're a guard, huh? And you specifically mentioned that you're my personal guard?

It was true, though. Gerrand was still a registered guard. He still had the uniform, the stones—even though he didn't wear them—and he still had all of the weapons they were commissioned to wear: a knife in a sheath that was strapped to his calf, the sword in another sheath at his waist, and probably more weapons that weren't visible. Guards didn't wear any armor, so they were trained in offensive tactics rather than defensive, which I thought was highly inefficient, considering that their job was to *defend* the palace from potential danger.

I discreetly got up from a sitting position and pushed Gerrand outside where we could have a private conversation. When I finally glanced at his face, he had an unreadable expression, which didn't help me figure out what I was supposed to say to him, so I just went with the first thing that burst into my head: "What on earth are you doing?"

His eyebrows furrowed. "I was checking out what Crevan was like. It's no big deal."

I was fuming. "Are you kidding me? Why were you so obvious? What if he finds out—"

"Finds out about what? Finds out that I never wear any of the stones, even though guards are supposed to? Finds out that you like me? Sure. *That's* what you're worried about because you're supposed to marry him. Is that it?"

"What?" I stammered. "No! I don't even—"

"You don't even like me? Is that what you're trying to say? Speak. Words."

"Yes! No! I . . ." I exhaled angrily. "I'm not supposed to like you. If you haven't noticed already, I'm going to marry *him.*" I pointed to the door in the direction of Crevan. "*That* is non-negotiable."

He was angry now too. I could read it in his tense expression. "Oh, so you're giving up on this, then?"

"That is *not* what I said."

He scoffed, shaking his head. "No, I get it. I just thought that you wanted this more. Apparently, you don't. Have fun with your prince."

"No! Gerrand!" I whispered harshly, shooting out and catching his arm before he could leave. "Why are you making such a big deal out of this? You don't get it. The marriage alliance is unavoidable. I have to do it. I'm obligated to."

He ripped his arm out of my grip. "And do you think that *I'm* obligated to do this? To break all of the emotion guidelines and talk to you informally? Do you think I'm *obligated* to do any of this? I'm risking *everything* for you." He paused. "Why can't you risk everything for me?"

With those cruel words, he took off down the hallway, taking my heart with him.

TWENTY TWO

The next morning, I found myself walking beside Crevan on the way to the meeting. "What do you think the detail planning session will be like?" I asked him.

"It will probably be our fathers, your uncle, and my mother arguing with each other and trying in vain to agree on the smallest details while we just stand in the background and watch."

I laughed. "As much as I don't want to admit it, you're probably right."

The sun hadn't risen yet, so nobody else in the palace was awake, not even the servants. But Raymon and Kadar had concluded that we were to have a planning session before anyone else awoke, to get it over with and maximize productivity. I didn't protest, but it had still been a pain to get myself out of bed without Akilah to help me, especially since I hadn't slept very well with my mind crowded with the events of the previous day.

Crevan continued speaking. "It isn't exactly fair. We're the people getting married. We should be the ones to decide everything."

I cringed. It was still uncomfortable when someone mentioned that the two of us were betrothed to one another. Even though people mentioned it about fifty times a day, I couldn't bring myself to think of Crevan as my future husband—at all. Even though I was almost eighteen, and that *was* the appropriate time to get married, this part of my life felt foreign to me.

"Should we? Would you want to decide everything?" I asked him.

"I don't know, but I certainly don't want everything arranged *for* us."

"That's a valid point."

We turned the corner and strolled down the palace hallway toward the private study room where we were meeting. It was one of the bigger study rooms, so I guessed there would be a mob of people inside.

At least Crevan dislikes the same things I do. We can suffer through it together

The two of us reached the door, and even through that barrier I could already hear sharp, hushed voices. Everyone was already snapping at each other, their words like cracking whips. *If they're already fighting, then this is going to be a long day.*

"It sounds like this has already morphed into chaos. Have you prepared yourself emotionally?"

He smiled. "I guess so. What about you?"

I held up my necklace of stones and put them on. "I have these. I'll be fine," I lied.

Crevan nodded, a little hesitantly, and pushed the door open.

The scene that unfolded before us was truly one of complete pandemonium. The first thing I noticed were fragments of red stone scattered across the carpet. Dozens of the shards littered the floor, glittering in the light of the chandelier like scarlet stars. *What on earth? Are those bits of ruby? Did a stone get smashed? That would certainly make sense, considering how furious everyone is acting.*

I dared to scan the rest of the room. The people we had expected to be there had arrived. Our family members, specifically our fathers, were bitterly arguing with one another at the very back of the room, practically spitting in each other's faces. That surprised me. King Raymon had been nothing but bright and relaxed since coming here. I spotted Cyrus shouting at a cluster of ambassadors from Tanum. Several officials from both kingdoms clumped near the sides of the room, snapping at each other and jabbing at pages in books. Queen Emerald sat in the corner of the room with a somewhat amused expression on her face. The table in the center of the room carried messy piles of books. Haphazard stacks of scattered paper and pens covered every inch of the tabletop.

As soon as we came in, however, everything ground to a halt. All of the people in the room turned to meet our gazes. A sudden comforting peace settled over the room, and a lone sheet of paper brushed off of the table and drifted to the ground.

"Well, this is certainly a bad step in the direction of kingdom unity," Crevan remarked.

Raymon cleared his throat. "Ah! Syona! Crevan! Thank you for being here! And you are quite right. I apologize. Things got a bit out of hand."

Crevan continued speaking, "I'm not even going to *begin* to imagine how this happened."

"Right." Raymon bent down and collected the papers on the floor. "I . . . may have snapped off Kadar's . . . stone, and things just spiraled out of control. *Anyway*, now that the prince and princess are here, I think we should get started—in a more civilized manner, that is."

"Thank you. Now, what have you agreed on so far?" Crevan asked.

I decided once and for all, at that moment, that Crevan would do all the talking for me. Even though he was mostly quiet and always swore that he didn't like attention, he seemed to have a way with words. Maybe it was just his natural charisma, but he could be persuasive if he wanted to.

He could be a great leader one day if he puts his mind to it.

"We haven't decided much of anything, except that the wedding colors are going to be blue and white," Raymon answered.

"Really? Blue and white?" Crevan turned to Kadar. "You *agreed* to this?"

"We both admitted that those colors are winter colors. They look good together. As long as we balance it out by making the bride and groom wear red and black, I think it's okay," Kadar explained.

"I'm fine with that," Raymon said.

"Great," Kadar continued. "Now, for the designs, I thought that we would do—"

I dared to speak. "Wait. Hold on. You just decided that without our input? If you didn't want us to help with the arrangements, you didn't need to invite us to come here or to waste our time. If you're not going to ask our opinion on anything, we'd better leave or go back to sleep because it's still early."

Everyone in the room, including all of the strangers, glared at me. They were certainly not used to the background princess sharing her opinion or interrupting people; that's for sure. *Why did I say that? I don't ever speak during events like these. Should I have kept quiet?*

"Then what would you like to wear for your wedding, *Syona?*" Cyrus sneered.

I thought about it for a few seconds. I certainly didn't want to wear red. I had worn red for altogether too much of my life. It would just remind me of the kingdom of Ashlon and the amount of pain it had caused me. Since I would most likely be staying in the kingdom of Tanum, at least for a little while, I wanted a color that represented a fresh start, just like the wedding date.

"May I wear white?" I whispered.

Cyrus snorted. "You don't get a say in—"

"Why not?" Raymon questioned. "Why can't we let her wear white?"

"Because we're not *going* to let her wear white," Cyrus protested. "Right, Kadar?"

"She can design her own wedding dress. It's fine with me. Set time aside for her to do that," Kadar eventually answered.

I breathed a sigh of relief. It would be more work for me, but I could control at least one aspect of the event.

"Fine," Cyrus huffed, "but make it quick. We only have two weeks."

"Which room will the ceremony be held in? Anything big enough to fit the number of people attending?" Raymon questioned.

"I don't actually know. I was thinking maybe the main hall? It's directly connected to the entrance, but we'll be able to fit plenty of people," Kadar explained.

"That would work."

"Wait," Crevan interjected. "I have a question. Is Syona going to wear her stones during the wedding?"

"I think it would be appropriate," Kadar responded.

"No. No. No," Crevan protested, stepping between Raymon and Kadar. "I want Syona to have access to her emotions. I want her to act like an actual human being, and I think she would agree if I asked her. She got to decide the color of her dress. Can I get a say in a few things like her?"

Raymon suddenly clamped his hand over Crevan's arm, eerily similar to what Cyrus did to me. He dragged him over to one side of the room and pressed him against the wall, speaking to him in a tense whisper. I couldn't hear what they were saying, but after silently glaring at Crevan for a few more seconds, Raymon calmly walked back over to Kadar.

"Sorry about that. I just had to remind my son of something. No big deal," Raymon smoothly explained.

It certainly didn't look like it wasn't a big deal. Crevan stayed pressed against the wall, looking scared and worried. The outburst had come out of nowhere.

Raymon's been nothing but elegant since he's arrived at the palace. Why is he so angry? Is there something I don't know? What does he have against his own son? I dared to scoot over to Crevan as the conversation continued on without me.

"We still haven't clarified something," Kadar pointed out. "What's happening to Syona after the wedding? Will she go to the kingdom of Tanum?"

"She's staying here," Cyrus snapped. "She has too many things to do."

"Come on. What's the most important thing she's doing here?" Raymon stepped forward and spread his arms, switching back to his confident, suave self. "Having useless political lessons? Let her stay with us for a little while—a month maybe. Then we'll send her right back. I think she'll enjoy it."

The king sighed. "Fine."

Excitement shot through me, but it was dampened by my worry for Crevan. "Um, are you okay?" I whispered to him.

He took a deep breath and his stressful expression melted away. "I'm completely fine. It'll be nice for you to come over to the kingdom of Tanum since winter will be over. By all means, come with us."

"What did your father say to you?" I asked.

"Oh, nothing important. Seriously. It's fine. We just don't have the . . . best relationship," he explained.

"Okay. If you say so."

"I promise. Nothing serious is going on between us."

He sounded absolutely sincere, so I moved on to another subject. "This'll be nice. I have my birthday the day after the wedding, too, so this all works out perfectly."

"Really? That's great! You'll be eighteen like me."

"I will, won't I?" *I'm going to the kingdom of Tanum. It'll only be for a little while, but I'll be able to leave this place, spend time with Crevan and Raymon, and not wear the stones for an entire month.*

On my birthday, I'll finally. Finally. Be free.

The planning meeting lasted for another hour before we were finally allowed to leave. The king thought it would last the entire day, but with Crevan organizing and streamlining everything, it went more quickly.

With everything decided and done, the advisors and planners gathered their things. Raymon was the first to leave, followed quickly by Crevan. As everyone else trailed out the door, someone tightly gripped my wrist.

"Where do you think you're going?"

"Out of this room?"

Cyrus twisted my arm so that I was forced to look at him. "Don't be smart with me. We need to talk."

"What? Do you want to get back at me for actually getting what I wanted?" I shot.

"No. I'm concerned that you may have forgotten what I wanted in the first place: a confession for being a Malopath," he snapped.

"That's not fair. I've . . . I've been doing what you asked me to. I'm a suitable heir, aren't I? If this marriage works out, a peaceful future is guaranteed for this kingdom."

"That's not enough. I still have leverage over you. I could expose you to the king right now, and you'd be dead by next morning. You have to do what I say."

"Fine! What more could you possibly want from me?"

"You can't go to the kingdom of Tanum after the wedding. You have to stay here. *That's* what I want."

That certainly shocked me. "Why?"

"I don't want you running off on an excursion. I want you to stay here so I can keep an eye on you."

So that you can control me, you mean. I get it now. You've given up on the throne. Now that I'm marrying Crevan, you'll never be a ruler over this kingdom. The best you can do is to make me miserable and decide everything I do. Is this what my is now, blackmail by the one person I can never get rid of?

"Fine," I relented. "I'll talk to Crevan and King Raymon. They like me. We can work something out."

He immediately released my wrist. "Thank you, Your Highness. I am *ever* looking forward to the time when you become a princess of Tanum." After giving me a mocking bow, he sauntered out of the room with that sly smile marking his face.

"Do you have your wedding dress designed yet?" Akilah asked me, strolling into my room and disturbing the silence I was enjoying.

I glanced up from my book. "Yes, but it's not going to be ready for at least another day. We're certainly cutting it close."

"What does it look like?"

"It's what you'd expect from me: floor-length, sleeves down to the wrists, high neckline, that sort of thing. It does have a few pretty designs on it, though, and I still have to wear all of the stones in necklace form."

Akilah chuckled. "Just be glad they didn't sew them directly into the dress."

"I guess so, and don't you dare suggest that idea to the king because then they'll do it that way. I haven't seen the dress, so that'll be one thing to look forward to tomorrow."

She leaped onto the bed beside me. "How exciting for you! Are you excited? I'm excited."

"This book is more exciting."

"Really? Seriously? You're getting married to a *prince*—a prince who is quite dashing, by the way. I like Crevan."

"You've only met him twice."

"Yeah, but in those few times, he's seemed pretty nice. He makes me feel good."

"He *is* sweet," I agreed.

"So." She came closer to me from behind. "What are you reading?"

I shut the book. "Don't you *dare* read over my shoulder."

She put on a sad face. "Fine. Are you at least reading it for fun?"

"Yes."

"That's good. I think you've had enough lessons and reading assignments to last you at least a lifetime."

Really. Huh. At least someone agrees with me on that. "Akilah?"

"Yeah?"

I allowed a few moments of silence before speaking again. "I just want to say thank you."

She seemed confused. "For what?"

I sighed. "For . . . putting up with me. I've been snappy with you several times over the years."

She waved her hand dismissively. "Oh, it's fine. I honestly don't care."

"Even if you don't, I just want to thank you for being a friend to me."

She smiled. "Aww . . . that was sweet."

This was getting awkward very fast. I decided to diffuse that feeling by being snappy to her again. "Well, appreciate it. I don't do sentimental things very often."

"Thanks." She tilted her head. "I forgot. When's the wedding again?"

"The day after tomorrow." I put on an annoyed expression. "Thanks for reminding me. I had just stripped that information from my memory."

"Oh, calm down. It's not like you have to stress about the one day in your life that actually matters and is incredibly world-changing."

I rolled my eyes. "Why'd you come in here in the first place—if it wasn't just to annoy me, that is?"

Akilah laughed. "The king just announced something."

"And he didn't tell me? Like *that's* new. He practically runs my life for me." I glimpsed down at my book, trying to sneak in a few more pages.

"Anyway, he's announced that to celebrate the wedding between our two kingdoms—"

"Oh. That's *actually* new. Have we ever officially celebrated anything?"

Her expression became serious. "Are you going to let me finish?"

"I'm sorry. Go ahead."

"To celebrate, he's going to put on a ball."

That certainly ripped me away from my book. "A ball? Like, a formal dance? I don't think we've ever had one of those before."

She tapped her finger against her chin. "I don't think so either, but they have them in the kingdom of Tanum—perpetually, even."

"Why? It seems like a waste of time and resources."

"It lifts morale. They have one specifically for winter, too. You know, to celebrate while they're being buried alive in all that snow."

I chuckled. "I guess that would make sense. We're hosting one? That'll be interesting. When is it?"

"The day before the wedding."

"Tomorrow?"

She nodded. "That's the plan."

"At least I'll have something to look forward to. Wait. *Should* it be something to look forward to?"

Akilah thought for a moment. "It'll be loud, and I'm sure you'll get a lot of attention, and there's dancing too."

"Then what makes you think I'll enjoy it?" I jokingly snapped, glancing down at my book again.

"Because both Crevan and Gerrand will be there."

I froze. "Sure, Crevan being there is an incentive but Gerrand? Why should I care that he comes?" I was lying through my teeth, but I didn't know if Akilah could tell.

"Oh. Is that over? I was under the impression that—"

"Nothing was ever between us in the first place. Besides, I have my amber stone now. I'm not supposed to love anyone anyway, even if I don't wear it all the time."

She continued speaking. "I just thought—"

"Nope."

Her face was skeptical. "The faster and more snappish your comments get, the more I'm convinced otherwise."

Maybe I did need to work on lying. "I admit it. What if I like Gerrand? I'm marrying Crevan, and I like Crevan too. It doesn't matter."

"But—"

I faced her. "But what? Aren't you like everyone else? Don't you think emotions are a curse? Shouldn't you discourage liking someone?"

"Yes, I should, but I've been with you for so long that some of your opinions are rubbing off on me," she explained. "And for the record, I think it's cute that you like both of them. Like . . . what do they call it in books . . . a love something? Love triangle? I can't remember."

"Stop it. I should stop talking to Gerrand and focus on Crevan. Thinking about Gerrand is just making everything more complicated than it needs to be."

"But doesn't he like you too?"

"I don't know! Maybe as a friend? I don't even know if we're past that point yet." *Yes. Yes, we are, and it's making everything a complicated, emotional mess.*

"He gave you the necklace back. He fixed your necklace."

"We've already discussed this. He was wearing an amber stone at that time, so it didn't count. Nothing counted back then."

"Can't you give *him* a chance, though?"

"No, because I'm supposed to marry someone else in two days. It doesn't matter who I like. It's never mattered who I like. I'm the princess. My life is never in my control."

I launched off of the bed toward the door. "I have to go. I have things to attend to. Stop talking. Now."

"No, you don't!" Akilah protested. "Come back! Please!"

"I'm done for now. Just leave me alone." Before she could chase after me and before she could change my mind, I pushed open the door and bolted down the hallway.

Keep your thoughts straight, Syona. Remember what's important. The day after tomorrow, you will marry Crevan, a sweet, sensitive boy who's everything you've ever wanted.

Afterward, I don't know. Maybe I'll do what Cyrus wants me to, or maybe I'll actually go to the kingdom of Tanum. Either way, nothing will be the same again, and I'll have Crevan to protect me. I'll be free.

So put all of this nonsense behind you.

TWENTY THREE

The ball would take place in the main hallway, right near the entrance. It was where the wedding would take place too because our small palace didn't have enough space for anything important. Crevan explained that the biggest room in *their* palace was the ballroom, and they used that for everything. We didn't have a ballroom because nobody ever threw balls in our kingdom. I couldn't recall a single instance in our kingdom's century-long history of anyone ever hosting a ball, even before the discovery of the stones. It seemed that since we were the branch kingdom, we were more interested in our reputation and gaining strength than having fun and spending precious time doing leisure activities.

We would make up for it now. Even though this had been on such short notice, the king tried to arrange things as best he could. Rumors circulated throughout the palace that they would have an orchestra, which would be hard to set up. Playing a musical instrument wasn't illegal, but it was generally looked down upon. I wondered how far they had to search through the kingdom to get that set up. The more and more I learned about this kingdom, the more I realized that it wasn't just a nation devoid of emotion but creativity and talent as well.

I guess you can't be passionate about something or love a certain skill set if there's no emotion involved.

Most of my family and most of the inhabitants of the kingdom were clueless about how to set up a ball, but the guests from Tanum gave us plenty of advice on how to make it all go down. From what I had heard in rumors and whispers of gossip, they had done a good job. Against my better judgment, I was actually looking forward to it. It would be a night of fun before I put my past behind me.

If I could just find something to wear.

"How about this?" Akilah asked, holding up another dress. It was one I probably hadn't worn or seen in years, and I knew why. It was a flashy bright pink.

"Nope. I don't want to—"

Akilah cut me off with a sigh. "Let me guess. You don't want to wear it because it's too attention grabbing."

"No. It's because I hate the color pink."

Akilah's eyebrows shot up. "Really? Wow. Okay. What colors do you like?"

"I really like red and purple, and are we expected to actually dance with people?"

Akilah laughed. "Yes. That's why it's called a *dance.*"

"But there's no emotion here, specifically love and happiness. Why would people want to dance with each other and have a good time?" I asked her.

"That's a valid point, but the people from Tanum said that we should give it a try, and they're attending too." She walked over to my closet and selected another dress. "How about this one? It's purple."

"Yes. Thank you. I'll wear that," I obliged, walking over to her and taking the dress. "Do I have to wear all of the emotion gemstones?"

"This isn't a formal event. We've never done something like this before, so I think you can get away with not wearing them all. I'd play it safe, but you can do whatever you want."

"Who's attending? Is there an official guest list?"

"You're driving me crazy. Do you have to ask so many questions? Do you have to know everything?" She sighed. "I guess that's something about you that'll never change, but I think everyone who works or lives at the palace is invited, including all of the guests from the kingdom of Tanum."

"You could go."

"Yes. Hypothetically."

"Will you?"

"Maybe." She shrugged. "I haven't thought about it very much."

"If you want to, you can. You're my friend. We can make that happen." I looked outside and caught a glimpse of the rapidly setting sun. "But we need to get ready *right now*, or we won't be able to go at all."

——⚬——

I had significantly lowered my expectations. Even though the people from the kingdom of Tanum were specifically directing us, I was skeptical. Our culture didn't value celebrations or anything sentimental, so I thought everything would be skimpy and plain.

That perception shattered the moment I glimpsed the spectacle below me.

From my position at the top of the staircase, I had a clear view of what it looked like, and it was nothing I had ever seen before. At least two hundred people had arrived, all dressed in bright colors and absolutely dripping with jewels. Only a small percentage of them were actually dancing, but the rest chatted to one another excitedly. I wondered how many wore their emotion stones because almost everyone appeared to be having a good time.

The lit chandelier reflected rays of light across the entire hall. That, combined with the white lustrous marble, made it appear as if the sun were sitting in the middle of the large hallway.

The sound of so many people talking at once would have normally overwhelmed me, forcing me to retreat to my room, but the music outshined the white noise. There, sitting near the entrance to the palace, was a full orchestra with at least a dozen people, possibly the only musicians in the entire kingdom. The cheery classical music sliced through the other sounds and rang clear. I would have been entirely comfortable with keeping my position at the top of the staircase and listening for hours on end.

Akilah waved her hand in front of my face, pulling me from my thoughts. "Hello? Syona? Are we going to go now? What are you waiting for?"

"I'm waiting to see if the officials kept their promise about not announcing my presence at this event."

"Why did you ask for that?"

"I don't want to deal with all of that formality. I only want to go down there and melt into the crowd and maybe have a good time."

"Okay. Well, it's already been a few minutes, and nobody's said anything."

"Let's go then."

I descended the staircase with as much grace as I could muster, which wasn't much. Akilah looked smoother than silk, gliding down the steps like liquid. I didn't think that was fair because I distinctly recalled spending three months of my life attempting to fix my posture. I should have been able to walk more gracefully than her. When I eventually made my way to the floor, I spotted Crevan immediately, waiting just beside the stairs. His eyes shone brightly like shards of colorful glass. He sauntered up to me and threw himself into an extravagant bow.

"Why, hello, My Lady. What a lovely evening it is to make your acquaintance."

I laughed, shaking my head. "Stop. That's already too much. If you're going to continue talking like that, I'm not marrying you."

He mimicked my expression. "You don't exactly have a choice, Princess. It seems you're stuck with me."

"You're speaking as if it's a bad thing," I said with a smile.

Crevan finally stood up and held his hands out to me. "I guess it isn't. Would you mind if I had the first dance?"

"You realize that half the people around you have never danced before, including me, right?"

He raised his eyebrows. "You've never danced before?"

I shook my head. "I already told you. The kingdom of Ashlon isn't in the habit of hosting dances."

"That can be easily remedied. I'll show you." He took my wrists and flipped them face up. "It's simple. Your left hand goes on my shoulder."

I reached upward and placed my left hand on his shoulder, ignoring the tingling feeling that sprouted in the pit of my stomach.

Crevan held out one of his hands to the side. "Then, your right hand holds my hand."

I reached out and folded my fingers into his, feeling the warmth of his skin.

"Good. That's the position. There are certain steps and different types of dances that you can do, but since you're a beginner, I think it would be best if we just sway to the music."

I did what he said, leaning on the balls of my feet in time with the music while Crevan gently led me, swirling across the dance floor. It was unnatural for me since I had no idea where to step, but Crevan knew what to do and covered for my incompetence.

He suddenly started talking, trying to be heard over the music. "We're getting married tomorrow evening."

"Yes," I responded.

"The two of us."

"That's usually how it works."

He bit his lip. "Are you okay with it? Are you okay with me?"

"Crevan. I don't have a choice, but even if I did . . ." I stared up into his face. "I really like you."

"Like or love?"

"*Must* you ask that question?"

He twisted his hand to gently spin me around, and my long dress swept across the stone. "Yes, I believe I do."

"I . . . I don't know. Maybe love?"

"I was wondering when you would admit it," he said, showing a coy smile.

I scoffed at him. "Oh, stop it. I can't believe you made me say that. You deserve a slap to the face."

"You would never dare harm His Royal Highness, right?"

I rolled my eyes. "Your arrogance continues to astound me. Am I really that readable?"

"Everyone is that readable, Syona, as long as you know what to look for. Like I said before, it's amazing how much you could pick up from just observing what's going on around you. With that, combined with your uncanny ability to think and draw conclusions, you could know anything you wanted to about the world. For example, I know you like to climb trees because—"

"Let me guess, because I like being outside in nature, especially in forests." I glanced down at my hands. "You saw me purposely touching the trees and not freaking out when I got dirt and sap underneath them, which means I'm used to that sensation. Did I get it? Is that it?"

"Yes. That and I directly asked Mareena about it."

I laughed. "Ha! You've been cheating this whole time! Everything you know about me comes from Mareena!"

"Not *everything*."

"Why are you telling me this anyway?"

He shrugged. "I ran out of things to talk about."

"*Already?*" I scoffed at him.

"*And* it's a useful technique that you can use later."

"Thank you, then."

"My pleasure."

I spotted a shadow out of the corner of my eye, and a few seconds later I felt a tap on my shoulder. I spun on my heels and barely managed to stifle a gasp when I spotted Gerrand standing next to me. He wore his guard uniform, same as always, but his necklace was missing.

Crevan's eyebrows furrowed. "Hello. Officer Raynott, right?"

Gerrand nodded. "Yes. Please excuse me for interrupting, but I was wondering if I could borrow the princess for a few minutes. I need to talk to her about official business."

Crevan's puzzlement was apparent on his face, but I knew he would cave in. "Yes. Certainly. I don't mind. Do you?"

It took me a second or two to realize he was addressing me. "No. I don't mind," I absentmindedly replied.

Crevan smiled. "It was nice dancing with you. You did great for a beginner." As he glided away, his fingers untwined from mine, and my skin became cold again.

I whirled around and faced Gerrand. "What are you doing here?"

His mouth creased downward. "I have as much right to be here as everyone else, and why were you dancing with him?"

"I . . ."

The song suddenly ended, leaving my ears reaching for a few ghost-like notes that were no longer there. A few people politely clapped, but another song abruptly started, drowning out the clapping.

I grabbed his shoulders and stared at the floor, trying to compose myself or to give myself more time to decide how to respond. "Stop. I'll explain everything," I promised.

"Please look at me."

I sighed and reluctantly glanced at him, at his brown eyes that were nothing like Crevan's. "Give me a chance to justify myself. We'll have a nice long talk, okay? Just not here. Not with everyone watching."

"Everyone's busy dancing or talking. I don't think anyone will watch us," he pointed out.

I shushed him. "It's also really loud in here. I can't concentrate that well." I skimmed off the dance floor, hoping that he would follow me. "Come. I know a good place."

CHAPTER
TWENTY FOUR

The view from my balcony was nothing short of spectacular. The sun's rays exploded outward into a mix of golden colors, hoping to earn the attention of onlookers for its last few minutes of life, like a farewell before the moon stole its place. The vibrant shades arched across the sky like a bonfire resting on the horizon.

Gerrand leaned over the railing and watched the scene laid out before us. "This is beautiful. It's like the whole world is on fire."

I stepped up alongside him, resting my arms on the railing. "It is. I love having a west-facing balcony. It's connected straight to my room too."

"Lucky you, getting to see this view every day."

I shook my head. "Not as often as I'd like. I'm almost always eating dinner or being lectured or attending lessons somewhere in the palace."

"At least you get to see it now."

"For one last time."

Gerrand immediately scrutinized me. His head jerked in my direction, eyebrows furrowed. "What do you mean *for one last time*? Are you leaving?"

"Yes. I'm leaving for the kingdom of Tanum right after the wedding," I informed him.

His grip tightened on the railing. "For how long?"

"A month."

He waited for a few seconds before responding. "That'll be nice, being able to take a break and go someplace new. I haven't had a break from this lifestyle in well over a year."

"Why don't you resign then? You could take a leave and spend time doing what you want."

"I can't resign. My family will never allow it. I'm nobility. They're mad at me for choosing this position in the first place, but I don't know what they'd do to me if I quit working altogether. Besides, I like being a guard. I like being of worth to people, helping and protecting them." He sighed. "I'm sorry. I guess that's why I'm bitter about this whole situation, the marriage alliance. I don't want to lose you. I don't want you to forget about me because I feel like owe you, like I haven't given you enough."

"Don't worry. I'll give you a chance to save me from danger sometime, like a guard should," I said with a smile.

"How could I possibly save you from danger? You're going to the kingdom of Tanum. There won't be any danger, and it's not like I can go with you. Wait! I can! I can run away to the kingdom of Tanum! That's what I'll do!"

I snorted. "You're taking impulsivity to a new level. That would brand you a traitor; then you wouldn't be welcome anywhere. It's a statistical certainty that the outer guard would catch you. Even if you do manage to make it past them, which is extremely unlikely, you'll stick out with your dark-colored eyes and skin. You look like an Ashlon."

"But I'm sure people switch kingdoms all the time! I've seen people from the kingdom of Tanum in the outer villages before!"

"Yes, but not in the palace city! You don't go into the palace city if you don't have permission or some legal reason for being there! This is quite possibly the worst idea you've ever thought of. Do you ever think things through?"

"I'm just trying to do what I want. I'm seeing what else I can do with my life."

"Fine. Mareena once said that everyone is a bird, born into their own type of cage. It's up to you to either work to find a way out or learn how to sing."

"Sound advice." He turned to stare at the sunset again.

"You can't be an official guard anymore since you don't wear the stones. Someone will find out sooner or later. So, your idea of following me to the kingdom of Tanum means you'd be choosing the first option: finding a way out."

"What about you? How are you dealing with your cage?" He started counting on his fingers. "Your mother died; your brother died; you have the pressure of your position; and now you're being forced into a marriage alliance." He glanced up at me. "Have you sung or found a way out?"

Not to mention the pressure of being a Malopath. "I don't know. I think I've found a way out, if having the marriage alliance is a way to get away from my normal life." *But it's both, in a way. I've learned how to sing. I've met so many people, and I've been able to develop a relationship with and spend time with people I love. I've made my life something I can enjoy.* "It's still hard. I love you, and I love Crevan. The two of you are amazing, and every moment I spend with each of you has been fun, but I can't ever be with you because I'm still supposed to marry Crevan tomorrow. I'm sorry. I wish that this could happen a different way."

He sighed. "I know. I know, Syona. I just . . . wish I could be yours."

"Not unless something happens to me or Crevan by tomorrow," I jokingly suggested.

"That *could* happen, couldn't it? I imagine the wedding couldn't happen if . . . let's say . . . the prince went missing. I'm perfectly capable of making that happen."

"You're joking, right?"

"What if you faked your death? Can you fake your death?"

I laughed. "Gerrand, you are too good for me anyway. You deserve someone better."

He scoffed at me. "Where did you get that idea?"

"Do you remember when you fixed my necklace?"

"Your pearl necklace? Yeah, I remember."

I studied his expression. "Why did you fix it? It probably took a lot of money, and you were even wearing your emotion stone necklace at the time."

"I can't remember exactly what was going through my head that day, but I just knew that it was the right thing to do. You cared about that necklace a lot. You wore it almost every day. It was special to you."

"See? That's why you're too good for me. You, Gerrand Raynott, are the bravest and most honorable person I've ever met. You always do the right thing, no matter what. You care immensely about other people, and you always have my best interests in mind. You were even willing to give emotions a try when I asked you to, something that any other Ashlon in the palace would immediately refuse doing and probably file a report to get me arrested for treason."

He stepped a little closer to me. "You're a good person too, Syona."

"Me?" I asked skeptically. "What have I done in my eighteen years of life that could be considered *remotely* honorable?"

"Maybe not honorable but certainly admirable. You stepped up to fill your brother's position when he died—not an easy task to do. You adapted and learned faster than I thought was possible. You were able to think on your feet and make smart decisions. You were brave enough to take a palace guard that you liked and expose him to the one thing that's against the culture of our kingdom. You accepted the marriage alliance and even managed to fall in love with the boy you're supposed to marry." He smiled.

"Only you . . . only you would complement me on that."

"It certainly makes your life easier; that's for sure. I . . . I like Crevan. He's a good person. You're a very lucky girl to be able to spend the rest of your life with him."

He slid a bit closer, and his fingers brushed over mine, sending tingles across the back of my hand and up my arm. Time froze and our faces inched closer and closer, but this time, my thoughts didn't protest. I drank in the experience.

"What are you doing?" I asked as I continued closing the distance between us.

"I'm giving you this one night, this one moment together, so you never forget me."

His lips brushed against mine, almost gently. It felt like the lightest sweeping touch, like a sprinkling of dust, and the world seemed to fade away. All that existed in my head was the heat and the feeling of his skin pressed against mine. It was more than a kiss. It was an image of the future we could never have. A flame was exchanged between the two of us, a simple representation of the thing we both wanted but could never have.

He lingered for only a moment before pulling away. "But you never did tell me something, not in all of our conversations."

"What have I not told you?" I responded, still reeling from what just happened.

"You've never told me why you care so much about emotions. You don't seem like that kind of person. Sometimes, you even like to remain detached from feeling so you can make unbiased decisions. Why are you, of all people, an advocate for something that a princess of Ashlon shouldn't tolerate?"

I backed a few inches away from him, mind racing. *He doesn't know. He hasn't figured it out yet. My secret's still safe. Should I tell him? Is there a reason not to? I trust him now. He deserves to know.*

I peered at his face. His eager expression told me he wanted to know the answer as badly as I wanted to share it.

Not now. Later and soon but not now. I can't. He still might freak out or get annoyed at me for not telling him sooner. It'll have to wait.

I placed my hand against his chest. "I can't tell you now, but I promise I'll tell you later. After I get to Tanum, I'll send a personal message to you explaining everything. I just can't give you the answer now. Do you trust me?"

He gave his answer without hesitation. "I do."

I sighed in relief. "Good. I promise that a couple of days from now, everything will be clear. All of the fog and mist will lift away. Okay?"

"Okay."

I smiled. "Thank you for giving me this one night."

He mimicked my expression. "Thank you for letting me give it to you."

I observed the sunset, seeing the last strands of light fade away into darkness as the sun dipped below the horizon. "I should probably go back inside. People might be searching for me."

"Goodnight then."

"Goodnight."

With that short exchange of words, I opened the door and slipped back inside my room. I tried to keep my expression neutral, but inside, my heart was singing a joyful song that I hadn't thought I'd ever hear again.

CHAPTER
TWENTY FIVE

I t was the day, the day all the inhabitants on the peninsula hoped would happen smoothly. Today was the day when a three-decade-long war would finally end peacefully. It was the day my life would change forever.

I knew I probably should have been accomplishing something, like inspecting my dress, scouting out the main hallway, or making some last-minute decisions. I *was* the bride, after all. I wasn't supposed to be so anxious that all of my muscles were tensing up or so terrified that I couldn't breathe well. I had plenty of advance time to think about this. Now that the day was here, right in front of me, I wanted to curl up forever. The one thing I *did* know was that I certainly wasn't supposed to be hiding out in my room, trying to escape from reality with my nose in a book.

But that was exactly what I was doing when Crevan found me.

I hadn't even seen him come in until he sat down next to me on the bed and gently pulled the book out of my grip. Then, he closed the cover and tossed it onto my pillow.

"Is reality that bad?"

I exhaled. "No, it's not. I'm sorry."

"Well, if you haven't noticed already, we're getting married to each other in around an hour."

"You don't have to remind me. I know."

He paused. "Are you okay?"

"I'm fine."

"Good." His hand brushed over mine, allowing the ghostly sensation of Gerrand doing the same thing to resurface.

"Why did you come here in the first place?"

"To make sure you weren't sucked into a book."

I stared at him, incredulous. "Really?"

"No. A little. Um . . ." He swept his hand through his black hair. "I wanted to ask you if we have to write vows or something."

"That's it? Honestly?"

"Yes. I know what weddings look like in our kingdom, but with yours, you know, not having emotions and all—"

"You have absolutely no idea."

"No, I do not," he admitted.

"How come you haven't already reaped that information from your environment?"

He threw his hands up in defense. "Cut me some slack, okay? I just thought it would be better if I asked you."

"It's very different. No, we don't have to write vows or anything. It's all pre-written. In fact . . . I don't even want to describe it to you. Just brace yourself."

"Is it *that* different?"

"Most marriages, if not all marriages, in the kingdom of Ashlon are done for personal gain. Marrying someone because of love is unheard of—shameful, really. It's to continue your family line or to gain money and support from people, reasons like that. It's all selfishly motivated. Ours is too, actually, so we're not breaking the trend."

"What? No, it's not. Is it?"

"It wasn't initially based on love. This was all arranged and very impersonal. A vast majority of all marriages in this kingdom are arranged, too. This entire event is to stop a war and ally two kingdoms, a kingdom that our king wants to ally with solely because he wants access to the Northern Forest. Selfishly motivated."

"Fine but you love me now that you've gotten to know me, and you realize I'm an amazing, charming princely person who's perfect for you."

"Wow. I . . . wow. That was awful."

Crevan started laughing so hard he collapsed onto the floor. It was a light, childish sound that dripped with joy.

"Stop being so arrogant and just relax!" I snapped at him, bursting into laugher too.

He recovered quickly and jumped back into a standing position. "You're right. Sorry. I'd better go. It's bad luck to see the bride before the wedding."

"We don't have that superstition," I informed him.

He rolled his eyes, pouncing over to the door. "Of course you don't. Your kingdom doesn't believe in anything."

"Hey!" I laughed. "Well . . . maybe."

His hand was on the doorknob, almost opening it before he pivoted around to face me. "Does Cyrus treat you badly that often?"

I froze. "What?"

"I was just wondering what problem you have with each other. It sounded like he's blackmailing you."

"Where did you get that from?" I asked, feigning ignorance.

"The conversation the two of you had after everyone left the planning meeting," he answered, smiling.

"You were eavesdropping on us?"

"Yes."

"Of course you were."

"I only heard some of it, though. Seriously. What problem do you two have?" Crevan asked again.

"It's fine. We just argue sometimes."

"It seemed a lot more serious than just arguing. Come on. I know you better than that."

"Do you now?"

"He can't get away with treating you like that. Why don't you defend yourself and stand up to him?"

"It's more complicated than that. I've never had any real power. Davin always defended me because he was the crown prince and could actually *do* something about it."

He tapped his chin. "Hmm . . . and do you realize that you're the crown princess and you outrank him, which means any blackmail he could potentially have against you doesn't matter anymore? He can't accuse you of anything."

"What? Really?" I asked.

He nodded. "Absolutely. I can tell that it'll be hard for you, but the next time you see him, try to stand up to him. You do have power. Maybe you've never used that power, but you *do* have it. Just think about it."

"I will. Thank you."

With those words, Crevan stepped outside into the hallway, and the door quietly clicked shut.

Then, unexpectedly—but also sort of expectantly—the door opened again, and Crevan's head popped back into view. "I have one more question. Who's actually marrying us?"

"Osion, the ceremonial official."

"Right. The drippy loyalist. At least you finally remembered his name. Thanks. I'll go. For real this time."

I laughed. "What? Where'd you get *that* from?" I tried to ask him, but he had already disappeared behind a closed door.

A solid ten seconds went by before I heard the clicking sound of the doorknob turning once more.

"Crevan! You're supposed to *be* somewhere!" I scoffed at him, exasperated.

He threw his hands up in defense. "Okay! Fine! Last question! In your version of a wedding, does the person say something about kissing the bride?"

There were a few moments of silence before I spoke. "That. Without a doubt. Is the stupidest question I've ever heard. You came back to ask me *that?*"

"Yes, in fact."

"No. That doesn't happen." I tilted my head, a smile creasing across my face. "Why?"

"No reason."

"What? Do you *want* to kiss me?" That image formed in my head, but I immediately extinguished it.

"Well, may—"

"*Go*, Crevan!" I shouted, laughing again.

"Okay! Okay!" Then he slipped out, and the door shut for the last time.

—————

When I finally opened the door a while later, I observed hordes of people rushing around in the hallways. They were sprinting, carrying things, and making hasty arrangements. All were yelling at each other if someone didn't execute something properly or weren't wearing ruby stones. It was, by far, the busiest the hallways had ever been. Servants and officials and messengers darted everywhere, trying to get to their destination as quickly as possible. The noise alone made me want to retreat and skip out on my own wedding.

I spotted Akilah in the crowd, running to me as fast as she could. "Hi, there," she said breathlessly. "How are you?"

"This is madness," I commented.

"Yes. It is," she answered. "Everyone's trying to get everything ready at the same time."

"This is supposed to be going on *right now*, right?"

"Yeah, so this beehive is probably going to last for a while."

"That's *lovely*." I stole a glance out my window at the painted sunset that was a harbinger of what was inevitably coming. "I'm the bride. I'm certain that I'm supposed to be *somewhere*."

"Yes," she stammered. "King Kadar and King Raymon sent me. I'm here to escort you to Mareena, who's going to help you get ready."

She led me through the crowd, the people hardly parting to let me by. The noise crawled into my ears and stuck there, and I would probably hear its echoes for a while. It made me shiver. I decided to distract myself by talking to Akilah.

"Akilah? Where do you live?" A stupid question but one that would lead to a long, information-filled conversation that would give my brain something to digest and store away.

"You've never asked that question before."

"I'm asking it now."

"I live here in the palace in a wing specifically set aside for all of the workers and servants," she answered.

"Do you ever see your family?"

"Well, no."

"Do you want to?"

"No."

I hadn't expected all of these negative responses, so I had no idea how to continue the conversation. "What are they like?" There was a story in her, something I had never bothered to learn until now, and it was probably something having to do with her intense dislike of sadness.

Akilah slinked up to a room and twisted open the doorknob, blatantly ignoring the question. "Here," she huffed. "This is where you're supposed to go, and I don't want to talk about my family so please don't bring it up again."

My thoughts raced, trying to discern why that topic made her so angry as I stepped into the room. It was smaller than I expected. In front of me was a full-length mirror, lit with rays of light from a window on the left wall. Several boxes of jewelry had been placed on surrounding counters and desks. White lights lit up the entire room, which gave an airy feel to it.

I smiled when I glimpsed who was there. Mareena smiled back at me, and she held her arms out in greeting. "How's my girl?"

"I'm stressed to the bone." I sped toward her for a quick embrace, and she allowed me to give her one. I was starting to like the physical affection.

"I'll leave," Akilah announced awkwardly before shutting the door behind her.

Mareena gave my hands an encouraging squeeze. "How are you? I can see that you've gotten through these past couple of months."

"They were interesting; I'll skip past the details," I finally answered. "Are you here to help me get ready?"

"Yes. We have about an hour, which may seem like a lot of time, but it's not much. Let's get your dress out. It's finally done."

She paced over to the closest on the right wall and slid the door open. With the contents exposed, I observed a glistening white wedding dress now basking in the light of the window.

I darted over to study it, running the soft fabric through my hands. "Yes! It's white like I asked."

"Cyrus was adamantly against it, but he eventually caved in. It was a surprise because nobody expected him to, but he let it slide this time."

I swept my hands over the soft folds of the long sleeves, and Mareena chuckled. "Yes. Be grateful for that and be grateful that it covers this." She took my left wrist and turned it face up.

Why do people keep doing that? And how are so many people finding out about it? I slid my hand out of her grip. "Come on! Seriously? It's not such a big deal. The skin is just a little red. It hasn't scarred or anything. How did you know anyway?"

"I've known for a while, and I've seen you do it a couple of times," she vaguely explained. "While I approve of you having a technique to control your emotions, I'm not in favor of self-harm. I advise something different, like this."

She flicked her wrist and a bracelet slid into view. It was plain with no charms. Even after all these years of knowing her, I had never laid eyes on it before. Composed of delicate silver links, it looked remarkably familiar, but what was it similar to? An association was triggered in my brain. I had seen these small silver links before. Someone had worn something staggeringly similar to her bracelet. I tried to dig around in my memories for the answer but came up empty.

She twisted it around her wrist. "This is how I can control myself. It keeps my hands busy. I can buy you something like this."

"Thanks." I stole another glimpse of the dress. "It's beautiful."

She clapped her hands. "Let's get you wearing it then. We don't have all day."

CHAPTER
TWENTY SIX

A s soon as Mareena arranged the finishing touches, she turned me around to face the mirror, and I glimpsed what I truly looked like. The lights in the room complimented the white outfit, making me practically glow. I paced in front of the full-length mirror, marveling at myself in the reflection and puzzling over how so much light reflected off of it. Even Mareena stepped back and peered into the glass to admire her work.

All of my requests had been fulfilled, just as I wanted. Petals of netted material were layered over the white skirt, brushing against my hands. The lightweight mesh fluffed up the dress, making it look bigger. The unique texture and design of the skirt made me feel like being wrapped in a cloud. It accented the top part of the dress, a simple white with no design so as not to take away attention from the intricate bottom half. Pearls lined the edges of the sleeves, which added an elegant touch to the outfit.

"You look beautiful," Mareena commented.

"Thank you."

"Now, let's see if I can do anything creative with your hair." She gathered up the strands that had fallen across my shoulders and started braiding them. "They didn't tell me to do anything specific. Do you have any preferences?"

"No."

"Crown braid it is. I'm going to weave some pearls into your hair so it can match your dress." She reached over and snatched a few things off of the desk; then she dragged a chair from the corner of the room so I could sit down.

We both fell silent as she worked. I continued to stare at myself in the mirror, drifting along in my thoughts like riding the swell of ocean waves.

"I'm really happy for you," she said.

"You are?"

"Yes." She stuck a few hairpins in her mouth and attempted to talk around them. "I didn't think you'd survive until your eighteenth birthday."

I laughed. "My birthday's tomorrow. Something still might happen."

Mareena snorted. "Don't talk that way. It's practically impossible. Nobody can touch you now. Besides, you've gotten so good at hiding your emotions that I can hardly tell you're a Malopath anymore."

"Is that a compliment or an insult?"

"A little bit of both," she mused. "But don't run away from that side of yourself, okay? It's not healthy."

"Yes, Mother," I said with joking disrespect.

In the reflection of the mirror, I saw her face twist into an expression of amused puzzlement. "Mother?"

"Aunt? Lady. Mareena. Lady Mareena. Princess Mareena? Fellow Malopath Who Is Also My Mentor Who's a Little Hard on Me Sometimes but I Love Her Anyway. What do you want me to call you?"

She continued twisting her fingers through my hair. They were expert, practiced hands. She had done this a thousand times over her decades of living in a palace. "Actually . . . Mother would do just fine."

Really? Mother? You're allowing me to call you Mother? I felt a tingling warmth spread throughout my body. *Thank you. That means a lot to me. You have no idea how much that means to me.*

"Will you be the one walking me down the aisle?" I wondered aloud.

"Yes." I felt the pressure of a pin sliding into my hair.

"Why?"

"I've been your sole caretaker for practically your entire life, haven't I?" She smiled. "Besides, your father didn't want to do it, so he asked me."

"Okay. Oh, wait. I haven't asked you this yet: how do you feel about this entire marriage anyway? You've been so tight-lipped about it. I don't know your opinion."

She sighed, her breath full of longing and exhaustion. "I've never liked the kingdom of Tanum or the war, so I guess I support a peaceful end to it, but I don't like the idea of you having an arranged marriage."

"I'm a princess. Did you think Kadar *wouldn't* arrange my marriage?"

"I know." She exhaled again, wearily. "Just be careful. There's not much we know about the royal family's true intentions."

"Crevan's okay. I trust him with my life. I promise."

"Good. Trust is hard to come by these days."

"He's nice," I said, trying to defend him. "I like him a lot."

"That's wonderful to hear." Mareena placed one last pin in my hair and stepped back to inspect her work. "What do you think?"

She had woven all of my hair into an intricate crown braid, threaded with strings of pearls that were the same shade as my dress. All was matched perfectly.

"It looks beautiful." I gently brushed my fingers over the braid. "I didn't know you could do this."

"I can. Be careful, though. It'll draw in a lot of attention," she said jokingly.

"I . . . I'm okay with that. I don't think I was meant to stay in the shadows my *entire* life. Sooner or later, something like this was bound to happen. I was trying to hide and not accept the truth, but I'm better."

I glimpsed a smile break across her face. "Do you want to wear a necklace?"

The change of subject was relieving. "Oh. Yes, actually." I gestured to the jewelry boxes laid out before me. "Is this from my room, or is it just standard jewelry?"

"Some of it is from your room. Why?"

I reached toward the half dozen boxes, pushing jewelry aside and scanning the pile. "There's something specific I want to wear. I won't consider myself ready without it."

"Then what is it?"

I spotted what I was searching for. Gently, I pulled the strand of pearls from the other necklaces, feeling the shape of the worn, off-white pearls. I draped it over my hands and held it out for Mareena to inspect.

"Oh, you love that necklace. It's your favorite, right? Is that why you want to wear it?" she asked.

"Yes." *That and because Gerrand fixed it for me. It reminds me of him, which would be considered slightly treasonous because I'm wearing it while I'm getting married to Tanum's prince, but nobody will know . . . besides maybe Akilah, but she wouldn't make the connection.*

I reached toward my neck and put on the necklace. The pearls matched perfectly with my dress and shone against my skin. Glimpsing myself in the mirror one last time, I turned to the door. "I'm ready now."

"Good." Mareena squeezed my hand. "Remember, you just need to get through this marriage, and then you'll be free. Don't forget what I've taught you, okay?"

"I promise." I squeezed her hands back and smiled. "I love you."

She smiled, her outer demeanor cracking. "I love you too, my girl, my beautiful Syona."

For old time's sake, I laid my fingers on my leg and tapped them twice, our secret signal for happiness, and Mareena did the same.

I reached over and twisted the door open to find Cyrus waiting. He was probably there to check if Mareena was done with me. He glared at my dress with obvious distaste in his expression. "You are absolutely dripping with pearls."

I wanted to snap back at him, but I chose a simple response: "Pearls are white. Should I change to something else?"

He sighed. "No. We need to get you moving. You're almost late. Everyone else is already there."

My legs wouldn't move. I couldn't make them move. I kept staring at Cyrus, Crevan's words repeating in my thoughts. *He's right. I'm the crown princess, the heir to this kingdom. I have the same power that Davin had. I've just never been assertive enough to use it.*

Out of the corner of my eye, I observed Cyrus sigh in frustration and reach to grab my arm. Physical contact always meant a heated lecture. That realization jolted me out of the haze I was in. I jerked my arm away from him before his skin could brush against mine. Before I realized what was happening, words rushed out of my mouth.

"Don't. Touch. Me."

Cyrus hesitated for a few seconds before scoffing. "What?"

I took a few deep breaths and turned to address Mareena. "Mareena? Could you please excuse us for a few minutes? I would like to have a private conversation with Cyrus."

Mareena looked confused and a little worried. She glanced back and forth between Cyrus and me before curtsying and reluctantly descending the staircase next to us, leaving the two of us alone in the hallway.

Cyrus immediately descended on me. "What are you trying to do? Do you think talking to me in your stupid, timid voice will make me change my mind about anything? I bet you haven't even talked to Crevan or Raymon like I asked you to."

His sharp tone of voice made me reconsider doing this, but I took another breath and tried to focus. "I'm not *going* to talk to Crevan or Raymon. You can't make me obey you anymore."

He laughed at me. "Really? Do you think this is a joke? I can do anything to you. Your life is in my hands. I'll always have power over you."

It took everything I had, but I forced myself to step closer to him. Since I really wanted to get back at him, I spoke with the same mocking tone he had used during all of our conversations. I also quoted all his pointed phrases that I could remember: "I sincerely apologize, but I'm just concerned that you may have *forgotten* who I really am. Allow me to refresh your memory for you. I'm royalty. Malopaths have never surfaced in the royal family or even in nobility, and they never will, or did you forget that? I apologize. I didn't think you were *that* stupid." I somehow relished the expression of fierce anger that twisted across his face. "Maybe you took advantage of my ignorance of my true authority in the past but not anymore. You can't accuse me of anything. I am Crown Princess Syona of the kingdom of Ashlon, and my position outranks *everyone* in the palace except the king, including you. You have to do what I say." I couldn't help but smile as I threw his own words back at him. "So . . . you are dismissed. Go."

Cyrus stood frozen in shock, like a statue. Not one of his muscles moved. He certainly wasn't used to the invisible princess talking back to him.

I won't make it easy for you to control me anymore. I have power that you've never let me use, and it's power you have to respect. I'm not the same girl I was a few months ago. I have Crevan and Gerrand with me. I was thrown through a trial by fire and survived. That takes strength, and even you have to admit that.

I waved my hand at him like Davin used to do. "Oh, and I don't want you at my wedding either. I'm sure the king doesn't specifically need you to be there."

Cyrus clenched his teeth. "You—"

"Go. Shoo. Don't make me late."

He curled his fingers into fists and sent me a glare that could have melted the flesh off my bones. The glare lasted for about a minute before he spun around on his heels and stalked away.

I let out a breath I didn't know I'd been holding.

I made my way to the top of the staircase and paused to peer at the scene below. People crowded the stone floor like the day before, but it wasn't a dance taking place. It was a wedding—*my* wedding. It made me dizzy all over again just thinking about it.

In the main hallway, several rows of wooden benches were packed with people. Some were from the kingdom of Tanum, but most were from Ashlon. There must have been twenty benches on both sides of the hallway, set up in rows and perfectly spaced, each decorated with blue and white flowers. The banisters were wrapped with those flowers too. How they had gotten them in the middle of winter was a mystery to me. In between the benches was a long red carpet that traveled the entire length of the hallway up to a small stage in front of the benches. On the small stage were two people, Osion and Crevan. They were both dressed nicely and facing the crowd.

I spotted Mareena lingering near the top of the staircase. She immediately turned around, and her face lit up. "You're alive! How did it go? What on earth did you two talk about?"

I shrugged. "I followed some advice; that's all. But I don't think he'll be bothering us anymore."

Mareena sighed in relief. "That's amazing. I'm so proud of you." She glanced at the crowd below us. "Are you ready to go?"

"Yes, I think I am." I reached into the pocket of my dress and produced the emotion stone necklace I was expected to wear. I clasped it on and breathed deeply, closing my eyes.

This is it. This is the climax. Once you go down there, your life will change forever.

Words resurfaced in my mind, familiar and haunting. They were words I hadn't thought in months: *Nobody cares. Nobody pays attention. You are invisible.*

Not anymore I'm not, and I don't think I'll ever be again.

Time to accept it.

Making sure Mareena's hand was in mine, I slowly descended the stairs.

CHAPTER
TWENTY SEVEN

I reached the base of the marble steps trying not to collapse under the weight of everyone's stare. I made my way to the beginning of the red carpet. Mareena and I exchanged a glance with each other before I nodded, and we strolled down the red carpet with everyone's attention completely on me.

I surveyed the crowd, taking in the scene before me—until my eyes locked onto Crevan's. He looked at me with the cutest expression of anticipation I had ever seen, and a burst of euphoria flooded through me. I loved him. I loved Crevan. I would be overjoyed to spend the rest of my life with him. The marriage alliance, which could have been an absolute disaster, had turned into a blessing once I realized the true nature of my future husband. I couldn't have asked for a better prince to marry.

Once we reached the top of the steps on the stage, Mareena gently took my hand and placed it in Crevan's, our skin brushing against each other. This was a tradition we had decided to resurrect for the occasion. Then, she retreated to the side of the carpet to watch.

The prince leaned down to whisper to me. "I'm trying to learn what this is like. There's no veil for the bride, no flowers, and no music?"

"Right."

"You are a princess to a kingdom of cynics."

I risked cracking a grin, hoping he wouldn't realize that the emerald I wore should have blocked that emotion. "Maybe."

He glanced down at my necklace with a confused expression. "Shouldn't it . . . be impossible for you to feel happiness right now?"

I can never find a way around you, can I, Crevan? I scrambled for an excuse. "They're . . . fakes . . . normal, unenchanted stones."

He looked impressed. "You managed that? Good for you, then."

Directly after that quick exchange of words, Osion stepped up and lifted his arms, silencing straggling conversations, including ours.

"This is a great day, a day to be celebrated. It's a day that the people of both kingdoms have waited decades for. We are not only recognizing the uniting of two people but also the unification of two kingdoms: the kingdoms of Ashlon and Tanum. It signifies the start of a new era, an era of peace, trust, and prosperity. From this point, henceforth and forever, these nations will share the peninsula and all of its resources, including both the Northern and Southern Forests and access to this kingdom's mines. These specific trade agreements will be negotiated tomorrow morning by the two kings, King Raymon and King Kadar.

"Tomorrow, after negotiations, Syona will also leave with the rest of Tanum's royal family. We have given her time to learn about their kingdom. We will bid her and our new allies a fond farewell. Now, vows will be exchanged." He faced me. "Please repeat after me."

I sighed internally, knowing what he would say. It would be painfully objective and unemotional as it had been in every wedding he officiated. I cringed each time I had to attend a wedding in the kingdom of Ashlon.

Just say it. Repeat it. Force the words to come out of your mouth. Get this over with, and then you'll be free.

"I, Syona Ashlon."

Great. My full name. "I, Syona Ashlon," I repeated.

Osion droned on: "Do promise to obey and respect him and to develop a relationship based on trust and honesty."

I withheld a snort: "Do promise to obey and respect him and to develop a relationship based on trust and honesty."

"To uphold this marriage for the sake of my family and the benefits this brings to them . . ."

Fine. That I can say truthfully. I know how much this means to our kingdoms. "To uphold this marriage for the sake of my family and the benefits this brings to them."

"To wear an amber stone in his presence to prevent myself from being emotionally compromised, to remain detached from love and all sentiment, and to respect this event by never marrying again if he dies."

Ha. Sorry. I've already broken that rule, and I don't think I'll ever follow it. "To wear an amber stone in his presence to prevent myself from being emotionally compromised, to remain detached from love and all sentiment, and to respect this event by never marrying again if it so be."

As I was repeating this, Crevan stared at me with a slightly confused expression on his face, as if he were appalled by these statements.

When I finished, Osion nodded and switched to Crevan: "Prince Crevan, please repeat after me."

He still appeared confused but gave a reluctant nod and recited: "I, Crevan Westbay, promise to respect her and form a relationship based on trust and honesty. To honor her family and provide for her. To uphold her wishes with the emotion stones and refrain from love and to respect this event by never marrying again if it so be."

Crevan repeated all of these statements without a moment's hesitation.

"Good. Then Prince Crevan of the kingdom of Tanum, do you take Syona to be your lawfully wedded wife?"

"I do," he agreed, with the hint of a smile on his face.

Osion turned to me. "Princess Syona of the kingdom of Ashlon, do you take Crevan to be your lawfully wedded husband?"

I glanced at Crevan, only a foot away from me, still holding my hand from when Mareena had placed it into his. It might have been inappropriate to have the husband and wife touch each other during the ceremony, but I didn't think that anyone cared by this point.

My eyes wandered around the room, staring at the crowd before me. I opened my mouth to say the words when I spied something that made me stop cold.

Gerrand.

He was leaning against the wall at the very back of the room, staring intently at me. I hadn't even expected him to come, but there he was. Our gazes locked, and I tried to read his expression as best I could. I suddenly realized that too much time had gone by and everyone in the audience might think something was wrong.

Please, I pleaded with him in my mind, *what do you want me to do? I don't want you to be mad at me.*

His face suddenly broke into a somber smile, and he gave me a slight nod.

I mimicked his smile. *Thank you.*

I faced Crevan again, gazing into *his* eyes. They were green instead of brown. They were bright and full of anticipation. They showed anticipation of the freedom that would await both of us after this moment: me, freedom from the emotion stones; him, freedom from expectations.

Both of us free. Together.

"I do."

"Then I officially pronounce you husband and wife," Osion announced.

I could have imagined it, but I thought I heard a subtle sigh coming up from the audience.

Osion waved his hand. "Bring out the rings, please."

Mareena, from her place to the side, produced two silver rings from the palm of her hand. They were simple as rings in the kingdom of Ashlon always were. Crevan's was just a silver band with a few darker carved lines around the edges. Mine was a copy of his, but the top sparkled with a trio of diamonds.

Crevan leaned over to me. "You didn't tell me there were rings. I wasn't expecting that. It's a nice surprise."

"Well, rings are only used in royal or noble families. Anywhere else, they're considered a waste of money."

"That doesn't change anything. I still like it."

I took the ring from Mareena's outstretched hand and slid it on my hand. Crevan, taking the hint, did the same. It fit perfectly on my finger, but the cold metal burned against my skin. I wasn't used to wearing rings.

Osion nodded with approval. "I now solidify the alliance between the kingdom of Ashlon and Tanum. The royal families are now permanently connected. Syona is now henceforth and forever considered a princess of Tanum, with the royal family being subject to all the rights and responsibilities of her being in that position. Crevan is also henceforth and forever considered a prince of Ashlon." He took a breath. "The ceremony is over. I dismiss the two of you."

Crevan and I glided off the stage in near-perfect synchrony. As we continued walking down the red carpet, I heard polite, scattered applause, which was more than I expected. A normal wedding didn't mean much, but a royal one was a bit more of a spectacle.

As I kept walking, joy flooded through me. It was *done*. Finally, finally, nothing could stop me. I could feel my chains unlocking and clanking to the floor.

Crevan caught me staring at him and smiled again. "What are you thinking right now?"

"I'm thinking that . . . I love you. I'll always love you, and I don't think I'll try to hide it anymore. You are amazing."

"Ha. I'm glad you think so." He slipped his hand into mine and leaned closer to me. The physical contact was unexpected, but I welcomed it. It gave me a rush of energy and sharpened my senses.

As we exited the main hallway and wound through one of the smaller branches, we found ourselves in seclusion. Crevan stopped me and scanned our surroundings, checking to see if we were truly alone. Then he sat down on the marble floor and rested his head against the wall. I did the same, scooting up right against him. I rested my head on his shoulder and drank in the warmth of his skin. In that moment, with my back against the wall and pressing myself against another person, a person I loved, I felt protected.

I felt safe.

And again, for old time's sake, I used the simple, familiar way of expressing myself. I laid my fingers on the marble floor and tapped them.

CHAPTER
TWENTY EIGHT

I couldn't sleep. The celebrations and festivities had ended hours ago, yet I couldn't sleep at all, which was weird. I usually stayed up so late that I fell asleep in only a few minutes.

Tonight, though, was different. My mind sped around like a racehorse, and I could not calm myself down. All of the soft things around me felt unusually uncomfortable. My mattress, my blankets, I cringed every time anything brushed against my skin. My temperature fluctuated every couple of seconds, making it impossible to even remotely relax.

After a couple of hours, I gave up and bolted upright in bed, exhausted and tired of my restlessness. Crevan had decided to sleep in his own room for that night, which was good because he would not have tolerated my weird sleeping habits. The sweaty curls of my hair fell over my eyes, and I pulled them back with a flick of my wrist. I buried my face in my hands and sighed. I wasn't going to fall asleep—not tonight, at least.

Might as well do something.

Even though every muscle in my body ached and I felt like I would collapse to the floor at any moment, I threw the blankets aside and rose on uneasy feet. The carpet felt soft as I peeled a blanket off of my bed and flung it around myself.

From the near darkness of the corridors, I could determine that it was long past midnight. Even the guards knew I was always asleep at this hour because only one candle burned. The flame was weak but burned steadily. I snatched it off of the wooden mantle and made my way into the darkness. The small light danced in my hands, threatening to flicker out of existence.

I knew where I was going now. It was somewhere I felt I could sleep or at least calm down: Davin's room.

I found the door easily. I could locate the hallway blindfolded. The room was familiar now as I had visited several times after discovering it again. I entered and gently set the candle on the bedside desk as I sat down on the mattress. I scanned the dark room and imagined again what it would have been like to see Davin in here. I wondered what he had thought about when he'd sit in his room with his books. It comforted me somehow, being in his room. It was probably the closest I could get to him.

"Hi, Davin," I said to the shadows. "How are you doing?"

Talking to nothing should have seemed crazy, but somehow it was helping. I could feel the coiled strings inside of me starting to unwind. "I'm the new heir now, if you didn't know."

Silence.

"I'm a Malopath too, if you didn't know that either, but I'm doing okay. The first few months of being crown heir were a little shaky, but I think things are better now." I glanced down at my left hand. "I, um, married someone today. His name is Crevan. I think you'd like him. He's a lot like you but less outgoing and more reserved. The war's over now, too. Oh! Guess what? I stood up to Cyrus today, just like you always did. I probably won't have to deal with him anymore. Good, right?"

The stillness in the air was so thick I could've fallen into it and disappeared. "I miss you. I wish you were here."

The blanket wrapped around me was warm and soft. I could sink into it, just like the quiet atmosphere that surrounded me. Suddenly, all of the exhaustion that I should have felt suddenly rushed up to greet me. My eyes drooped. I lowered my head to the pillow below me, and my thoughts slowly drifted into nothingness.

—⁘—

The palace was supposed to be as silent as the grave in the early morning. Not a soul should have been awake before dawn, not even the servants who rose before everyone else to get ready for the day. It broke the curfew rules, and no servant or guard dared to break any rules in the kingdom of Ashlon, which is why I shouldn't have been awakened to the loud sound of pounding feet.

My eyes opened, and I strained my ears to discern the source of the noise. It was the distinct sound of several people sprinting down the hallway, their footfalls echoing so loudly that everyone in the palace could probably hear it. I heard a quick exchange of words, several quick shouts produced by unfamiliar voices and structured in the way guards would give orders to each other.

Why would palace guards be running and shouting at each other? It's the middle of the night. Is there some kind of emergency?

Then there were more voices, loud and jumbled voices, maybe a few hallways down from where I was. I estimated a dozen speakers, their words all clamoring at once. The sound of pounding feet continued, and it was coming from all directions. When I glimpsed shadows pass under the crack of the door, I bolted upright in bed.

Untangling myself from the blanket I had wrapped myself in, I leaped off of the bed and onto the floor. The carpet muffled my footsteps like I was stepping on moss. The atmosphere around me shifted somehow, like the shift in air pressure when a thunderstorm was coming. All of my intuition whispered to me that something was desperately wrong. This wasn't normal. I could feel the cold air condensing against my skin as I advanced toward the door. My heart pounded, trying to escape. My breathing turned shallow.

As I reached the door, a realization struck me and went sizzling down my spine like lighting with the thunderstorm: *Why hasn't anyone woken up yet? The sound of that many people sprinting around and shouting should be deafening to the people in that other hallway. It's loud enough that everyone should be up by now.* I pressed my ear to the door. *Why am I not hearing familiar voices? Where is everyone?*

With my attention tuned into the sound, I could finally discern what they were saying: "Spread out! Have you taken care of everyone in this hallway? Is everyone in the palace out of commission?"

A bit of information wormed through the walls of my mind and into my conscious thoughts. I *recognized* that voice. That was *Raymon's* voice. The guards running around were from the kingdom of Tanum. *What are they doing in the middle of the night? Is this an attack?* I opened my eyes and glanced at my hands pressed against the wood of the door and at the ring that glittered on my finger. *The alliance. We're supposed to have an alliance. The wedding was yesterday!*

"Yes, sir. We've searched all the rooms that we knew had people in them. Everyone has been incapacitated."

Incapacitated, my mind echoed. *So they're breaking the rules of the freshly laid alliance. Why? Whenever I talked to Raymon, he seemed overjoyed that our kingdoms were doing this. Why take the time and resources to orchestrate an elaborate marriage alliance only to break it the day after?* My thoughts paused for a few seconds, dissecting their words for meaning. *What did they mean by 'incapacitated'? And how did they do it so quickly? It only sounds like a dozen of them. A dozen against all of the guards in our palace? Impossible.*

"Good. Where's the royal family?"

"Lord Cyrus is dead, and we just found King Kadar's room."

"The king is still alive? Good. Hand me that knife. I want to kill him myself." His words were almost a growl, seething with anger.

The door became freezing to the touch. My breath caught in my throat as I slid down to the floor. The cold air constricted me. A tsunami of emotions crashed down on me, inviting me to drown in them. *Raymon . . . wants to kill my father? What about everyone else? Who else have they killed? That's not possible. None of this makes any sense.*

"We captured Lady Mareena, but we still haven't located Princess Syona. She wasn't in her room."

My brain was struggling to work, but I still understood those words.

"What?" he barked. "Why didn't you tell me this sooner?"

"I—"

"Find her. Now."

A small ray of clarity broke through the clouds. *They haven't found me. That's why I didn't know what was going on at first. I wasn't in my room. I was supposed to be in my room, but I'm in Davin's room. That's why they didn't search here.*

I clenched my fists. *I still have some control over the situation. I can help. I can do something.* I stretched my stiff legs and twisted open the doorknob as silently as I could. Peering out, I scanned the corridor. It was deserted. I stepped into the hallway, eternally grateful that I wore shoes with soft fabric. *I need to find someone, anyone I know. Maybe I can help them and fix this. Mareena. Did they say that they have Mareena? She can help me.*

Amongst all of those thoughts, two questions kept resurfacing.

Why did they kill my father, my family?

And what do they want with me?

CHAPTER
TWENTY NINE

The palace was dark. The sun had just started to rise, casting a yellow glow over the hallways but not chasing away all of the shadows. There was no unnatural light: no candles, no fireplaces. In a rush to take over the palace, they didn't pause to light the hallways. Apparently, they had accomplished their task, according to their conversation, in less than half an hour and with only twelve people.

It seemed impossible.

Yet when I turned the corner into the main branch of the hallway, I saw that it had been done.

There must have been twenty people—guards, servants, and various others—clustered on the floor near the walls. Their dark shapes were almost disguised by the shadows that surrounded them. I darted over to one of the people. He was lying limply on his side with his arms outstretched in front of him. His eyes were closed. He looked dead. All of them looked dead, but they were still breathing and had no visible wounds. I could see the gentle rise and fall of their chests. I glanced up to scan the rest of the hallway when I saw something that turned my blood cold.

Akilah.

I could see her black braided hair. She was in front of a window, lying in a pool of white light, looking just the same as all the other people in the hallway. She curled into herself, all of her muscles tense.

I rushed over to her, inspecting the scene and trying to discern what was making her like this. As I came closer, I saw one thing that wasn't normal. She was crying. I could see streams of tears traveling down her face, reflecting in the light like liquid silver.

That was strange on its own. Akilah never cried. She always wore a sapphire. That was the only stone she ever wore for some strange reason. I reached for the chain around her neck and pulled it out from underneath her clothing so I could see it better. The single sapphire strung on the chain slid along the necklace and into the palm of my hand. When it came into view, my eyes widened.

It was *glowing*.

It glowed a light that was the exact shade of the sapphire. That, in itself, was normal. Stones often glowed when the person wearing them felt an extreme version of the emotion it was supposed to block. I glanced back at the tears freely streaming down Akilah's face. The stone wasn't blocking her sadness.

Without thinking about what I was doing, I grasped the necklace in my hand, snapped it off her neck and threw it across the hallway; the chain skittered across the floor like a rock skipping on a lake.

Akilah revived instantly. Her eyes snapped open, and she tried to scramble to her feet, latching onto the window ledge to pull herself up. She had a desperate, pleading expression on her face.

"Whoa. Whoa. Stop." I grabbed her shoulders and forced her back into a sitting position. "Are you okay?"

Akilah's dazed eyes focused on my face, and she immediately brightened. "Syona!" She sighed with relief. "I'm so glad to see you here! I need to tell you something. When I—"

"Stop talking. Get down," I ordered her. I could hear the quiet echo of footsteps approaching. Both of us pressed ourselves against the floor in the shadows just in time to witness a Tanum guard turn the corner and enter the hallway.

He looked the same as any: blue jacket trimmed with black and layered over a white shirt. He had several weapons, and his eyes were wide and alert, scanning for threats. He could be a guard from our kingdom if the colors were different. He stopped in the center of the floor and surveyed the hallway, eyeing all the shadows and the still forms of people lying on the stone. Akilah and I didn't dare to breathe.

Another sound suddenly pierced the silence of the corridor. Light footsteps skimming over the marble floor; someone else was approaching. I tried to move as little as possible as the person came into view. It was a servant girl, like Akilah. Her short brown hair was rumpled and messy, like she had just woken up.

She eyed the Tanum guard just as he spotted her. "What's going on? Is everything alright? I heard voices, and I thought something was wrong."

The Tanum guard smiled and held out his hands palms up to appear non-threatening. He slowly prowled toward her. "It's okay. Everything's fine. We're just doing some emergency training drills. We didn't mean to wake people up."

The servant tilted her head in confusion. "Why would you be doing an emergency drill in a palace that isn't yours, and aren't you leaving for your own kingdom today?"

The guard sighed. "You're wearing a stone, right? Good, of course you are. You're an Ashlon." He flicked his fingers at the girl, and the sapphire strung on her necklace flashed brightly. She let out a gasp and dropped to the floor like a stone.

The Tanum guard paused only for a few seconds to glance at the girl lying on the floor before he continued stalking down the hallway. As he left, I could hear him mumbling. "Sheesh. That excuse worked with the other servant girls."

"Is that what happened to you?" I whispered to Akilah.

"Yeah, but it was with a different guard." She pressed her hands against the sides of her head. "Oh, my head is splitting open. When he flicked his fingers at me, the stone started glowing and I felt so, so sad, sadder than I've ever felt in my entire life." She shuddered violently. "I felt so hopeless that I didn't want to do anything anymore. I collapsed against the wall, and then you found me."

"Aren't the stones supposed to make you not feel that emotion?"

"Yes, I was thinking the same thing. Do you know why this is happening?"

I shook my head. "I don't know. If I had more information, I could draw better conclusions, but right now, I have nothing." I waved my hand at the scene before us. "Besides what we just saw."

"Do you want to find other Ashlons? We can try and figure out why this is happening along the way."

"Yes." I took her hand, and she let me pull her off of the floor.

We continued to sprint down the hallways, searching for anyone alert. I inferred that the stones were causing this, but we couldn't find anyone else who was conscious. There wasn't a single person in the palace who wasn't wearing at least one stone.

Why is this happening? my brain sang repeatedly. *Okay. Review the facts. Break it down. That's what you're good at. They were able to take down the guards and capture the palace with only a dozen men because they exploited the stones, which is probably the most efficient way possible. Everyone wears the stones, and the Tanum guards are somehow using an extra ability to control the emotions of each wearer. That means they knew that the stones could do that, which is an ability that nobody else knows about.*

How long have they known about the stones? How long have they been planning this?

The possibilities were disturbing.

As we turned into another corridor, the two of us spotted something at the same time, another guard from Tanum, pacing along the edge of the very end of the hallway.

"There's another one. What do you think we should do?" Akilah asked.

I frantically looked around, searching for a hiding spot. My gaze fell upon a door a few yards from us. It could have been a small guest room or a supply closet, but I didn't care. It was a way out.

Akilah spied it at the same time. She threw open the door and gestured with her head for me to get inside. I didn't need any encouragement. I leaped into the shadows beyond the door, and Akilah rushed in after me, shutting the door and plunging both of us into darkness.

I pressed my fingers against the wooden walls. This was indeed a supply closet. I didn't know what it held, but it was a place to go. I continued running my hands over the textured wood, relying on my sense of touch instead of sight.

I only did that for a few seconds until my fingers brushed against something warm and soft. Skin. Another human being who definitely wasn't Akilah. I would have screamed, or at least yelped loudly, if the person hadn't spoken first. "I'm sorry. This closet is already occupied. You might want to find another hiding place."

I swiveled my head in the cramped space. "Gerrand?"

"The one and only. How is everybody?"

"Gerrand!" I angled myself to face him. "Are you okay? Is everything okay?" I traced my fingers down his arm until I found his hands, and I squeezed them hard.

"I'm good. Besides being in a small closet with two other people, I'm good."

An immature, impulsive part of me realized I was in a cramped closet with a boy, but I smashed the thoughts immediately. I had other things to worry about. "Do you know what's happening?"

His voice had a hint of sadness in it. "Well, I wanted to hear your opinion first."

"For goodness' sake. Does everyone think I know everything?"

"You are the person most likely to have figured out something miles before everyone else," Akilah commented from her side of the closet near the door.

"Sorry. I don't know. I wish I did, but I don't. Only a few theories. Sorry."

"Well, great. If Syona doesn't know, then we're really in trouble." Gerrand said with exasperation.

"Stop it." I snapped my fingers to get his attention. "You're smart too. Figure it out. Walk us through what happened."

"I was patrolling with everyone else, and then one of the guards from Tanum came into our sight and did something with his hands. Immediately after that, everyone around me just collapsed. Nothing unusual happened to *me*, but I did the smart thing and dropped to the floor with them. Then, he left. After he was out of sight, I got up and—"

"Hid in a closet? Really?" Akilah asked with disbelief.

"Yes. Cut me some slack, okay? Do I have to remind you that you two did the same thing? The best theory I can come up with so far is that it has something to do with the stones since I was wearing non-enchanted ones. That's the only difference between me and everyone else."

"Yes, I think so too. Somehow there's another setting or some property of the stones that inflates people's emotions to the point where they're incapacitated. I don't know how that came to be or how Raymon found out, but that knowledge was really useful for this attack."

"Wait. Attack?" Akilah whispered. "Attack? This isn't an attack, is it?

"They killed my father and my uncle," I said, my voice almost breaking. "So, yes, it's an attack."

Akilah and Gerrand didn't react. Though I couldn't quite see their expressions, I assumed they were both dumbfounded. I continued before they could start speaking, "I also overheard them saying that they have my aunt, Mareena, and . . . I don't want her to get hurt. I need to get out there and find out what their intentions are. Okay?" This time my voice really did crack. *They can't. She's the only one I have left. She's practically my mother. They can't. I won't allow it.*

"Okay," Akilah finally said. She brushed against my arm reassuringly. "Be careful."

"Stay here," I commanded. *I love you guys. I can't let you get hurt too.* "Stay. Here."

"Seriously? Why?" Gerrand complained.

"Because if you die, I'm going to hunt you down and kill you."

He scoffed at me. "That doesn't make any—"

"It's not supposed to make sense."

"Ha! Syona's saying something that doesn't make sense! When has that ever happened? You would know, Akilah."

"Nope. Never. This is a first," Akilah replied.

I rolled my eyes, even though the darkness obscured everyone's vision. "Stay." Before they could talk me out of it, I opened the closet door, darted out, and closed it again. In the illuminating light, I observed that their expressions showed disappointment, but I didn't care. I started walking, this time toward the sound of the voices.

After a few steps, I spied something that made my heart leap out of my chest. Crevan was pacing down the hallway in the exact spot the guard had previously stood. He kept swiveling his head and inspecting the corridors, like he was searching for something, but my brain missed that piece of information as I streamed toward him. Emotions flooded over me. I could trust Crevan, even though his kingdom had betrayed us. He would help me, no matter what. I *knew* him.

When I came into his field of view, his eyes widened. I rushed over to him and yanked his arm, shaking it desperately as I slid to the floor. "Crevan! What's going on? You . . ." I bit back a sob. "Your father, he—"

Crevan squeezed my shoulders. "Syona, what are you doing here?"

"What are you doing? The alliance . . . your guards killed . . . I—"

He sighed, snapping his eyes shut. He clenched my shoulders tightly, like I was a lifeline for him. "I'm sorry. I'm really sorry."

My voice choked with emotion. "For what?"

His expression contorted, like he was trying not to cry. "I told you that my father wanted to merge the kingdoms, Syona. He's always wanted to merge the kingdoms. We just needed to find out how. We just needed a way how."

I was getting frantic. "What? What are you talking about?"

Crevan sighed one last time, swiveled his head to the side, and shouted as loud as he possibly could. "I found her! She's over here!"

Nothing made sense. My perception of reality distorted, like a cracked mirror. "What? What are you doing?"

Tanum guards started pouring in from all sides, filling my entire field of view as if the kingdom had buried me alive. The pounding of their feet was the only thing I could hear. Two of them hooked onto the underside of my arms and jerked me to my feet, sending a burst of pain through my shoulders. I hardly maintained my footing and my shoes slipped on the smooth stone floor. I couldn't fight; I was too confused. The burning intensity of my attention was focused directly on Crevan.

"Crevan! Stop!" I protested. "Why are you doing this? How are you doing this? How can you control the stones? What's wrong with them? They don't control people's emotions! They only take away emotions! What did you do to them?"

Crevan shook his head with disbelief. "You don't get it, Syona. The stones could always do that. We didn't change them in any way. The only reason we knew about it was because we were the ones who made them in the first place. The kingdom of Tanum. *We* did."

CHAPTER
THIRTY

I t made perfect sense. It made a perfect, awful sense. So many things I had puzzled over were now explained. The new perspective and the new information let my brain break through the secrets. Connections were made. Conclusions were drawn. My mind assembled all the pieces and truth finally came crashing in.

The stones were discovered five years into the war in one of our silver mines. They were cut gemstones, thousands of them, enough for all the inhabitants of the kingdom. Just sitting in chests. Everyone thought we had found buried treasure. We brought then to the surface, made them into necklaces and realized they were enchanted, emotion sucking, addictive. It spread through the kingdom like wildfire.

In the craze, nobody, not even once, questioned where they had come from or how they were enchanted.

Raymon's interest in Malopaths and Crevan's shying away from talking about the stones and the history of his kingdom now made perfect sense in such a horrific way. The stones were a way to control us and manipulate our emotions so they could easily capture our kingdom. They had all the cards the entire time. We played right into their hands.

They roughly shoved me—forget about being royalty—to the branch of the hallway near my room where a dozen Tanum guards stood in a half-circle around Mareena, who knelt on the floor. She glared up at Raymon as he loomed over her. I would've cried out with relief if I hadn't had the wind knocked out of me from being jostled around. She was alive, my aunt, my Malopath sympathizer, the only surviving member of my family. If she were to die, I would die with her.

But she was *alive,* and that's all I cared about.

They yanked me into the center of the circle of guards and forced me to my knees alongside Mareena. We were so close I could have touched her. I moved my eyes to glance at her expression. Her muscles were stiff, but that fear didn't manifest on her face. She stared up at our captors, completely calm.

I tried to mimic her by slowing my breathing, but my lungs had a mind of their own. I couldn't calm down no matter how hard I tried. The one thing that terrified me more than anything in the whole world was the unknown, when my brain couldn't figure out what was going on. This was completely unfamiliar territory.

Raymon peered down at us with such a condescending expression that I felt like a child. "So. We finally found you. You were hard to track down. You weren't in the place we thought you would be."

I returned his gaze. "How long have you been planning this?"

"How long has it been? Thirtyish years? Thirty-five? Thirty-six? Longer than the war has lasted, certainly—before the war, even." His face creased into a mocking smile. "I'm sorry. I just can't seem to remember the exact details."

"Was the marriage alliance just an excuse to get into the palace?" I whispered.

"Well, yes, but everyone in your kingdom was so cocky. They thought we had completely good intentions when we suggested the idea. Even if we didn't, they figured that we would never be able to overpower them in their own palace, surrounded by their own guards. It seemed audacious and impossible." He opened his hand, revealing a necklace with a sapphire threaded on it. "But it was not impossible with this."

We didn't know the stones could do that. Why would we expect an attack if we had no idea that the stones could enable someone to manipulate our emotions? That's not fair.

He stalked closer to me and leaned down, his eyes full of scorn. "You thought you had everything figured out, but you didn't suspect anything. At all! You believed the fake stories everyone in your kingdom believes. You say you're so smart, but you're not."

I watched someone appear from behind Raymon, a flash of black and green coming out from an adjoining hallway. Crevan stood behind his father, appearing almost as his shadow. Part of my heart leaped when I saw him, but my head put a pause on my emotions. He had sold me out a few minutes ago. I wanted to see him as he truly was—a traitor—but my brain kept unearthing tender memories of him. I couldn't bring myself to think that he had turned on me.

Raymon faced him with a smile on his face. "Ah, Crevan! So glad you could join us! Would you care to do the honors?"

I was getting more flustered than I wanted to be. "How did you create the stones in the first place?"

The king shook his head. "So many unanswered questions."

I wanted to speak more, but I felt Mareena's firm hand on my wrist, squeezing me to silence.

Crevan stepped into the middle of the circle, in front of the guards. "I'm sorry you two, but . . ."

No. Crevan. Please. Don't. My thoughts went unspoken as he fastened a sapphire necklace around my neck, the cold metal burning my skin. I wished it was painful, to punish myself for being so stupid, but it wasn't. The only thing that was somewhat painful was that insufferable faint humming sound, the origin of which I still hadn't figured out. Crevan put one on Mareena too, and all I could do was watch.

I knew what was going to happen. He would activate the other setting of the stone, the one that inflated and manipulated emotions instead of purging them. In a few seconds, I would feel sad, hopelessly and despairingly sad. I would then sink to the ground, wanting to die, where they could do anything they wanted to me.

Crevan flicked his fingers at the two of us, making me flinch.

But absolutely nothing happened besides my heartbeat shooting upward like an arrow. For only a split second, the humming sound increased to an ear-splitting volume, like I was sticking my head into a hive of bees, but that was it.

Crevan spoke it first before my mind could think of it. "You're both . . . Malopathic."

"Yes," Mareena confirmed, the first words she had spoken since they had thrown us into this situation.

Crevan stared down at me, and I could see it in his eyes that everything had clicked together in that moment. As he figured out the puzzle, clarity flooded his features. "How did I not figure it out sooner? I'm so stupid. Everything you've said, the rule-breaking, the willingness to not wear the stones, everything. The only thing that stopped me from believing it was the fact that you're royal. How . . . royalty? Surely it couldn't—"

"Tell me *exactly* how this happened, and I'll let you live," Raymon hissed, cutting off his son.

Mareena was as frantic as I was; the barrier that usually surrounded her emotions had crumbled to pieces. "I don't know anything. Nothing. Neither of us knows anything."

Raymon clenched his teeth. "What about your parents? Do you know anything about your parents? Names, age, origin? Do you have any useful information?"

"Why do my parents matter?" Mareena asked, stress apparent in her voice. "We don't know anything!"

"Tell me!"

Mareena threw her hands up in submission. "My sister and I never knew anything about our parents. We were adopted. Our parents died when we were very young. I don't know anything."

"Why did your sister marry the king?" Raymon demanded, a question that seemed to come from nowhere.

"It was arranged!" Mareena yelled at him. "The only reason why Ionda married the king was because we were adopted into a noble family and he chose her, but we were never told anything about our origin. Nothing. I swear."

"Is that all you can tell us?" Crevan asked, his voice calm, unlike his father.

Mareena exhaled. "The only thing I got from my sister was this." She held up her wrist, exposing the simple chain bracelet she had shown me—appearing as plain and innocent as ever, but when Raymon's eyes fell on the bracelet, his face paled. He jumped backward like a cornered animal, as if that simple piece of jewelry was the most dangerous thing in the world.

Crevan's expression hardened as he peered down at Mareena. Then, he faced his guards.

"Kill her."

My mind had hardly registered the words before one of the guards unsheathed his sword and slashed it across Mareena's throat.

CHAPTER
THIRTY ONE

The world shattered.

A strangled shriek escaped me as another guard jerked me out of the circle and restrained me with his arms. A wave of confusion and terror exploded inside me. My veins turned to ice and splintered to pieces. The image of Mareena's final moments replayed itself over and over, seared into my mind, taunting me. The sound of the sword slicing through the air echoed in my thoughts.

"*Let. Me. Go!*" I screeched, the words sharp as knives. My nails found the man's flesh, and he abruptly released me. I frantically scrambled over to where Mareena lay.

Her brown hair had fallen over her face, and I quickly brushed it away. I peered into her brown eyes. Her eyes, once full of light, were now dull and lifeless. Life had been ripped from her.

Needles stabbed at the back of my eyes, and hot tears streamed down my face. I took a shuddering, emotion-filled breath as I clutched her hand, a hand that didn't squeeze back. This wasn't a nightmare, though I wished it were. My fingertips grew numb and tingling as my mind broke, rejecting reality.

I refused to glance down at her neck, but I knew what it looked like. The image remained there at the back of my eyelids, appearing each time I closed them. Never forgotten. Never forgiven.

My thoughts echoed like the palace hallways. *You failed, Syona. She's dead.*

"Check the records." Raymon's voice gave the order to the guards. "See if there were any dissenter incidents around the time she was born, about three and half decades ago."

Another voice, one I didn't recognize. "We don't keep records of that, and most of the traitors aren't even accounted for. We can't keep track of all the people who sneak between kingdoms."

"Check anyway! There must be something!" someone snapped.

My muscles shook. The tears kept falling, splattering against the marble. I drank in the warmth of her skin, warmth that I knew would fade away soon. My eyes fell on the bracelet dangling from her wrist, a simple piece of jewelry but one that had condemned her. I snapped it off her wrist and tucked it into my pocket. I didn't know if they let me take it or just hadn't seen me do it. Crevan's face entered my field of view.

My voice was a ghost. "Kill me, please. You've killed everyone else."

He winced. "We can't."

"I have nothing to live for anymore."

"You're too important. Sorry."

A full ten seconds went by. I counted them in my head, each one a small eternity, ticking like a clock. "Did you ever love me?" Stupid. A stupid question to ask in that moment of complete vulnerability.

He didn't answer but simply turned away so I couldn't see his expression.

I didn't say anything more, but I felt so many negative emotions. Betrayal. Complete disbelief. *You were the one who gave the order to kill her. You were the one who did it. I hate you.*

I was full of conflict. I wanted to hate him, but my feelings for him barred me from doing so. Previously spoken words kept surfacing in my memory, the beautiful words that had passed between us, that I thought we were both relating to:

I just don't like talking to people that often. I'd rather be by myself and sit in the background. Does that make any sense to you?

I observe. I think. I listen. Just. Like. You.

We're more alike than you might realize or care to admit. Any heartache, any trouble you've ever been through, I will know what it's like. I'm sorry that life is so hard on you.

It wasn't possible that someone so empathetic and relatable would give an order to kill someone.

It wasn't possible.

Surprisingly gentle hands untangled me from her body and drug me away. Something with a sickly smell was pressed against my face, but by then I was already fading.

―――

My dreams threw me into the past, reliving a memory that was now painful:

Her stern expression morphs into a smile. "I'm really happy for you."

"You are?" I try to turn around in the chair, but I can't. Not with her holding my hair. You can practically hear the eagerness in my voice.

"Yes." She sticks a few hairpins in her mouth and tries to talk around them. "I didn't think you'd survive until your eighteenth birthday."

I laugh, something I want to do more often. "My birthday's tomorrow. Something still might happen."

She snorts. "Don't talk that way. It's practically impossible. Nobody can touch you now. Besides, you've gotten so good at hiding your emotions that I can hardly tell you're a Malopath anymore."

"Is that a compliment or an insult?" I don't want to seem like I'm not human, but it happened to be a matter of survival.

"A little bit of both," she muses. "But don't run away from that side of yourself, okay? It's not healthy."

"Yes, Mother," I say jokingly.

In the reflection of the mirror, I see her face twist into amused puzzlement. "Mother?"

It's a risk. Mareena's sensitive to her sister's death. She usually doesn't want to be called Mother, saying it's disrespectful to Ionda. I try to counter it. "Aunt? Lady. Mareena. Lady Mareena. Princess. Princess Mareena? Fellow Malopath Who Is Also My Mentor Who's a Little Hard on Me Sometimes but I Love Her Anyway. What do you want me to call you?"

She continues to weave her fingers through my hair. "Actually . . . Mother would do just fine."

It took me a long time to drift back to reality. Maybe my subconscious brain didn't want to return there; it knew that in the real world, my family was dead, my friends were missing, and the people I thought I could trust had betrayed me.

Mareena. Mother. Mareena. The two words echoed in my thoughts like a voice far away, intertwining so tightly that they were synonymous with each other.

They had murdered her.

No. *Crevan* had murdered her. In *front* of me.

My eyes snapped open, and I bolted upright, breathing heavily. I tried to untangle myself from the memory. My hair fell into my eyes and across my face, but my hands immediately reached up to brush it away. Sweat drenched my face. I angled my neck back so I could stare up at the ceiling. It was a light tan color with a swirling texture.

Wait. Where was I?

Light flooded in from a source on my right. I turned and saw a stained-glass window on the adjacent wall right next to me, but the curtains were blue, not red like I was used to. I was sitting on a bed. I was in a bedroom, and based on the color scheme of my surroundings, it was a bedroom in the kingdom of Tanum.

"Oh, good. You're awake. It's been so *boring* with nobody to talk to."

My head shot to the side, toward the sound where I found Raymon stretched across a sofa. Blue to match the colors in the room, the sofa was tucked into the back corner near the door. He draped over it like a curtain, hands folded behind his head. His eyes were dazed, vaguely staring in my direction. He looked relaxed, like he always did. Like he didn't care.

I snapped off the necklace I still wore and chucked it across the room in his direction.

Even though he appeared completely relaxed, his hand shot into the air and snatched the necklace before it hit the ground. "I advise not doing that. These are expensive. Do you know how much effort it took to create them?"

"You don't deserve *any* cooperation from me," I hissed.

"We do, actually. This is on diplomatic grounds. You are in a neighboring kingdom."

"Diplomacy is nonexistent at this point," I seethed, clenching my fists.

"That may be, but you were given time to visit the kingdom of Tanum. Even though the alliance is broken, you remain bound by that original contract, which was on diplomatic grounds. This is your vacation! Isn't it exciting? Now, are we going to have a conversation like civilized people, or do I have to bring some guards in here to restrain you by force?"

I hated how calm and slow his voice was, as if he were explaining something to a child. He was minimizing the situation. Slices of anger shot through me. My world had been destroyed, reduced to burning splinters. I hated him for it. There was no way he could distort what had truly happened. A fire smoldered inside me, waiting to burst out.

"I'll talk to you."

"Good."

Needles pricked at the back of my eyes again, but I refused to submit to them. I would not cry. "Why did you do all of this? I deserve to know that."

"Ah, that's the question of the century. Well, I didn't appreciate you Ashlons when I found out you split from my kingdom in the past. I mean, we were oppressing your race and all, but I thought it would just be better if you were with us again." He clapped his hands together, making me flinch. "So, when the previous king died and I came to power about thirty-five years ago, I kept thinking, *How can I get them back? How can I get the kingdoms back together again?*"

I despised the way he explained it; his voice was high and mocking, like he wasn't taking any of this seriously.

"Then all of us got to thinking: what if we start a war between the two kingdoms? It was easy enough to do as there was already a resource problem. It was only a matter of time. Then we created these . . . stones." He held the reflective sapphire in his hand. "Stones that take away emotion. Stones that can control emotion. It was a foolproof plan. You do have to appreciate the genius of it. Wars cause devastation and destruction. People want to feel numb in the middle of a war. We created them, stuck them in a convenient place, and waited. It didn't take long for you to find them and discover what they could do, and they spread all over the kingdom."

"But what about the other setting that makes it possible to manipulate the wearer's emotions?" My fists squeezed so tightly that my nails jabbed into my skin—a familiar feeling.

"Ah, yes. That was so we could control everyone's emotions and change them to total hopelessness or apathy. We knew it would be easy to waltz in and take the kingdom from a people crushed by despair. Unfortunately, we didn't expect so many—how do I put this—*dissenters* from our kingdom. Obviously, these traitors settled down and started families with people from yours. Malopaths are people who have *just* enough of our blood for the stones not to work. They started popping up everywhere. Fortunately, your father actively hunted them down and killed them, which took care of that problem. Unfortunately, we didn't expect you and your aunt to be one. That's for sure."

It made sense. It clicked. We were two different races of people. We had different traits and appearances. Mareena and I had already inferred that being Malopathic was a trait passed down in families, but we didn't know how it came to be or how it worked. But the two races intermixing? *That* I could understand. *I have Tanum ancestry. Mareena knew almost nothing about my grandparents, but one of them must have been from Tanum—or both. That's why royal people have never been Malopathic.*

Oh. A flash of memory and inspiration came to me. *That's why they wanted to know if there were any dissenters at the time of Mareena's birth. They were checking to see if . . . Oh.*

It was a small amount of satisfaction, finally knowing my origin, and it sapped away some of the pain I had been feeling. It was a single ray of light in an overcast world.

I started talking again. "If you could take the kingdom that easily, then why did you bother with the war lasting thirty years?"

"We couldn't just go in and capture the kingdom, even with the stones and all the control we had," he mused. "If we had done that, the people of your kingdom would always have the drive to rebel and split apart again. It wouldn't work. No. To gain their loyalty, we couldn't do it by force. We had to do it . . . politically."

"The marriage alliance," I whispered.

"Good girl." He nodded, a little patronizingly. "We figured that, sooner or later, we would have heirs and your father would have heirs, and we could take the kingdom subtly through an alliance, through marriage. Crevan is a prince of your kingdom now, which means he can rule." He stared down at his hands and the volume of his voice dropped significantly. "And maybe I just wanted to get into the palace so I could kill the king with my own hands."

I didn't understand the burning hatred he held for my father, and he probably wouldn't tell me if I asked, so I shot seething words back at him. "That means you don't have any power. Crevan does. He'll be the king. Not you."

Raymon snorted. "You think Crevan has any real power? He can't do anything. Not if I don't let him. Besides, even if you throw out technicalities and quote as many rules as you can remember, it doesn't matter. As long as we have you in our kingdom, you can't do anything." He huffed, possibly annoyed that I had thrown off the rhythm of his monologue. He then smiled a dark smile. "Anyway, for my plan to work, your kingdom could only have one heir." He folded his arms behind his head again. "And that was easy enough to do."

I should have expected it, yet the world came crashing down on me all over again. When I spoke, my voice was steel: "Davin didn't die in a hunting accident."

He had the audacity to chuckle. "No, of course he didn't, and I couldn't believe how simple it was. All we had to do—"

I leaped off of the bed and onto the floor, fuming. "Don't. You. Dare. Don't tell me how easy it was to kill my bother. But do explain why you chose me as the heir and not Davin."

Raymon was a bit ruffled by my sudden outburst, but he maintained a smooth composure. "You were female. I had to use Ashlon's female heir since I couldn't possibly risk marrying off one of my useless daughters. And I liked you. You seemed smart and quiet, easily controllable . . . if you want me to be blunt."

I clenched my teeth so hard my jaw started hurting. "I am not easily controllable." *Not . . . not anymore.*

He stood up, and I resisted the urge to back away from him. "You keep telling yourself that, but you are. You've been like that your whole life, and you're never going to change." His face relaxed. "But if it makes you feel any better, you are my favorite daughter."

My blood turned to icicles. He was trying to manipulate me, and I hated it. "Stop it. I'm not your daughter."

"You are, though, by marriage. You're also the last surviving member of your family. You have no friends, and you're alone. Our kingdom now has complete control over yours." He stopped advancing toward me. "I'd better go. You seem . . . unstable."

"No! You haven't told me everything!"

He didn't listen to me. He paced to the door and opened it in one fluid motion. "I'll be locking the door behind me if you're wondering that too." He closed it with a confirmative clicking noise.

I rushed over to the door and started pounding my fists on it. "Wait! Why do you want the kingdom of Ashlon? If I knew, maybe there's a way we can work this out! Why did you hate my father so much? What did he ever do to you? How . . . how did you create the stones in the first place?" I grasped at the doorknob, but it was indeed locked. "Wait! Come back!"

But he was gone, leaving me with a pile of never-ending questions.

Never asked.

Never answered.

CHAPTER
THIRTY TWO

I was expecting Crevan to come in too. It would be poetic. I knew he wouldn't wait long to see me. It would be nagging at the back of his stupid but intelligent and observant mind until he did. I was dreading it, but I felt like I needed it. That was the only thing I could decide on, that I needed to talk to him and find out how he truly felt.

When the door opened and I saw his beautiful and terrible green eyes, I was ready—as ready as I ever would be.

"I hate you," I whispered under my breath, tucking my knees to my chest to feel more secure. It didn't work very well.

He grimaced. "I know. You should. I'm sorry." He shuffled over to the bed and stared at me from a standing position.

His response startled me, but I quickly tapped back into my anger. "You're *sorry?*"

I got up on my knees and swung my fist as hard as I could in his direction, though I knew he would be expecting it. He snatched my wrist and stopped me before I could hit him. "Yes. I'm sorry." His voice stayed remarkably calm for what I had attempted to do. "Now. Are we going to have a civilized conversation, or—"

"You're exactly like your father," I spat.

He squeezed his eyes shut and looked away. That hit him harder than I expected. "Yes. I'm exactly like my father. He forced me to be exactly like him. Are you ever going to give me a chance to explain myself?"

"What happened to the Crevan I knew?" I asked, tears coming to my eyes.

He clenched his teeth. "That Crevan's still there, just smothered by what everyone wants him to be." He released my wrist. "You think your life is bad by being a Malopath? How about having your entire life written out for you before you were even born?"

He stood up, never taking his eyes off me. "You have a good imagination, Syona. You can probably imagine being told your father's plan for your entire life. Imagine being manipulated, being crushed by the expectations. He looked away, squeezing his eyes shut again. "I remember them telling me about a princess in another kingdom whom I would have to marry. Then, at eighteen, I had to go to the kingdom of Ashlon and see this princess for the first time."

His words were airy and breathless. "It was so painful to see how smart you were and how fragile you were. I could hardly bear the knowledge of what we were going to do to you and your family, how it was going to *break* you."

"You killed her. You killed Mareena when you didn't have to."

Wrong thing to say. Crevan immediately faced me, eyes blazing. "I *did* have to. We had to make sure you were the only person left in your family. That was *specifically* part of the plan. My father was *right there*."

"Raymon controls you," I said aloud. "He threatens and manipulates you."

He turned away from me, but I saw tears streaming down his face. "Yes. He does."

A complicated mixture of sympathy and hurt swirled inside of me. I tried to smooth it over. "Why are you here, Crevan, besides trying to make me feel sorry for you?"

He immediately stood up straighter. "My father wants you to appear in front of the people of your kingdom and . . .calm them down, basically. We can control them with the stones, but he just wants to make sure there's no political unrest."

"What are you doing to the kingdom of Ashlon right now?"

He exhaled and brushed his fingers through his hair. "Sending more guards in, trying to control the situation, spreading the news of what happened."

"Do you really think they'll stay with you?"

Crevan stared into my eyes, seemingly wiping away his emotions. "Well, we have their queen, and as far as I can tell, the people respect you."

I'm the queen. I'm the queen of the kingdom of Ashlon. It's a reality now. Everything that I hoped wouldn't happen did. I'm the queen of an entire kingdom, a kingdom that needs my help, a kingdom that they're invading. Ashlon is a kingdom with thousands of people, and I'm the queen of it.

"I won't do it. It's my kingdom, Crevan. You can't take it." The words *my kingdom* sounded wrong in my mouth, and I immediately regretted saying them.

"We have already. We're just trying to make the transition as smooth as possible." He spread his arms beseechingly. "You have to. Do you want my father to be upset with me?"

I recalled the times Raymon had gotten mad at Crevan. There weren't very many. He probably wanted to hide their true relationship, but he had still been very direct and harsh with him. "I. Don't. Care." I forced the words out of my mouth.

"Fine. Then I'll go." He shuffled back to the door.

"Were you the one who killed Davin?" I suddenly asked.

"No. It was just some hired guards. Nothing special. We made it look like an accident, smoke and mirrors," he casually replied.

"You're just like him."

He actually seemed confused. "Davin? How am I like Davin?"

"You both have conflicting personalities. You're torn between who you want to be and who you have to be. You're two-faced." *And Davin was kind, gentle, charismatic, authentic, and easy to talk to. He protected me from Cyrus, just like you. I should hate you. I should. You destroyed my life.*

He dared to take a few more steps toward me. "I do what I have to, Syona. You can't blame me for that."

"You had a choice," I snapped. "Go. I don't want to see you again."

"No, I don't. I've never had a choice," he protested.

"You . . . you can't *kill* someone I love right in front of me and use your *father* as an excuse for forgiveness!" I shouted. "Leave. Right now."

He cringed from my words. "I—"

"*Leave!*" I snatched up a vase on the desk and hurled it at him. A tan-colored, plain-looking object, it sailed through the air and exploded against the wall, scattering the shards everywhere. He flinched but retreated and left the room.

I felt like I wanted to cry, but there was nothing left, which was good. I was sick of crying, but the sadness still lingered like mildew clinging to my brain. I wanted to get rid of the feeling. I wanted it gone. It was a weakness.

I heard Mareena, in my thoughts, talking to me, a gentle whisper: *Don't bottle up that side of yourself. I know it's slightly counter-intuitive, but the worst thing you can do is to pretend your emotions don't exist at all. If you do that, you're just as bad as everyone else.*

Don't wish not to have emotions, I thought, adding to her words. *They make us who we are.* I took a few deep breaths, pressed the back of my head against the wall, and prayed I would wake up from this nightmare.

I paced along the floor as it was the only thing I could do. I wondered when my shoes would wear holes in the carpet. I didn't know how much time had passed, but the sun had sunk below the horizon and out of sight. All its warmth and light had disappeared, plunging the world into darkness. Even though the temperature was appalling, I still forced my legs to move my shivering body across the floor as I searched for a solution.

The thick blankets on the bed were probably warm, but I refused to touch them. A few servants had come by to bring me food, but I hadn't taken a single bite. Starving and freezing myself probably wasn't helping me think of a solution, but I didn't want to be relaxed. I needed to be alert.

I finally submitted to the pleas of my aching muscles and sat down. To still feel productive, I thought through a list of objects I could access—not much to name. They had probably stripped the room before placing me here because it yielded nothing useful. Besides a few blankets, a simple plate with food, and the sapphire necklace that Raymon had left on the sofa, the room was quite bare.

Anger spiked through me. *Come on, Syona!* I shouted at myself. *You're good at thinking through problems and finding connections. That's the only thing you're good at, but it's enough. You're smart enough to find a solution. You treat life like a big set of puzzle pieces to fit together. Put together the pieces! You need to escape and get the kingdom of Ashlon back.*

I sat up straighter. *Think of it this way, you're trying to escape from a high tower. There are two possible exits: the window and the door. The door is locked. That's the most logical way to escape—through the door—and that's why they lock it.* I looked up. *That leaves the second option, the window.*

I climbed to my feet and inspected the window panes. They didn't appear to be locked or latched. I pressed my fingers against the cold glass and pushed. The wind shot through the window and filled the room, but I chose to ignore it.

They could have locked the window, or enforced it somehow, but they chose not to. That was probably a safe bet because no sane person would ever go through the window. I stared down at the dizzying drop below. *It's too easy to fall.* The wind howled with a vengeance, daring anyone to attempt that method of escape. It smashed itself against the bricks of the tower and flooded into the room.

Bricks. The wall is made of bricks. I peered downward at the uneven spacing of the stones; the bricks were not perfectly aligned in stacks. The texture was rough, with the edges of the bricks sticking out slightly more than usual. I suddenly saw possible places for my hands and feet while climbing.

Nobody would attempt it or expect it because it's not logical. I don't think Raymon considered this option. Even if he did, he wouldn't think that the crown heir of the kingdom of Ashlon would know how to scale brick walls.

I leaned out farther. *I haven't climbed anything in a while, though. It's been a few years. These certainly aren't the ideal conditions to relearn, but I think it's my only option.*

After hesitating a few more seconds, I climbed backward out the window, grasping the window ledge with my fingertips and angling my toes to seek traction on the slippery bricks.

CHAPTER
THRITY THREE

I dug my jagged, torn nails into the mortar and prayed I wouldn't lose my grip and plummet to the ground.

The wind laughed at me, catching my hair and tossing it in every direction. The curled strands brushed against my eyes and mouth, pulling my focus away from the important task at hand. I carefully shifted my weight, removed my foot from the divot in the stone, and lowered myself to the next available ledge. It was a guessing game. I had to blindly search for a lower brick that was rough enough to provide traction.

I pressed my body as close as I could against the wall. My muscles were tense and sore. I couldn't feel the tips of my fingers, and my tendons were stretched to their absolute limit. My lungs only allowed me to draw breaths in short, staggered gasps. I clenched my teeth so tightly I thought they would break. My hair continued to whip around me as I slowly and painstakingly climbed downward.

The cold was unbearable, sucking the little energy I still had. Shadows cloaked around me and hid me from view but sucked away any heat. I had never felt so exposed in my entire life. My teeth chattered, but I couldn't hear the chattering over the roaring wind. I gave up, and I closed my eyes. I didn't glance down to see how far I had left to go. I just knew that I had reached my limit and couldn't go any farther.

I glanced downward and saw that the ground was only ten feet below me. The muscles in my arms and legs were so fatigued that I knew I wouldn't be able to climb all the way. Could I make the drop? I let my fingers slip from the gritty stone, and I accidentally cried out as I fell. The wind whipped around me for a split second before my feet hit the pavement. My knees buckled, and I landed backward on the pavement.

It took a few seconds for me to register the situation. *I'm alive. I made it, and I don't think any of my bones are broken either.*

I tried to stand up, but I could only manage to push myself into a sitting position. I rested my head against the stone wall and allowed myself the luxury of deep breaths. *I escaped, yes, but I don't know what I'm doing. I could be caught at any moment. Guards are probably patrolling the palace, maybe they even heard my yell, and I don't have any strength left.*

As if my thoughts controlled my life, I heard the sound of footsteps on cobblestones—two people, from the frequency of the sound. The noise was loud, which meant they were running and coming directly toward me.

I exhaled. *Fine. Take me. I'm tired, and I'm certainly not in any condition to evade recapture. I don't know why I tried to escape anyway. It was hopeless in the start.*

The two people rounded a corner and suddenly came into view. I expected to see a pair of Tanum guards, even Raymon and Crevan themselves.

But no. I saw the frantic expressions of Gerrand and Akilah.

I almost screamed again. All of the stress and tension melted out of me, and I felt like crying. Finding my two allies, alive and in this kingdom with me, was an absolute miracle.

They looked like they needed help, too. Gerrand's brown hair was rumpled and messy from the wind. He wore a faded black jacket, but that was all that shielded him from the cold. Akilah's hair had pulled halfway out of its long braid, and her face was smeared with dirt. She wore a tattered red cloak that flapped wildly in the fierce currents of air.

They both immediately noticed me. Akilah darted forward first. "Syona! How did you get here?"

"Um, I escaped?" I answered. "How did *you* get here?"

Before Akilah could answer my question, Gerrand shoved past her. "Are you okay? Are you hurt? Did they do anything to you?" His expression was still full of concern, even after everything that had happened.

"I'm okay." I managed to say before I threw myself into his arms. I embraced him as hard as I could and rested my head on his neck. I didn't want this to end, having my head nestled against him. I never wanted to leave him. I never wanted to stop touching him. Ever. I felt such an enormous wave of relief that I collapsed again.

"Hey!" Akilah shouted. "You didn't answer my question. How did you get down here?"

"I went through the window and climbed down."

She peered upward at the tower I had been in. "That's high."

"Yes. I'm completely exhausted."

Gerrand laughed. "You did that? You were so modest when you said you climbed trees when you were a kid. *That's* impressive."

"How did you get here?"

"It's a long story," Gerrand began. "When we finally came out of the closet, the people from the kingdom of Tanum were gone, so we figured they had taken you with them. We came all the way here to rescue you."

"You didn't get caught? Two Ashlons have been sneaking around this palace and you haven't been caught yet? Didn't I specifically tell you that going to the capital would be suicide?"

"We were *very* sneaky, and Gerrand found an abandoned cellar where we've been hiding out," Akilah interjected. "And almost all of the palace guards are actually in the kingdom of Ashlon. They're sending most of their army into our kingdom to seize control. From what we could tell, everyone submitted pretty quickly. There's so much confusion. Nobody knows where you are, and the Tanum guards can manipulate everyone's emotions anyway."

"Why would people care about where *I* am?"

Akilah's face was somber. "You're . . . you're the queen, Syona."

I exhaled angrily. "I . . . I know I'm the queen, but . . ." I saved myself by immediately changing the subject. "Raymon revealed some pretty shocking things to me. He and Crevan were the ones who made the stones. They've been planning it from before the war. This entire wedding alliance was a ruse to combine the kingdoms and take over."

"Wow," Akilah said faintly. "Really? I kind of figured the marriage alliance wasn't supposed to be an alliance, based on what they've done so far, but I didn't know that the people in the kingdom of Tanum made the stones. That's surprising. How did they do it?"

I shook my head. "I don't know."

Gerrand reached forward and grabbed my shoulders, forcing me to look into his eyes. "Look, Syona. We can't think about that right now. We need to focus on getting your kingdom back. That's all that matters."

I sighed with frustration. "How are we supposed to do *that?*"

"We hide out for a while and try to formulate a plan. I imagine you can do that. Anything that comes from my brain will probably be a bad idea, but we can wait them out in this kingdom, or we could go back to the kingdom of Ashlon and try to gain supporters to lead a revolution. The stones are Tanum's control over us. If we free the people from the stones, their control is broken, and the kingdom will be ours again."

"That's a lot of speculation. Are you sure we can do this?" I asked him.

"Think of it this way: I'll finally get the chance to protect you from danger, just like what you said on the balcony. I've never actually saved someone before while not having my emotions muted, so I'm looking forward to what it makes me feel!"

"I . . . I still don't think I can do *any* of that." I fished the sapphire out of my pocket and clutched it in my hands. "I'm not worthy of being a queen. I wasn't even a good princess or a good Malopath."

Akilah and Gerrand both stared at me, shock written all over their expressions. "You're a *Malopath?*" Gerrand cried.

"Yes. I'm sorry for not telling you before," I said sheepishly.

"But—" Akilah started talking.

Gerrand shushed her with a wave of his finger. "Syona, we'll help you through this. You're a Malopath. It explains so much about you. But if you *are* one and survived in the palace for eighteen years without being executed, that has to count for something."

I squeezed my eyes shut. "We're in a terrible situation right now. What if we fail? What if all of this is for nothing? What if I cry and get my heart broken?"

"Crying is human, and hearts are made to be broken over and over again. That's the joy of it. It's both beautiful and confusing. I've learned that emotion isn't good or bad. It's just a sensation that allows us to experience life to the absolute fullest. Even if there's sadness and fear in your life, you can always balance it out with happiness and love." He smiled. "It might seem hard, even impossible, but we are both here for you, and we'll be able to get through this together."

"Who . . . who said that? Someone from the kingdom of Tanum? Mareena? Because there's no way those were your own words. You're not poetic enough for that."

Gerrand rolled his eyes. "At least you're able to joke around."

"Thank you, though. I needed that. That was sweet, coming from a former Ashlon guard."

"I'm glad you agree with me." He pointed to the necklace in my hand. "Now smash the sapphire. It doesn't work on you anyway."

I scoffed at him. "You're just getting back at me for smashing your amber stone, right?"

"No," he immediately replied. "Maybe. Yes. Just please do it for me."

"Seriously?" Akilah whined. "I want to use that!"

I turned to her. "Even after knowing what they actually do? What *is* it with you and sapphires?"

She sighed and shook her head. "I'll tell you later. Smash it if you must."

I unthreaded the stone from the silver chain and placed it on the stone street in front of me. With help from Gerrand, I stood up and lifted one of my feet off of the ground, positioning it over the stone.

If you do this, there's no turning back. As soon as you run away with them, you'll be a fugitive for the first time in your life. You'll be trying to overthrow a kingdom that has control over thousands of people, and your only help is a former guard and a teenage servant girl.

That's impossible.

But I've always been faced with the impossible. I was a Malopathic princess who survived in the kingdom of Ashlon for eighteen years. I even got the two people I love most in the world to take off their stones. I have two new friends who will always help and support me, against all odds.

Mareena's gently spoken words washed into the current of my thoughts. It was what I needed in such a crucial time like this one: *Cherish your emotions. Take those private moments by yourself and laugh. Cry. Get angry. Think of the people you love.*

Try to accept that it is a part of who you are.

My foot came down, smashing the sapphires into the street. The blue shards broke away, glittering in the light.

My sadness disappeared with it.

EPILOGUE

Crevan burst into the guest room, smashing the doors against the walls. The throng of guards accompanying him spilled past the doorway and into the room, inspecting the scene laid out before them.

Chunks of the tan-colored vase Syona had thrown rested at his feet. The window was open, and the curtains were blowing in the wind. The window panes had shattered, probably thrown against the outside wall by the force of the wind. The rug on the floor was scuffed and unthreaded, as if someone had paced on it for hours.

It was a mess. *That* upset him the most, not Syona escaping. He had expected that. He knew that they wouldn't be able to hold her for long. She was too smart, something he admired about her.

Now that he was thinking about it, he couldn't decide whether to root for her or be panicked.

The choice was easy a second later, though, when his father materialized behind him, seemingly out of nowhere. He could feel the hairs on the back of his neck stand on end, and all of his muscles tensed up. Not many things scared the prince, but his father definitely made the list. King Raymon was a tyrant to his family. He always had a plan formulated in his head. If all the pieces fit and people easily executed his desires, then he was bright and easygoing, the most carefree person in the world. But if something was out of place or he wasn't completely sure that his desire would be fulfilled, well, that was different.

Crevan feared his disappointed, vengeful side more than anything.

"*Where is she?*" Raymon bellowed from behind Crevan.

One of the guards winced, almost stumbling backward. "We don't know, Your Majesty. Our information is very slim. We came to the scene with it looking like this."

"Find. Her. Or I'll hunt you down and kill you myself."

The guard nodded and scurried out of the room, eager to get out, as anyone would be when Raymon was in this state.

The king clutched Crevan's shoulders and jerked him around to face him. The prince flinched, wilting under the burning intensity of his father's gaze. Crevan had no will anymore. His father had stripped that away an eternity ago. His intentions had to be completely aligned with Raymon's, or he would suffer the consequences.

"You know her better than anyone. Where would she go? Surely you have some information for us to use. Tell me. Now!" he demanded.

A pawn, that's what I am. I'm shuffled around in my father's game and used when convenient.

"She escaped quite recently."

"How can you tell?" Raymon snapped.

You're doubting me? Even after all this time and after all the times I've been right? "She spent quite a bit of time in this room, even after I left. Scuff marks on the carpet and rug prove she paced for a while before finding a way to escape."

"And what was the way of escape?"

"She went through the window and climbed down."

The disbelief in his voice was insulting. "*Climbed* down?"

"Yes, I told you before. She climbed a lot during her childhood: trees, vertical walls. If anyone could do it, she could. The brick layering on this side of the palace is also slightly uneven, providing her with footholds and places to grasp."

Raymon folded his arms, finally intrigued. "Is she going to be alone?"

"No. I'd expect three of them: Syona, her servant, Akilah, and her personal guard, Gerrand. They care about each other. They'll try to meet up and go on the run together. Maybe Akilah and Gerrand have already found their way into the kingdom of Tanum. What they'll do after that? I'm not really sure."

Raymon clenched his teeth, making Crevan flinch again. "No. That's not going to happen. I won't let it happen." He reached up to his neck and ran his fingers over the metal chain he always wore, a habit that surfaced whenever he got nervous. "Set up a perimeter around the kingdom. Nobody's going in or out. Get some guards and set up a search party. We'll find them. We're finding them by tonight." The king suddenly fled down the hallway, screeching for his advisors.

With his father gone, Crevan could breathe a little easier. He was in good standing with him, for a while anyway. Since Raymon's plan with the emotion stones went so well, there wouldn't be any punishments. But Syona was an uncertain variable. Even though it would be extremely hard for her to stop his father's plans, she could still wreak serious havoc.

Everlee abruptly appeared in the doorway, scanning the room with interest. "What happened here?"

"Syona escaped," he responded, deciding to keep it simple.

"Oh, good," she said in her cheery, quiet voice. "I liked her. She's a lot like me."

Crevan glanced over at Everlee to study her expression. Crevan had good observation skills, one of his strengths. He could study someone's face, an event, or a scene, and immediately infer the truth about the situation. He was pretty accurate most of the time, which was one reason his father continued to keep him around.

He didn't know very much about Everlee, though. In fact, he didn't have the foggiest idea of what she did on a day-to-day basis or how much she knew about their plans. It was always between Raymon and Crevan only. But it was a big palace with countless opportunities for eavesdropping, so she *could* know. If she did know the secret of the stones' creation, she could tell someone, but Everlee had a reputation of being well mannered and soft-spoken. Maybe she wouldn't do anything. Everlee *never* did anything.

Crevan, however, did do things. He cringed as memories flashed through his mind. *The things I've done! The things my father has made me do. I've had to plaster on a face of stone and pretend it's no big deal.* He recalled painfully the order he had given to kill Mareena. *I'll probably have that image in my head for the rest of my life.*

The prince exited the room and started rushing down the hallway. *I can't choose what side I want to be on. I still love Syona. It's hard not to. She's unlike everything in my life. Nothing about her reminds me of anything related to the kingdom of Tanum or Raymon. Syona was my escape.*

I can't lose her. Not like this.

Crevan glanced back at the empty guest room, recalling the conversation he had with her. *I have to support my father. Always. That's the one thing that can never change. I'll always have to be by his side and do what he wants me to, but I could root for Syona on the inside. I can secretly support her, at least for a while.*

After all, it's her kingdom, and he shouldn't have the right to take it away from her.

ACKNOWLEDGMENTS

Wow! Thanks for reading a book written by a teenage author, and getting to the very end so you can see all the amazing people who supported me throughout the entire process.

I'm grateful for my unofficial writing group, Kayla, Jane, Anna, and Kylie. They were my cheerleaders and gave me tons of helpful advice. I loved talking on the bus about dragons and magic and avenger movies. They were the ones who convinced me to turn this story from an epic fantasy adventure into an indoor romance. I'd never have written a love triangle if it weren't for them. Thanks, guys. I'll get you back for that someday.

I have eternal thanks to my family, especially my parents, who stubbornly never gave up on me and gave me all I needed. Thanks to Angie Fenimore, Randi, and the Calliope inner circle group who were the ones that kickstarted this whole project and led me to the pitch meeting, and all my beta readers like Becca, Jaycie, and Jess. Thanks to Morgan James Publishing for taking a gamble and accepting my manuscript and to the editors who fine-tuned it.

I appreciate all my English and creative writing teachers who put up with me writing stories that were so much longer than the maximum of three pages and my incessant habit of reading during class, and thanks to all the librarians who I've harassed mercilessly by checking out two or three books every day.

This book was written and edited while I listened to a combination of Lindsey Stirling songs and anime soundtracks. And thanks to all the writing advice, sketch comedy, show reviewing, and animation channels that I watched. This book would have completed months faster if you didn't exist. Thanks for reinforcing my procrastination!

ABOUT THE AUTHOR

Sarah Humpherys lives in Lehi, Utah and is a die-hard fantasy nerd that can't stop talking about dragons and anime. She is trying to get through high school by burying herself in Japanese TV shows and creating her own worlds and characters. She does make friends, but only with people who can stand her habit of constantly talking during movies to critique the plot, her memorization of the How to Train your Dragon Wikipedia page, and a monologue explaining why Doctor Strange is obviously the best avenger.

Connect with her online at sarahhumpherys.com

A free ebook edition is available with the purchase of this book.

To claim your free ebook edition:

1. Visit MorganJamesBOGO.com
2. Sign your name CLEARLY in the space
3. Complete the form and submit a photo of the entire copyright page
4. You or your friend can download the ebook to your preferred device

Print & Digital Together Forever.

Snap a photo

Free ebook

Read anywhere